DEADLY NIGHTSHADE

JOSS STIRLING

FROST WOLF

Copyright © 2018 by Joss Stirling

First published 2018 by Frost Wolf

ISBN: 978-1-910426-26-5

DEDICATION

With thanks to Hannah Jayne Adams, Jessica Allen, Sarah J Andrews, Niamh Brown, Andrea Navarrete Caliz, Vicki Cawley, Lex Chortlon, Aisling Coffey, Alana Collins, Jessica Cottee, Rachel Decruz, Magdalena Eifert, Lucy Gardner, Maud Grefte, Kirsty-marie Hill, Hannah Hesketh, Alice Hitchcock, Mia Hoddell, Maria Høilund, Sarah Beth James, Heidi Jørgensen, Andy Grey Komuro, Melisa Kumas, Rachel Langford, Laura László, Lydia Lubben, Bethan Main, Janely Marcial, Linsay McGarva, Lilly Moore, Jimena Patiño, Carrie Phillips-Davies, Debbie Pinzon, Gisele Sabrina Presti, Carlotta Rudolph, Claudia Schnaible, Frances Smith, Lucy Jane Spreadborough, Vicci Stamp, Martha Stevens, Alicia Swann, Lou Turner, Jade Underhill, Nivetha Vamathevan, Chelsea Van Gompel, Ines Verbesselt, Jemma Vial, Giana Villalva, Anna Williamson

1

HELLO AGAIN

Have you ever felt so totally different from everyone else in your world? I don't mean little things like you've got braces, follow an obscure indie band, or that you get hiccups when you laugh. I'm talking about something major that sets you apart. Something that makes you a freak in other people's eyes.

Welcome to my life. This one – at least for now.

THE OLD-FASHIONED WALL clock in the English classroom hadn't moved in the last half hour. The hands were refusing to release us into our weekend like a stubborn parole board turning down every plea for mercy.

Please let me go. I've been good. Mostly.

Parole denied. Suck it up, kid.

Miss King clicked through her slides on *Frankenstein*, effectively killing the subject on the wall screen after Mary Shelley had brought it to life with her lightning bolt of a book.

I doodled a thundercloud in my homework planner. I

met her once, Mary Shelley, I mean. She was reading in St Pancras churchyard (that's in London), perched on the grave of her founder-of-feminism mother, Mary Wollstonecraft. Poor woman died giving birth to her. Seriously gloomy now I think about it. You could say Mary Shelley had all the makings of an Emo – moody, angst-ridden, mind a maze of dark places. Very cool.

'Linny, stop gazing out of the window and pay attention.' Miss King threw a paper dart at me. She had these lined up on her desk, a little silo of rainbow missiles, thinking this made her discipline methods surprising and therefore effective. She should've seen what they threw in the 1810s.

I unfolded the paper and spread it flat on the desk.

'Did you hear anything I've said?' the teacher asked, crossing the classroom to retrieve her decommissioned torpedo.

'Possibly.' My reply, though inadequate for the teacher, was truthful. I had probably heard variations of everything she said in the last two hundred years since *Frankenstein* was published.

'By daydreaming the lesson away, you will never achieve what Shelley did by nineteen, which was how old she was when she came up with the idea for her novel.'

I would never see nineteen. 'Maybe she only wrote it because there wasn't much else to do?'

'What?'

'Mount Tambora erupted in 1815 and the ash cloud meant we had no summer for a few years.' It had been bitterly cold. I could still remember the itch of the chilblains that never cleared up and the hunger as harvests failed.

Miss King took a step away from my desk. These odd moments of mine have the effect of unsettling the teachers. I think they all consider me scarily unstable but it does earn me useful space. 'Then you can write about that in the essay I'm setting for homework.' The class groaned as the bell finally rang for the end of the day. 'I want you all to discuss how the scientific ideas of Shelley's day influenced her story. Those of you who were listening know where to look for more information. Hand your essay in next lesson. Linny, you can stay behind and copy Sian's notes as you appear to have been away with the fairies for the last hour.'

A few of the more sycophantic pupils chuckled. Miss King hadn't a clue what she was talking about. Fairy abduction was not something to turn into a joke.

Sian leaned over and slid her book in front of me, one of her copper-colored curls falling on the page like a question mark. 'Bad luck, Linny. I'll see you in the common room later, okay?'

'Okay. Thanks for the loan.'

'No problem.' My friend picked up her bag and joined the exodus, swept along in the flood of students. I took up my pen and began copying her neat page of notes while Miss King sat with bent head, marking work from junior students. This was so pointless. I knew all of this stuff first hand. I gave up. Tapping the end of my chin, I began sketching a leafless tree in the margin of my pad, enjoying the scratch of the ink pen nib with each stroke. It was like doing calligraphy. I've developed a very distinct style of handwriting over the years. The roots spread and spread, forking into a structure bigger than the branches. When you look at an oak, you don't think about the tiny little connections underground that produced it – not till it blows over and these are exposed to the light. Even then many of them are left in the ground. How long would it be till the next gale rattled the forest? It was so painful to remember, but then, I was accustomed to pain. Better to face it.

I got out my diary from my school bag and opened it at the first entry – an account of the very first uprooting I had experienced.

Miss King looked up and I pulled Sian's English book over my diary and pretended to take notes.

Sian's parting words clung in my mind. Bad luck, Linny – she hadn't used the words lightly. She had great respect for fortune of all kinds. Bad luck was what brought me here. To be more precise, a curse. I expect you've heard about them in fairy tales. But did you pay attention? Here comes my paper dart to land on your desk. The old word for fairy was fey. My history is a fey tale.

Fatal.

2

THE DAY I DIED

1st *January*
It's my fifteenth birthday today but I won't see sixteen. As soon as I remember, I always write down why I died that first time so long ago. I'll write it again here in full so there is a record of it in my last year this time around. Maybe I'll give this diary to Sian when the time comes so at least someone understands everything. I've already told her most of it.

It was a perfect autumn day, the kind where the skies are so blue you feel you are floating upwards into them, weightless. The leaves were fringed with gold, the trees gleaming with the magic that belonged to a younger world in ancient Ireland. My mother and her court were riding in the wake of Father's hunt. She preferred not to be there for the kill of deer or wild boar, enjoying herself instead by hurdling logs and jumping streams. I can picture her now, scarves fluttering, head thrown back, laughing with abandon as Wren, Finch and I cleared a fallen tree.

'Well done, girls!' she cheered.

Wren and I rolled our eyes at each other, thinking our mother's enthusiasm embarrassing in front of our friends in the household, but little Finch giggled, showing the gap in her front teeth where her adult ones were yet to grow through.

It felt wonderful to be alive that day.

Then, deep in the forest, the horns sounded as the hunters changed course. Their cries came closer – they were on the track of something that got the dogs howling and yipping with excitement. My mother signaled for us to fall back off the trail – my father could be single-minded about the pursuit and would only be sorry after the event that he had spooked one of his ladies' horses.

There came a crash from within the holly bushes and a white stag erupted into our midst. Horses reared away from silver antlers. My sight played havoc with my senses. I couldn't quite see the stag for sometimes it seemed to be pure energy, a burst of lightning flickering up from the ground. What was this creature? From another world than ours, surely? One thing was clear though: it was as shocked by us as we were by it. As I struggled to control my mount, I caught a glimpse of startled wide eyes, brown like polished oak, almost human in expression. As it fought to find a way through panicked horses, lowered antlers snagged Finch's skirt. It wasted vital seconds as it jerked free. The tug forced my little sister from her saddle, but then the stag was gone. Wren leapt down but Finch was already back on her feet, rubbing her behind.

'What was that terrible creature, Linny?' Finch asked, freckles quite marked against her pale skin.

The dogs poured into our clearing, baying in their deep voices. My father and his hunters followed.

By sudden instinct, I was filled with dread. Something awful was about to happen.

'Father, stop! Don't kill it!' I shouted.

He turned in his saddle, periwinkle blue eyes alight with high spirits. He was surprised to see his family near, so lost had he been in his hunt.

'Faint heart, Linnet? That's not like you.' He spurred his horse on. 'That stag will make fine venison for your sixteenth birthday feast!' His voice faded with the drumming of the hooves.

'I don't want you to kill it – not for me!' Desperate now, I kicked my horse in pursuit, though I had little hope of catching my father on his stallion while I rode my little mare. I reached the hunt just as they brought the stag to a halt at the edge of the great river. The creature stood at the edge of a cliff above the water, flanks quivering, sides foamed with sweat. Couldn't they see it was not the kind of beast you should hunt? It was pulsing with power; I could sense the energy rolling from the animal despite its terror.

'Please, don't!' I screamed.

Too late: my father's arrow flew through the air and struck the stag deep in the socket of the left eye. Its legs buckled and the hunters let out a victory shout.

'No, no!' I whispered, choked with pity for the stag.

Made frantic by the hounds snapping at its hooves, the creature found a last burst of life and tried to leap the river. Impossible. It crashed into the water and was swept away by the swift current, much to the anger of dogs and hunters alike.

All the sparkle drained from the day, the light chilled and the colors dulled.

'Don't you feel that?' I asked hoarsely.

'Feel what?' My father shook his head, dismissing my protest. 'Men, find that stag. It can't have gone far.'

Though the banks were searched for many miles, the body was not found.

.   .   .

THAT NIGHT AT THE CASTLE, the mood was somber. My father still fretted about the loss of his prize. He rejected my complaint that they should never have hunted such a creature. He'd seen nothing special, he told me, just an albino stag. As a result, I wasn't talking to him. Finch had been more badly hurt in her fall than we had first thought. She had her ankle bandaged and was perched on my mother's lap. Only Wren tried to be normal, smiling at the servers and those of the household sitting below our table. You could always count on Wren to think of others and try to cheer everyone up.

Abruptly the dogs all rose from the rushes and fled to the kitchen door, barking and scratching to be let out.

'What the blazes?' marveled Father, seeing his favorite wolfhound desert him.

The double doors at the far end of the hall crashed open. A chill wind blew through the room extinguishing all candles. Even the fire in the hearth blinked and went out. The dogs stopped barking and fell to whimpering. I clutched Wren's hand.

A man stood in the entrance. Dark power snaked from him and I was sure that he could strike out at any of us, bring the whole castle down if he wished.

'Linny, he's Sidhe, I just know it,' whispered Wren. She had been taking lessons from the castle mage so knew more about the hidden world of the fey than any of us. She started sketching protection charms with her fingers but they winked out like sparks in a rainstorm.

The man stalked down the central aisle, spurs ringing at his heels, and only then did I notice that he was accompanied by others of his kind. They fanned out and took positions along the walls, covering us all with their bows and arrows, young men, impossibly handsome but with cruel expressions.

My father rose. I could see his hand shaking in the folds of his tunic but his voice was firm.

'What is the meaning of this? Who are you?'

'King Cynewald?' The man spoke the name like he was throwing daggers at my father. Built like a bear but moving smoothly like a wolf, the newcomer had a mane of shaggy white hair and a robe that looked like it had been woven from frosted spiderwebs. A pattern of bird footprints in silver thread decorated the trailing hem. And his eyes – his eyes were almost entirely black and filled with hate.

'I am he.' My father bowed his head, one king to another. 'And you?'

'You know who I am. I am king of my people as you are of yours.'

My father's eyes turned to the armed men at the sides of the hall.

'Those are my sons, those that survive.' The interloper gave the last word a bitter twist. The Sidhe were famous for their wars with each other; rarely did they visit the human world.

My father tried the only course open to him when pitted against the magic of the Fey King: diplomacy. 'Why come you in such battle array, your majesty?' His voice sounded falsely hearty. 'There is no need, surely? Will you not join us in our meal? I have no quarrel with you.'

The man raised his hand, showing he held a naked sword under his cloak, curved like a boar's tusk but much, much longer. 'But I have one with you, human king. You killed my hart.'

My father raised open hands in a sign of surrender. 'The stag was yours? Then I apologize for I did not know.'

You should have done, Father, I thought. The fey king's eyes flicked to me then back to my father. It was almost as if he could hear me.

My father's hands went to his golden belt, thumbs hooked in the chain, trying to look at ease before his court. 'In my defense, I should point out that the creature was on my land. A man is free to hunt in his own kingdom.'

The Fey King did not blink. He pressed his fist against his chest, hand shaking. It was shocking to see such emotion from a Sidhe; they were said to be cold to the bone, creatures of ice and snow, not warm blood. 'You killed my heart.' A deadly quiet descended that not even the dogs dare interrupt with their whines. 'For that you will pay dearly.' His gaze went to us, my sisters and me. 'I lost that which I loved most. You will know pain like mine threefold. Each of your daughters will carry a curse. They shall know death, silence and bitterness, just as I know them.'

'No!' protested my father, but the Fey King silenced him with a slice of his hand. My father clutched his throat.

Horrorstruck, my gaze met the Sidhe's black eyes. The injustice was huge, like a stone lodged in my throat. That Fey King's anger was turning on three little girls, was it? He was despicable. But what could we do against such hatred?

I stood up, daring him to do his worst. No one would say the daughter of King Cynewald met her fate as a coward. I'd force the Fey King to see me. Meeting my eyes, the man adjusted the grip on his sword hilt but then hesitated. Was there a moment of doubt? If so, that spark was extinguished quickly. He smiled. Awaking from their horrified trance, palace guards rushed towards him with shouts and drawn swords. His sons disarmed them far too easily, weapons clattering to the ground. We were outmatched, powerless against their magic. The king swung his sword. Violet light erupted like a viper from the end, slithered across the floor, leapt and struck me full in the chest. I screamed as a black flood of curse magic filled me, making my sight fade, my whole body hurt. I crumpled, bones humming to an ugly discordant note.

He turned next to Wren.

'Please, just me,' I begged. I tried to crawl to him to grab the hem of his cloak in supplication but I no longer had the strength. 'Let me be enough.'

He ignored me. Wren was so quiet as the curse hit her. Only the barest whimper escaped. She swayed but did not go down.

'No, no, not my little one!' cried Mother, trying to block his view of Finch but to no avail. His power forked and flickered. My little sister gave a shrill cry like a fox cub caught in a trap.

'You beast!' I hissed, pulling myself up from my knees. My father was there, supporting me. I could feel him shaking with rage. 'You devil!'

My father hushed me, fearing further magical punishments.

'It is done and cannot be undone,' declared the Fey King. 'Come! We are avenged.' He swept out, taking his sons with him.

Silence fell in the hall as the door slammed shut, broken only by my mother's sobs as she cradled Finch.

'Linnet? Wren?' My father gathered his two eldest daughters in his arms.

A cough racked me. Already my limbs felt weak. 'Father?'

'What's happening to Linny?' cried Finch. I was relieved that she sounded unhurt. Wren's cool hands went to my forehead and brushed through my unbound hair. A clump came away in her grasp. She gasped.

Finch gave a cry of distress. She scrambled from Mother's lap and clawed at my gown. 'Linny, stop it. You've gone grey. You can't be sick!'

My mother gently pulled her away. 'Careful with your sister.' She knelt beside me. 'Oh, my dear love! Cynewald, please, do something! Our little songbird.' She touched my face, fingers coming away wet.

Tears also on his cheeks, my father hugged me to his chest, then lifted me in his arms. He threw back his head and howled. 'Devil take all Sidhe and their kin!' He swung round. 'Guards, if any linger in my kingdom, kill them on sight.' He strode towards my chamber to lay me on my bed. 'Linnet, I'll find a way to break the curse, I promise!'

That was the only promise he made me that he did not keep.

3

GREEN DRAKE

Finally released from detention with Miss King, I trudged through the snow back to our house. Anger burned in my chest, the usual result of rereading my diary. I should set it aside. It only ever made me furious at the unfairness of fate.

Fortunately, I had the weather to distract me. I had to hunch against what was becoming a blizzard. Green Drake Academy prided itself on its grounds and old buildings but, with an east wind blowing off the Atlantic, I missed a city school where you never have to set foot outside. I went to one of those once upon a time, a girls' school in Boston. I think that might've been my favorite. We played lacrosse, wore tartan skirts and said 'gosh' and 'darn' if we were feeling really daring, like characters out of *Little Women*, our favorite reading. This time, my parents decided that I would benefit from an exclusive boarding school just outside the town of Owl's Head, Maine. Any further north and we'd be in Canada. If you went out the school gates you could go left for the miles of sand dunes and iron-grey ocean, or right for the long bleak road to the nearest civilization in Rockland. I didn't get to go home often.

I kicked a rut of ice, sending frost shrapnel flying.

My younger brother and sister, by contrast, went to a school in New York, walking distance from our apartment in SoHo.

Draw your own conclusions.

The wind shifted to the northeast. Feeling a tingle on the back of my neck that wasn't caused by the weather, I glanced behind. The main school building crouched dragon-like, pinnacles on the roof a row of spikes along the spine. With a very little imagination, you could picture it transforming, lifting walls of wings to take flight over the whale-road, as Irish poets used to call the sea. Cold biting, I squinted ahead out of my little serpent coil of scarf, charting my course by the door to my school boarding house, glimpsed through the sideways snowstorm. The entrance to Crowthorne House was painted crimson and had a wreath of holly circling the crow knocker. It looked almost festive. I made the final dash, grappled for the knob in mittened hands, and shut the door smartly behind me. Ice slipped off my shoulders and from the folds of my scarf as I removed my outer layers in the entrance hall. The snow landed on the tiled floor, clouding the star pattern.

The housemaster, Mr Huntsman, came out of his study, which was strategically placed by the front door so he could keep an eye on our comings and goings. He was a tall man without a scrap of spare flesh on him, halfway already to skeleton.

'You forgot to swipe in, Linny,' he said.

'Just getting to it, Mr Huntsman.' I pulled off my mittens with my teeth and yanked the school identity card out from the neck of my jumper. I pressed it against the reader on the wall and heard the familiar beep. Technology and I often don't get on. I was lucky it registered me half the time. I think it knew I shouldn't be here.

Mr Huntsman checked his tablet computer. 'Good, that's everyone accounted for – except the new boy. He must've been held up by the storm.'

I kicked off my wet shoes and slipped into my indoor ones that waited for me under my coat peg. 'New boy, sir?'

Mr Huntsman was already returning to his study with its rows of books on butterfly collecting and jewel-like cases of specimens. 'Everyone has to be new once.'

'Not me,' I murmured.

The noise from the common room broadcasted where most of us had gathered on this stormy evening. First, I made a trip up to my bedroom to change out of uniform. One of the good things about this era are the clothes. It might be the first time that I have ever been completely comfortable. I took advantage of it now, picking out soft grey pajama pants and a hoodie with a pouch pocket in moss green. The rules have become so relaxed it is acceptable to wear these kinds of clothes in the dining room when it isn't a formal dinner. The staff drew the line at amusing animal onesies and novelty slippers but you could get away with almost anything else.

I ran a quick brush through my hair then bundled it up into a ponytail. The ends were wet and beginning to curl but I couldn't be fussed to get out the hairdryer. It would be warm enough downstairs for it to dry off naturally, doing what always felt a little like a magical trick of going from black to mid brown in the process. As a last thought, I hung up my damp uniform on the closet door. It was a privilege to have a room to myself and I have become quite tidy as a result – no sisters or classmates that I had to fight for space.

High un-shuttered windows in a workhouse – my sister coughing in our coffin of a bed – my arms around her thin ribs, trying to keep her warm....

I closed my eyes, banishing the memories.

I'm here. Warm. Safe. It's now, not then.

But sometimes I can't tell the difference.

'HEY, Linny, you're just in time,' called Sian as I entered the common room. She was exactly where I expected to find her, on the sofa hugging a tasseled cushion, legs curled up. 'Hilary's just been in an accident and Harry is on duty. They are so going to get together!' Her enthusiasm helped drive out the cold ache in my chest. Sian had an inexplicable love for the early evening hospital soap, *Blue Light*. Even her usual knitting project was abandoned – Sian had a thing for colorful craft knits like my scarf. I was slightly anxious about what creation might be in her patchwork bag destined for a Christmas present. It didn't look like another scarf.

'Bor-ring!' howled Jack, flopping back on the couch at right angles to Sian's prime TV spot. 'Linny, make her turn over. I'm missing the football replays from last night's games.'

I raised an eyebrow in his direction. 'Some would question your definition of boring, Jack.' He knows I prefer soccer to football.

He grinned at me, hazel eyes bright with teasing mischief. We both were well aware that we would find toads in our beds if we tried to change the program. I slumped down on the sofa cushion next to him.

He slung an arm around me as I rested my head on his

bony shoulder. Ours is a spiritual brother-and-sister thing. 'Sian said Miss King kept you behind again.'

'She doesn't like me much.' I toyed with his phone, adding crowns to our selfie. My cell was always on the fritz. Besides I didn't have anyone to message; almost everyone I loved was here.

'Who would? You're just so weird.' He took his phone back and posted the image on our message thread. Sian's phone buzzed but she was too caught up in the drama to like the image.

'This from the boy with the antique Megadeth t-shirt inherited from his dad and skinny ripped jeans.'

'Weirdoes of the world unite. We have nothing to lose but...our chance at ever being voted Prom King and Queen.'

'God, can you imagine that? The world would crumble if that ever happened.'

Blue lights flash on the screen as Hilary is rushed to hospital where the gorgeous Harry is waiting in his scrubs.

'Almost worth being in a car crash,' Jack observed as the doctor swept in to pull Hilary back from the brink of death. It suddenly no longer felt amusing. I knew what that was like all too well.

'So, Jack, how was your day?' I turned away from the screen.

In the year above me, Jack had picked classes in Music, Math, Drama and Photography.

'Not bad. I've started composing a piece. It won't be much good or anything...' His voice trailed off. His music was important to him and I thought him really talented. His teacher didn't share my estimation.

'It's going to be great, you moron.' I poked him in the ribs. 'Come on, play me a little of it.' I towed him over to the upright

piano in the corner of the room, put there in the early twentieth century for jolly community singing. We kids didn't have
many alternatives for amusing ourselves then. We perched
side by side on the piano seat and Jack played a little of the
melody. It was a haunting tune, a scatter of brittle high notes.

'I'm going to add a harmony on lower notes, a little hesitant but more positive.' He felt for a few notes with his left.
'Something like that. It's supposed to balance out.'

'What's it called?' I repeated what he had just played. I
had been taught the piano some time ago and somehow
never forgot.

Jack blushed. He always said his tendency to redden was
a bane of his life. 'I was going to call it "Linnet's Theme", if
you don't mind.'

A lump formed in my throat. No one had ever written a
song for me. 'I'd be honored.' I wondered if that was how he
saw me: this uneasy mix of spikiness and something I guess
you would call endurance. If so, then he totally got me.

'Well, thanks. I just wanted to cheer you up, you know?
So, moving swiftly on,' he laughed at our joint embarrassment, 'I'll work on it over the weekend and play you more
next week.'

A gust of exasperated laughter erupted from a group
playing cards over at the games table. Charlie, a prefect in
Jack's year, was raking in the winnings, mostly from the
freshers who still foolishly thought they could beat him. He
had an unerring instinct for poker. Normally a happy-go-
lucky person, once in a game, his eyes became shark-cool
and his teeth bared in a ruthless smile. The transformation
was both fascinating and a little scary. School rules were
that we aren't allowed to wager so the tokens used are
promises. As a result, Charlie has never had to do a chore
since joining Green Drake.

Charlie looked over and saw me watching. 'Hey, Linny, fancy your chances today? I must've used up all my luck by now.'

I slid off the piano stool. 'And find myself cleaning your muddy football boots? No thanks.'

'One day I'll persuade you to change your mind.' He got up, pocketing his winnings. 'Sorry, guys, if Unshakeable Linny's not going to join in, no more tonight.'

Jack put down the lid over the keys. 'He never invites me to play.'

I nudged him. 'That's because you lost so many times to that bloodsucker when you were both freshers that he feels bad about taking advantage of you. He has moved on to new victims.' I mimed biting his neck, making him laugh.

The theme music for *A&E* wailed across the room. Set free from the TV spell to rejoin us, Sian came over and sat down on Jack's knee, looping her arms around his neck. 'What were you playing, maestro?'

'Oh, nothing. Just a tune I thought up.' He glanced at me, signaling that it was too soon to expose it to anyone else, even Sian.

'Can you be a complete angel, Jack, and help me with my assignment?' Sian was taking Music despite the fact that she didn't have a musical bone in her body. I often wondered about the choice but her replies were always evasive.

Jack rolled his eyes. 'How long till dinner?'

'An hour. Pretty please?'

'Fine. I'll give you some pointers, Sian, but I'm not doing it for you.'

Sian sprang up. 'You, Jack Burne, are just the best friend ever!'

I cleared my throat.

'Joint first position, of course, with Miss Linnet Grace here.' She dragged him away to the study, which was supposed to be a little quieter than the common room.

That left me at a loose end. Sian and Jack were my only close friends. I looked around for a safe place to retreat. Going back up to my bedroom just seemed lame. The card players had moved on to backgammon. Some girls in my year were gossiping by the fire and didn't look open to the idea of me joining them. Maybe I should grab a newspaper and settle down to catch up on world events?

I was halfway to my goal when the door opened and Mr Huntsman entered. He clapped his hands.

'Crowthorne, a moment of your attention, please!' The noise level dipped and finally reached mute. 'I want to introduce a new member of our house, Quinn Ramsay. He'll be in Junior Year.' A boy stepped out from behind him, flipping back what looked like a black cloak until I realized it was just his coat over his shoulders. I hummed an ironic little *da-da-dah* in my head to match his dramatic entrance.

'Hi, Quinn,' murmured a few in the room.

Mr Huntsman cleared his throat. 'Unfortunately, his arrival was delayed by the storm so he wasn't able to join you in class today and get to know you that way. As it's now the weekend, I was hoping some of you would take him under your wing until Monday. Right, do I have any volunteers?'

Quinn surveyed the room like General MacArthur would a battlefield, completely unembarrassed by this awkward introduction. None of us were quite sure what to do. He just looked so daunting.

'Thank you, Linny.'

What?

'If you wouldn't mind showing Quinn over to the dining room, making sure he gets his bearings?'

How had Mr Huntsman interpreted standing arms crossed in the middle of the room as volunteering? But he hadn't left me any choice.

'Fine. Welcome to Green Drake.' I tucked my hands in my hoodie pocket to eliminate the chance of contact.

A pair of blue eyes came to rest on me and I got a slight nod.

'So, over to you, Linny. Oh, and er, a couple of house points for hospitality, I suppose.' We stopped getting excited about house points after a few months in High School but a few die-hards present gave a whoop until rapidly hushed by their savvier friends.

Mr Huntsman hurried back to his study, leaving me to cope alone.

4

QUINN

'Okay, so you'd like the tour?' I asked as the noise started up again. Everyone was watching us, but they were all pretending to be doing anything but that. I could see the girls by the fireplace preening and assessing. Quinn wasn't good-looking in the usual way, nose a little too narrow and long, fly-away hair (I was being picky) but somehow the combination with the elegant dark clothing and gold ring in one ear worked just fine.

'What's your name again?' Quinn took his coat off and folded it over his arm. I was on the short side for a girl of my age, which gave him at least a head's advantage over me. But he would rapidly find that small bad-tempered people like me do not make very good recruits if he carried on with his lord and master act. He was only a year older than me, not even a senior.

'I'll show you where to hang that up. It's Linny, Linnet Grace. I'm in the year below you.' I headed out to the pegs, not convinced he was going to do anything so humble as to follow me, but he did. 'There's a spare hook there.'

'So I see.' He didn't hang up his coat.

'For your...you know.' I nodded down at his arm.

'I'd prefer to keep it with me. So, what do we do now?' He flashed a charming smile that failed in its purpose. He leaned against the coat rack, the huckster's beguiling stance I recognized from many years of experience. *I have a bridge to sell you...*

I wasn't buying. 'Whatever you like.' He was rattling me though. Why, oh why, was I spending any of the time left to me on stupid moments like this? 'Do you want me to give you the tour or was that all Mr Huntsman's idea?'

'It was his idea but, yes, I want the tour. He's already shown me the house and my room. What I really want is to go outside.' He was putting his coat back on.

'In the snow?'

'In the snow.'

This was one strange boy.

'Fine.' Sooner we did this, the sooner it would be over. I kicked off my indoor shoes and got back into my still damp snow boots. 'This is completely insane, of course, but it's not like it really matters.' If I died of hypothermia it would just speed up the approaching unhappy ending. 'I don't know how much we'll see, but that's what happens if you choose to start school in the middle of winter up here. It snows. A lot.' My coat appeared behind me, held up by Quinn. 'Oh, thanks.' I moved away swiftly and opened the front door before he got any more gentlemanly manners past me. The sideways blast had become a gentle downward fall. It actually looked quite pretty now and I could see some students from Eaglestone House engaged in a vigorous game of snowballs, reminding me of a scene by the Boston artist, Childe Hassam. He'd painted me once, in the late nineteenth century. A good memory. The picture's in a museum somewhere. 'Okay, let's get this done.'

We set out. I was expecting Quinn to walk alongside me but instead he followed behind. It was all rather absurd. I stopped at the gate to Crowthorne. 'I expect you've already worked out that the houses where the boarders live are arranged around this green – like a little village of peasants attached to the great house.' I pointed across the sports fields to the main building. 'That big hall with the pointy bits is the dining room. They serve dinner there from six to seven thirty.'

'I know. Mr Huntsman gave me a timetable.'

Like me, Quinn wasn't wearing gloves and I noticed out of the corner of my eye a silver ring on his right hand. It was engraved with a pattern of what looked like bird footprints or arrows. It snagged on some memory but I couldn't pin it down. The air was so freezing my brain wasn't functioning properly. I slapped my hands on my sides, trying to shake off the icy feeling. It had to be dipping well below freezing. 'So where would you like to go first? Library or gym? Music practice rooms? Or I could show you the other houses? I suggest we end up at the dining room so we don't have to make the journey twice.'

'I'd like to walk around the boundary.'

'You're joking?'

'I'm not.'

'But that's, like, over a mile I think.' He didn't argue but I found myself saying. 'Fine. We'll do that then.'

Being a curious type, I had already explored the grounds thoroughly since coming to the school. There were areas that few students went as they had been left for the wildlife. I had some favorite spots but I wasn't going to show him those. Instead I took him where he wanted to go. The wooded path that followed the boundary wall was only ankle-deep in snow. The bare trees reached overhead, tangles of twigs and leaves where squirrels had built their nests. Snow settled on the skyward side, white-highlighting the branches. Little pockets collected on the bumps and furrows of the trunks. Holly filled in the gaps under the canopy making it difficult to see far. By marching along as rapidly as possible, I was growing warm in all my layers. Quinn breathed lightly behind me, following me through the dell, across little bridges over icy streams, past glimpses of the wall between trees. I had the unsettling thought that he had positioned himself there so as to grab me, should I make a run for it.

Hello? This was not normal. I couldn't leave it unchallenged.

'Are you doing a Good King Wenceslas on me?'

'What?' He seemed surprised by my breaking of the silence. We hadn't exchanged a word for the first five minutes of our winter boundary walk.

'*Mark my footsteps, good my page, tread thou in them boldly.*' I sang the line from the Christmas carol. I do stuff like that.

'So, you're the king and I'm the page?' The thought made him grin, though I couldn't see why he found it so funny.

'It just feels, I don't know, weird to have you behind me.'

He lengthened his stride to walk alongside me. 'Better?'

It wasn't. Now I would actually have to speak to him. 'I guess.'

'I'm just used to walking in single file.'

I cast a look behind. I could only see one set of footprints. He'd really marked my steps, hadn't he? 'Where are you from, new boy?'

'Nowhere in particular, old girl. All over, you might say.'

Wasn't he the fount of no information? 'What brings you to our school then?'

'Well now, I suppose it was my father's choice. He'd thought I'd do better here.' A faint Irish accent was coming through. Either he was from an Irish-American family or came from the old country itself.

'And what do you think of it so far?'

'You mean since I got out of the car in a snowstorm, was marched into a room of strangers, turned over to a girl who would prefer to be anywhere else than here, and now told I don't walk right?'

That effectively shut down my attempts at small talk. I sped up to move in front of him. 'Sports ground to your right. Tennis courts by the library garden. You can see the sea around the next corner if you're tall enough to look over the wall.'

I kept on walking while he took advantage of the view-point. It was fairly easy to scale even for someone short like me as the old stone was host to all kinds of plant climbers – ivy, Old Man's Beard, even a patch of Russian vine – but I couldn't see the attraction of putting my face above the parapet for added wind-chill. Turning to check if he had had enough, I spotted him bury something in the snow on the top of the wall.

'That's not a good place to plant a seed.'

'Tell me something I don't know.'

Right, be like that then. His charm factor seemed to have dropped away with the temperature.

We walked on. Every fifty feet or so, my strange companion would pause and I'd just catch him stamping something into the ground, or pushing it into a crack in the stone or lodging it in a hollow of a tree. Finally, I had to ask.

'What are you doing?'

'Marking my territory.'

'Thank God then that you're not a dog.'

He didn't laugh, just looked at me with that amused, mocking 'are you really that much of an idiot?' expression he had perfected.

A bell tolled six over in the school chapel tower.

'Dinner. Are you hungry yet?' I blew on my fingers. My mittens were still melting on the radiator back in my room.

'I have to finish this.'

'Okay, but you don't mind if I go, do you?'

'I prefer you to stay.'

And once again I found myself saying, 'Okay then' when really I wanted to say 'no way, José'.

It took us, in the snowy conditions, nearly another hour to complete the circuit. I was flummoxed by my own inability to make a break for sensible indoors. An evening ramble was the last thing I would normally want to do on a Friday evening, even in these picturesque conditions. My stomach rumbled.

'Now can we eat?'

He actually smiled at my plaintive tone. 'All right. But first, come here a moment.' He turned me to face him. It was strangely like the prelude to a kiss but somehow I knew that wasn't what he had in mind. I flinched just as he pressed two fingers to my forehead, saying insistently. 'You will forget.'

I slapped his hands away. 'Hey, back off!' Memories were all that I had to carry with me – no way was he getting those.

The smile disappeared. Blue eyes burned now with intent. 'Relax, I'm not going to hurt you.'

I'd heard those very words from many mouths over the years – none of them had ever proved truthful. 'I said, back off!'

He began muttering a string of words, not in a language I recognized. Gaelic? I'd once spoken that so something older? The temperature dropped sharply. My bones ached in his spell's freezing grip. Ice crackled as icicles formed on branches, grew too heavy, dropped to the ground, all within seconds. Who...what was he? I had to get away.

Knee. Age old defense. One of the things a girl never forgets.

Somehow I managed it, bringing my knee up with a jerk. Quinn proved as vulnerable as every boy or man I'd ever incapacitated, falling forward in an agonized heap. He swore at me as he writhed on the ground.

'You can find your own way to the dining room, you... you creep!' I set off at a run, not sure how long he'd be out of action. I hoped he froze out there because when he did come in, I had a feeling I was going to pay for that.

5

WOLF'S CLAW

Thankfully I found Jack and Sian at one of the long tables in the baronial dining hall, lingering over their meal. The fan vaulted roof spread overhead like a stone version of the winter trees I had just left behind. I dropped my tray beside them. I had no idea what I had grabbed in the canteen, such was my panicked flight. When I did look down, I saw that I had picked a baked potato, not a good choice this late in the evening.

'Where's the new boy? Heard you were showing him around,' said Sian, looking over my shoulder, expecting to see him. 'Did you jinx him already?'

'Don't start. You know I don't do that stuff – that's your thing.' I rubbed my hands together, nails tinged blue. 'I've just had a really bad time with him. He is so freaky.'

'More so than us?' asked Jack with genuine interest.

'Yes. You won't believe what just happened.' I proceeded to tell them.

Sian's eyes grew wider and wider. 'He didn't! Go back and make sure you remember everything!' Sian made me describe in full exactly what Quinn had done, asking me to repeat certain details, such as the places in which he had dropped his 'seeds' or whatever they were.

Jack, however, was more disturbed by the fact that the new boy had tried to put hands on me at the end.

'You think he could do it? Hypnotize you?' he asked.

I moved the jacket potato away from the knobbly swamp of chili con carne. 'I think so.'

'So he's like a magician with a stage act? One of those guys who mess with your head?'

'Or he thinks he is. I kneed him and ran for it before he could try it again.'

'Why take you with him if he wanted to be all mysterious in the forest?' Jack fluttered his fingers in a way that was supposed to indicate world of weirdo.

'Good question. The circular walk is hardly a difficult path to follow. He could've gone by himself.'

'Uh-oh, look who's recovered from his unmanning.' Jack was gazing past my right shoulder. 'Everyone, pretend nothing's wrong. And, whoa, that is one burning look he is sending your way. So sad, I think he's missed last servings.' Jack didn't sound sad at all. 'But what's this? The chef has been persuaded to find him something after all – shame on her.' This was unheard of: Mrs Kermode was a stickler for keeping to her timings, scolding us that the staff had homes to go to.

'She's probably just giving him the new boy pass.' I tried a mouthful of potato but it was cold.

Jack clicked his tongue in disapproval. 'I think it's more than that. She's actually smiling at him and getting something out of the warming oven. Our new boy is a chef whisperer.'

Sian meanwhile had been fiddling with something on

her lap, plaiting some threads from her little pouch of odds and ends. 'Is he looking this way?'

'Not at the moment,' said Jack.

'Wear this for me, Linny.' She dropped a slender charm bracelet of multicolored threads on my palm. Several glass beads and strands of a dried plant were incorporated in the weave.

I spread it out. Over the years, she had given me many of these friendship bands. 'What's that leaf from?'

'Wolf's claw, or club moss. It should stop him working his trick on you.'

Jack grimaced. 'Sian, you are the most superstitious person in existence. You can't expect Linny to go around with a bunch of weeds on her wrist.'

'I don't know, it's quite pretty,' I interjected before they could get into one of their rational versus magic arguments. 'Thanks.' I slipped the bracelet on my wrist but to be honest felt no protective force field settle around me. Jack was probably right and that was all in Sian's mind.

'You won't be saying that when it brings you out in a rash,' Jack muttered darkly.

I noticed that Charlie had moved into the empty chair beside Quinn, followed by a couple of girls in their year. Quinn appeared relaxed but I could sense that he knew exactly where I was while I was in the room. From the glances sent in my direction by his new friends, it looked like I was one of the topics of conversation.

'Let's go,' I muttered.

'You've not eaten much,' remarked Jack. 'There's not much of you to start with.'

'Not hungry.'

Sian was murmuring under her breath as we hurried from the hall.

'What's she doing now?' asked Jack.

'One of her things.'

'She's lucky she's not born in the sixteenth century: they'd've burned her as a witch.'

'They hanged as many as they burned.'

'Lovely. You really are the source of such happy historical nuggets.'

'It wasn't a very funny time.'

Jack wound his Crowthorne scarf around his neck – dork that he is, one of the few still to wear it with pride. 'You always sound as if you take history so personally.'

I thought I'd better not reply to that. I share many things with Jack but he couldn't cope with the truth about me. I'd long since learned when to hold my peace.

I GOT BACK to my bedroom to find several missed calls from my mother. It was nice she had thought to ring. Normally she only duty-calls on a Sunday.

'Hi. Everyone okay?' I asked when she picked up.

'Oh Linny – thanks for calling me back. Yes, we're all fine.'

'Claire and Paul?'

'Yes, doing well at school.' She never gives me much in the way of details. It is like we are talking about distant cousins I only see once a year. Come to think of it, I hadn't seen my brother and sister since September so that wasn't far off the truth.

'Great.'

'I called because I've news. My work has asked me to go to Melbourne and we decided to take the chance to have a sunshine Christmas down under.'

'Oh wow! That's amazing.' It suddenly crossed my mind

that I had never been that far away when the curse was due to fall. Maybe, just maybe, distance would weaken it? 'When are we flying out?'

There was a slight pause. 'That's the issue, Linny. You're in High School now, with important tests coming up after the New Year, and it would mean missing a few weeks of school. Your grades will suffer.'

'I don't care about that.'

'But your father and I do. It's okay for Claire and Paul at their age, but not for you.'

'You're joking, right?'

'We've arranged with the school for you to stay over the holidays. We'll call on the day itself, of course, buy you something nice, and come and see you in January.'

Fury raced through me like a chain reaction as my reactors melted down. I could actually feel the heat of it spreading to my fingertips, which were trembling. 'Why, Mom?'

'Pardon?'

'Why are you doing this? You know that this is a bad time for me. I've never made a secret of it.'

'You're not still going on about that foolish premonition of yours that you'll be dead before you're sixteen? Don't be silly, Linny. Surely you are old enough to know that children can't imagine living beyond their youth? I couldn't think what life would be after the giddy age of thirteen when I was eight. It's just a superstition.'

'It's not.'

'Then think how much safer you will be in school rather than in Australia with all those snakes and sharks.'

She was making light of it. I wanted to throw something at her, much heavier than a paper dart. 'What's the real reason, Mom?'

'I've told you, you've got tests, grades to worry about.'

'You and I both know that I could take revision with me. It's something else. The least you can do is tell me the truth.'

Her tone turned sharp. 'All right then, if you must know, you scare your brother and sister, okay? I've had to sort out counseling for them because they are convinced they are going to die too. We want this to be a real family vacation – relaxing – without being haunted by talk of premature death. They won't recover if you're there prophesying doom. I'm sorry, but there it is. I have to think what's best for all my children, not just you.'

'Wow. I think that might be a first. None of my other parents purposely left me to face this alone.'

'There you go again – talking about us as if we are just one in a long line! Linny, you need help. Why won't you go to the psychiatrist appointments I've made for you? You're breaking our hearts.' I heard a sob as she gathered herself at the other end. 'Anyway, we've never been good enough for you, always falling short. It's difficult being your parent, Linny. You'll appreciate that when you have children of your own.'

I ended the call. There wasn't anything else to say, was there? Goodbye, Mom, goodbye, Dad. I hadn't handled this life well, blurting out far too many spooky things when the memories started coming back when I was about five. Memory acts like a dimmer switch, getting brighter and brighter until the recollections blaze. I think I was probably too much like one of those wide-eyed kids in horror movies, saying where I had died before and what grisly things had happened to others who knew me. My parents on this visit, Ryan and Sheila Grace, not the warmest of people in the first place, had not coped well. They cooled towards their cuckoo in the nest, transferring the love they could feel to the twins that followed me a few years later.

I sprawled face down on the bed and dropped the phone on the floor. That's probably why tech doesn't work well around me. I can't summon up the energy to respect it. Not that I expected her to call back. I was likely to be taking my leave this time alone. I couldn't ask Sian and Jack to give up their vacation. Death wasn't a unique enough experience to make it special for me. This was one of the ones I'd have to endure.

6

NIGHT SPELL

I woke suddenly at three in the morning. Broken nights aren't unusual as I approach the end; my tension grows like a fighter in a boxing match taking place in the dark, not knowing where the next blow will come from. This time the punch came from the window. An owl – a long-eared one, two tufts spiked up like devil's horns over molten circular eyes. It must've tapped its beak against the glass.

'Wretch, you scared me,' I whispered, resting my palm over my racing heart. It stared at me, then took off silently, swooping back to the pine forest.

A hand slid over my mouth. 'I've heard they kill their prey by biting them in the back of the neck.'

I gave a muffled scream, flailing to get free but the grip was firm.

Quinn laughed. 'Scared you? Sorry.' He wasn't. 'I'll take my hand away if you promise not to yell.'

A promise under these circumstances? It meant nothing. I nodded.

I heard a mocking sigh. 'You don't mean it.'

I was infuriated by the thought that I amused him. I grappled behind to find a vulnerable spot – throat, eyes – but he was keeping out of reach. The knee had taught him caution.

'But think what would happen if you did kick up a fuss. I'd be gone, I promise you, before anyone reached you. You'd then have to convince them the new boy had taken such an instant interest in you as to break in through a locked door.'

He had a point: I bolted it from the inside. How had he got in?

'And, sadly, the word is that people think you're strange. They'll put it down to a dream or wishful thinking. I'm very persuasive when I try and they'll be convinced I'm innocent. As I said before, I'm not going to harm you. Now, are you ready to keep your promise?'

For all his smooth words, I was afraid as well as furious. Life had taught me that fights with a bully need to be picked very carefully. This wasn't the moment or place. I nodded, this time meaning it.

'Good.' Quinn moved out from behind me and sat cross-legged on the end of my bed. He wasn't in his nightclothes but wearing a white shirt, and black jeans. All he needed was a red sash and a dagger gripped between his teeth and he'd make the complete stage pirate. He certainly had a pirate's ruthlessness.

'You're crazy. I hate you.' I reached for the light to supplement the moon's glow. I then recalled that I had also drawn the curtains before I went to sleep. They were open now.

'Leave the light.'

My fingers paused on the switch, but then I over-ruled

his objection and pressed. Nothing happened. 'You've done something to it?'

'Have I?' He drummed the fingers of one hand lazily on a knee.

'It was working earlier.'

'Maybe I did then. Forget about it. I need to talk to you.'

I curled my knees to my chest and looped my arms around them. 'You're not supposed to be in here.'

'I go many places I'm not supposed to.'

'I want you to leave.' My brain was running through all the lessons I'd learned about how to deal with this kind of situation and couldn't come up with a helpful match. Just get it over with, seemed the best advice.

'I will, but I have to say something first.'

'Hurry up then.'

He leant back against the footboard and straightened his legs, now crossed at the ankles. His bare toes were near my feet but that didn't make him seem the least bit vulnerable. 'I'm sorry I scared you earlier.'

'You're scaring me now.' In fact, I felt more angry than scared. I'd had enough of people today.

'I'm sorry for that too. If you'd just let me start over.'

'Not interested.'

'I miscalculated – I shouldn't have picked you.'

'I thought Mr Huntsman picked me?'

'With a nudge from me, yes, he did. You were the first person I saw that seemed to...fit my requirements.'

'Hard luck. I don't. Not in a million years.'

'You paid me back.' He gave a wince that was supposed to be humorous.

I didn't rise to the bait. 'You deserved it.'

'Not where I come from.'

'And where is that exactly? Boston? Dublin?'

He rubbed his chin, assessing me. 'I've spent time in both cities, yes.'

'But you're not from either of them.'

'No – and that's irrelevant. Are you Irish too? I can't hear an accent.'

I have been. 'No, I'm American. Look, as much as you might enjoy pajama parties with unwilling participants, can you just get on with what you need to say and leave already?'

'Okay, darlin', I'll get on with it.' A flash of that vagabond's smile and the Irish thickened in his voice. Straightening, he began murmuring again in that odd language of his. Cold seeped into the warm bedroom, smelling of starlight and winter woods. With my palm over my right wrist, I gripped the bracelet to my skin.

Go away, my mind whispered. What to do? I let my eyelids droop, hoping he would think that his method was working.

'Did you tell anyone?' he asked in a coaxing tone.

'No,' I replied softly.

'Good girl. It's almost a shame,' he murmured, reaching out to tuck a tendril of hair behind my ear. 'Sorry, darlin'. No harm. You won't remember anything past the hallway. Lie down and sleep.'

I paused, then shuffled down in the duvet as if in passive obedience. Two fingers touched my forehead. 'Finished.'

I waited to hear the door click but there was no noise. I waited some more until my body was screaming at me to check he'd really gone. Gingerly, I opened my eyes and scanned the room, every shadow by the closet, every dubious space by the window. All appeared empty. I fumbled for the light but it still didn't click on. Then I remembered that I had disconnected it to charge my phone.

Swearing, I replaced the plug in the power outlet and finally had the light I craved.

It was okay now. He was gone. And he thought it had worked. As long as he believed I knew nothing, he would leave me alone.

SATURDAY MORNING BREAKFAST was usually a thinly attended event as many chose a lie-in over pancakes and cereal; Sian and Jack always did. There would be no lingering in bed for me though. I hadn't slept again after my nighttime visit and itched to get out of my room. I felt so uncomfortable in a house containing Quinn. I hurried across the school green to the hall to join the people who were up and about, wanting normality around me. Questions circled my brain. How had he got in through a locked door? Was his chanting real or playacting? If real, had Sian's bracelet deterred it? Or was it a form of hypnotism to which I was resistant? What was he really doing in the school?

One thing was clear: I'd have to pretend that I had forgot everything that had passed between us last evening and night.

Entering the dining room, I discovered I'd made another miscalculation. Quinn was already in occupation; his court, for that was what it looked like to me, was growing as more and more Crowthorne students and a few from Eaglestone joined in. I could hear them planning a day of amusements for him – water polo, pool in the games room, movie in the evening in the little theater students could book out when not needed for plays or concerts. They were really rolling out the red carpet for him. The head boy from Falconbury House moved his tray to sit opposite Quinn when someone got up to go. That just left Hawkfield untouched by Quinn mania. Maybe I should put in for a house transfer? No point, I mused, there wasn't enough time left to make it worth it.

Using the broad frame of one of the football team for cover as I moved through the canteen, I fixed a plate and chose a seat at the far end of the room near some freshmen who were too intent on trading football stories to notice me. It was hard to shake the feeling that this time was going to be particularly difficult – I have developed a sixth sense for how well it would unfold. Term ended in a week. The school would empty and I'd be here alone waiting for the Grim Reaper. I suppose a few staff would still be on site and they'd make an effort to see I was looked after by someone – at least nominally – but unless other students had been abandoned by their families, I'd essentially be Robinson Crusoe stranded on a cold island of a school campus waiting to die.

What would the school do when they discovered a boarder dead on 1st January?

As if my thoughts had summoned her, the deputy head came into the hall.

'Linny, good, I'm glad you're awake. I need a word with you after breakfast? I'll be in my office.' A slim African-American lady, she held herself like a column supporting the school roof. It was impossible to imagine her unbending.

'Yes, Mrs Rainbuck.'

She headed back to her room. It must be Mrs Rainbuck's weekend on duty. No lessons, but the school was open for sports on Saturday mornings. I could see that the long-distance runners were fueling up with a cooked breakfast so some students clearly intended not to let freezing temperatures deter them.

Threading my tray of uneaten cereal in the rack for dirty

plates, I followed the deputy head out. I glanced up to the
top of the room. Quinn lounged back in his chair, peeling an
orange with his long fingers while keeping the rind in one
piece. With a grin at his admirers, he coiled it on the table to
form the empty shape of the fruit once more.

'Mrs Rainbuck?'

'Linny, take a seat.'

I sat down on the chair across the desk from her. The
long tree-lined drive stretched out behind her, marred by a
few tire tracks. Staff cars, four-wheel drives only, lined up in
the nearly empty parking lot.

She laced her fingers together on the manila file in front
of her. Her nails were painted silver to match the color of
her hair which had gone prematurely white. 'Have you
spoken yet to your mother?'

'Yes.'

'She rang me yesterday and explained the situation. I
said we'd be delighted to have you as our guest over Christmas. Mr Huntsman will be staying over the holidays so
Crowthorne will be open. His daughter will be visiting him.
You won't need to move out.'

I nodded.

'And we'll make sure you have fun during the break.
There will be four other students staying on – another in
your house and three Chinese students from Hawkfield.
Mrs Bailey is arranging a trip to see a circus in Rockland.'

I hated the circus – or at least the modern form of it.
Without the excitement of big animals, a circus is just a
dance show, at least that's what one of my old dads used to
say. I guess it is less cruel now though. Maybe it was time I
updated my views? Still didn't mean I had to like it. 'Is that
optional?'

'Of course!' Mrs Rainbuck shuffled the papers on her

desk awkwardly. 'And on Christmas Day itself, one of the staff will invite you to share the meal with their family. We've not worked out who yet.' She meant that they hadn't roped in a volunteer as yet.

'That's very kind, but I really don't need looking after.'

'You will because there's no food service in hall that day.'

'I can microwave something.'

'Dinner will be provided – as will other fun opportunities.' She announced this with the finality of an auctioneer bringing down her hammer on a deal.

'Is there anything else, Miss?'

'Not for the moment.'

I got up. 'Just out of interest, who else is staying on in Crowthorne?'

She swung in her chair to open a filing cabinet, already moving on to more important matters. 'The new student, Quinn Ramsay. Didn't I say?'

7

JUGGLING

Jack was playing the grand piano in the music room when I got back to Crowthorne. He was still in his pajamas, hair stuck up on end, pencil tucked behind his ear – composing mode.

'You missed breakfast, Jack.'

'Hunh.'

I wasn't going to get much sense out of him. 'Where's Sian?'

He made a note on the stave. Work on my theme looked like it was going well. 'Said she had to research something so went to the library to use the computers.' The Wi-Fi is notoriously feeble in Crowthorne House, particularly on a Saturday with everyone trying to use it at once.

I hovered behind him, wanting to tell him about my scare of the night before, but how would that go? *The new boy broke into my room and tried to wipe my memory again.* Jack would be furious and would show it when he next met Quinn. I could only keep my friends safe if Quinn believed what I'd told him: that I'd not spoken about our trip around the boundary. Mentally, I zipped my lips. This situation wouldn't last long enough to matter all that much. 'I'll see you both later then.'

'Yep.' Jack ran through a phrase, took it down a semi-tone, lost in music land.

I went into the common room. It was curiously empty, which suited me. I picked up the paper I'd never got to the night before, curled up in a saggy armchair and began to read, selecting items about places where I used to live. Occasionally I'd come across names of descendants of people I once knew.

After fifteen minutes or so, the front door banged and voices chattered in the hallway – excited about something. I picked out a phrase or two.

'Snowball fight at midday. On the sports field.'

The fresh fall was sending everyone into hyperdrive. I folded the page to read about a boy chess champion from Queens. I think I knew his grandmother. She'd been a smart cookie.

Students trooped into the common room en masse, Quinn carried along in their middle. They settled, crows in a wheat field, on every available surface as there were not enough seats to go around.

'We've an hour before the fight. Cards anyone?' asked Charlie. 'Quinn?'

'What's your game?'

'Poker. Do you play?' Charlie was already shuffling the pack.

Quinn lolled back balancing his chair on two legs. 'No. Never had the chance. Dad's not into gambling.'

'I can show you.'

Letting Charlie teach you was like allowing the wolf to instruct the lamb how to make meat pie. I hid behind my paper, ready to be amused.

'Maybe later. Not sure I have the concentration for it now. Here, can you do any card tricks with that pack?'

'Like what?'

Quinn took them and flipped the cards in an arc, one hand to another.

'Cool! Can you do any others?'

Quinn just grinned. He fanned the cards out then snapped them shut. When he opened them again, every other card had turned around, creating a new pattern.

'How did you...? Wow.'

Quinn closed the pack. 'Hey, darlin', breathe on this for me?' he asked the girl crowding his elbow. Giggling, she did as he asked. 'Perfect.' When he opened the fan, the cards had gone back to face the same direction.

'I've never seen anyone do that before,' admitted Charlie.

'Wasn't me that time. It was my lovely assistant. What's your name, sweetheart?'

'Genny.' Genevieve should know better than to put on that airhead giggle: she was the best in our year at Chemistry.

'It's Genny who has the magic touch.' Quinn replaced the pack on the table.

'Seriously, how did you do that?' asked Charlie.

'Ah, that'd be telling.'

'Yeah – so go on.'

'Can't. It's a secret. Handed down from generation to generation in my family.'

'You're like, what? Members of the Magic Circle?'

'More like circus performers, always on tour.' Quinn shrugged as the students murmured appreciatively. 'You should see my brothers. They're way better than me at tricks.'

I laid the paper aside, meaning to slip out. I noticed that he hadn't said they *were* circus folk, just that they were like them, but I don't think anyone else had realized the difference. I'd been in a circus once too, in the heyday of such things in New England at the turn of the century – twentieth, I think, just before the Great War.

'Can any of you do anything?' Quinn asked. 'Any tricks?' He reached out and pulled a gold coin from behind Genny's ear – a chocolate one. He gave it to her.

'No way, not like you,' said Charlie.

'Everyone can do something when you apply a little persuasive power. They're just waiting for the chance to be made to show it.' Quinn went to the door. 'How about a game where no one enters or leaves until they do something – a corny joke, dance move, anything?'

The suggestion was met with cries of mock despair and laughter. Why was he doing this? I wondered. It was an uneasy form of leadership to push people out of their comfort zone. The common room was supposed to be for all of us; entry and exit wasn't in anyone's gift. I didn't want to be caught in this net so stayed in my seat, hoping I was invisible.

'I can walk on my hands,' offered one younger boy, proceeding to demonstrate. He got generous applause.

A girl in senior year came in carrying a mug of coffee. Charlie took it from her.

'Show us what you can do, Helen,' he urged her.

She looked around the ring of faces. 'What do you mean?'

'In or out you have to do some kind of trick or talent – Quinn's new rule.'

'Just for this morning, darlin',' Quinn reassured her with his megawatt smile.

'Oh, okay then.' She belted out the first verse of a power ballad. Helen was the star of most school concerts.

Quinn punched the air. 'Yes! That's what I mean. I knew there were hidden depths to all of you.'

She retrieved her mug. 'Not so hidden in my case. Quinn, isn't it? You're new?'

I didn't want to be here any longer, not now Quinn had turned it into a three-ring circus act.

'What about you, darlin'?' He had noticed me edging my way to the other door leading to the study.

'No, not playing. I can't do anything.'

'Linny, isn't it?' He clicked his fingers as if just remembering my name. 'You showed me where to hang up my coat yesterday.'

I looked down. 'Yes.'

'Everyone can do something. Look at Alfie and Helen.' He waved to the first two of his star turns.

I took a step towards the door but now a couple of boys were blocking it, grinning back at Quinn.

Charlie shook his head. 'Bad choice for a victim, Quinn. Linny does not join in stuff. Maybe her talent is being a fantastic Not-Joiner-Inner?' The suggestion was met with laughter. I appreciated that Charlie was trying to let me off the hook.

'Ah no, the punters won't pay to see that. Tell us a joke, Linny.' Quinn was using his coaxing voice but I didn't feel like falling into step to amuse him.

'Linny? Be funny?' guffawed Charlie. The thought of me cracking a joke had the laughter redoubling.

I was feeling very angry now. This was supposed to be our space, not just Quinn's.

'This is dumb. You all make fools of yourself over him; I don't want to.'

'Spoilsport. Then a quick dance move? Everyone has one of those.' Quinn did a spin and a sideways slide to arrive at my side. It was met with whoops and whistles.

'Lin-ny! Lin-ny! Lin-ny!' The others began chanting, thumping tables and the top of the piano.

I met Quinn's eyes. For all the smiles he gave everyone, there was something cruel about his expression. The coldness of a bird of prey.

'You're a bully.'

'Ow! Now she's hurt my feelings!' He appealed to the crowd. 'And I thought it was just a bit of fun. All I wanted was to see what everyone was made of.'

'Satisfied?'

'That you're made of no fun? Why, yes, I suppose I am.' He turned away, dismissing me.

I'd show him. Angry beyond words, I grabbed the fruit from the bowl on the table and began juggling. 'Throw me another,' I said tersely to a stunned-looking Charlie. Scrambling he picked an apple and tossed it to my right hand. It joined the circle. 'Another.'

'Now this is more like it!' Quinn leaned back against the sofa, arms folded.

'Catch, circus boy!' I threw one of my six objects at him, snapping him to attention. He didn't drop it but tossed it lightly back to me. I threw another, then another, more rapidly. He juggled them.

'Charlie, give her more,' he ordered, having to concentrate now.

Charlie raided the mantelpiece and added a couple of fir cones to our display.

A space cleared around us. Neither of us could stop now as we had too many objects whizzing in the air in a complex crisscross pattern only we understood. Why was I doing this? I was showing off a skill that I had kept private this time round. I didn't like people to know my full range of eclectic talents.

'Do you know the fountain?' Quinn asked.

My reply was to send the objects shooting up at the same moment he sent his. We swapped sides and resumed our pattern.

'How about this?' Charlie threw a cushion at me, which flopped to the floor before I could get my fingers to it. My side of the pattern collapsed, oranges and apples hitting the carpet. 'Oops – my bad!' moaned Charlie.

'You should see what I can do with knives.' I tossed the cushion at Quinn and left before anyone could stop me.

A LITTLE TAP at the door heralded Sian's return.

'Hey.'

I rolled over onto my stomach, legs waving in the air. 'Hey yourself. Where've you been all morning?'

'In the library.'

'So studious?'

'Yeah.' She entered, Jack at her elbow. 'I was looking up boundaries. It's a complicated subject.'

Quinn didn't seem to respect any of mine. 'I bet it is.'

'Will anyone come with me to see what he planted?' asked Sian, looking between the two of us.

'Seriously?' said Jack. 'We get only a couple of days off where we can hibernate in this snug warm house and you want to go back out in that? I love you, Sian, I really do, but not that much.'

'I'll come. I think I can remember exactly where he placed a couple of them,' I replied, forcing myself to get up off the bed.

Jack groaned. 'You're making me look bad. I suppose I'll have to go too now.'

'But we have to make sure he doesn't see us,' I warned.

'Don't worry – I checked,' said Sian. 'Everyone's caught up in the snowball fight.'

Out on the boundary walk, snow had continued steadily to build. The seeds Quinn had dropped on the ground would be impossible to locate. I took my friends to the patch of wall that I remembered well from the evening before. With Jack keeping watch, Sian and I hauled ourselves up on the ivy to the top and brushed off the snow. A little dark blue berry nestled between the stones. I reached out to pick it out but Sian stopped me by grabbing my wrist.

'We can't touch it.'

'Why? It's just a berry.'

'Yeah, but a berry from the deadly nightshade plant – and put there with a powerful incantation. The berry itself is poisonous; with the spell it's lethal.'

Deadly nightshade. I'd once, many centuries ago, worked in a convent herb garden. Sister Francis, our plant expert, called it by its Latin name, *Atropa Belladonna* – *Atropa* after Atrope, one of the thread-cutting fates of Greek mythology; *Belladonna* because the drug made your pupils dilate attractively – until it killed you, that is.

The last thing I wanted was to trigger another curse so drew my hand back. 'Why did he put it here?'

'To make a royal enclosure.'

I smiled bitterly. 'A what? Like for the Queen of England? Hats, heels and champagne at the races?'

'No. Not for that kind of royal family – for the other-world type.' Two frown marks bracketed the top of her nose. 'And I should've said royal defensive wall.'

'You're pulling my leg?'

'No, Linny, I'm not.'

'You're going to tell me it's part of your woo-woo stuff, aren't you?' I'd always tried to avoid that over the centuries seeing how much harm it had done me in the beginning.

She shrugged helplessly. 'Would you prefer me to lie? It looks like we've just taken delivery of a member of what we call the Sidhe, the fey folk. It's pronounced 'sith' but spelt s, i, d, h, e.'

I knew them far too well to need her guide to pronunciation. 'This isn't good.'

'I think Quinn must be Fey royalty.'

'My number one enemy?' I began to laugh in despair. 'I only have a few weeks left. I'm always gone by the time I reach my sixteenth birthday on 1st January. Regular as clockwork – bolt from the blue, terminal illness, unfortunate accident – I think I've sampled every way of dying but suicide. And now this time they've come to enjoy the show.' That explained his tormenting of me in the common room. He was playing with me, like a cat a mouse. Hadn't the Sidhe had enough of revenge by now?

Sian carefully buried the berry again, patting the top flat. 'I don't think he knows.'

'Hey, what's keeping you two? I'm freezing my butt off down here,' called Jack.

We ignored him. 'What do you mean?'

'I found out today from my research that the charm requires a male and female presence to work.'

'You mean he was using me to do his spell thing?'

'Yes. But it would've been much easier to pick another girl, not one who would've learned to resist mind tricks over the years. One of the younger ones would've been much easier to influence.'

'But he didn't.'

'No, and now he'll be wondering just why you were able to push him away. Maybe he thought you were younger? I take it he was exerting some pretty heavy-duty power?'

I remembered the unnatural chill that had gone deep into the bones and nodded.

'And the circle is set. I can't do anything to him while he is inside it.'

'Come on!' wailed Jack.

'But your bracelet worked, well, like a charm.'

'What do you mean?'

'Don't tell Jack, but Quinn tried again last night but I held him off with it. I let him think the forgetting spell had worked though.'

Sian shook her head. 'That doesn't sound right. It shouldn't work against him, not with the circle in place. None of my powers should.'

A snowball hit me in the small of the back.

'Look, you might think it fun to sit up there like a couple of robins on a Christmas card but I'm turning into a human popsicle.'

'Okay, okay, we're coming down, whinge-bucket!' said Sian, pushing herself off the top and landing lightly in the drift of snow that had gathered at the foot of the wall.

I stayed for a moment, facing the fretful sea. The salt meant that snowfall melted and the beach was clear where wave met sand, a pale-yellow strip between water and the dunes. That's what my life had become – a fragile clear space before I left firm footing again and joined the boundless possibilities of my next wavelike return.

I was so tired of this existence, too experienced even to hope that the arrival of a Sidhe would make any difference. Whatever he or anyone else did, I'd remain hundreds of years old but never more than fifteen.

8

SNAKE OR SPIDER?

That night, after lights out, Sian and I retreated to her room to discuss my situation in more depth. We couldn't do it in front of Jack – he just didn't believe in anything that couldn't be explained by reason so charms and curses were well beyond him.

'You know you were the first person I'd told about the curse in...' I ran my past lives through my head in quick review, 'in about five hundred years.'

Sian was sewing a scarlet and silver square onto the knitted patchwork rug – one of her many craft projects.

'You were bound to come across someone like me eventually.'

'It'll be a long time before I do again, I expect. There are so few of your kind left.'

'But plenty of imitations, I know. Mom says the same. How do you think it will go this time?' The advantage of Sian's upbringing was that she knew the power of Sidhe curses, and accepted that a small-time charm worker like her would never be able to counteract them. Her attitude was a comfort as I'd been through the cycles of frantic attempts to break the curse before and had no energy for that any longer, even with a helpmate.

'I don't know. Illness was most often the cause in the past but modern medicine makes that less likely. Doubtful that I will be shipwrecked or set on by highwaymen.'

'True.' She smiled at my gallows humor.

'Though I suppose a plane crash might've been on the cards had my mother booked me a flight with the family.'

'What do you mean?'

'My parents – and the twins – they're going to Australia for Christmas.'

'But they'll be back for New Year, surely?'

'Apparently not.'

She dropped her rug on the floor and came to kneel in front of me. 'Oh, Linny, I'm sorry.'

'Don't be. Maybe my mom has a point. I've not always been the only one to die.'

'Where will you be then?'

I shrugged.

'Here? Alone? No, no, we can't have that. I'll stay. I'll tell Mom that you need me. She'll understand.'

Mrs Willowbrook didn't entirely approve of Sian's friendship with me. Her kind, what centuries ago we used to call hedge witches or wise women, survived by not attracting attention to themselves from the Sidhe. Fey magic nobility did not appreciate ordinary humans muscling in on 'their' territory. Having me die on her daughter's watch would bring a spotlight to bear on Sian – and that might expose the Willowbrooks to their foes, especially now Quinn was in residence.

'Sian, there's no need. I'm used to it.' That was a lie: I never got used to it. 'You can't risk your family.'

Sian bit her lip. 'I'll talk to Jack.'

'Don't involve him. It'll be bad enough as it is without him being the one to find my body. I couldn't do that to him. I'll be fine. Maybe I'll just go to sleep and not wake up, at least not for a few decades?'

'You promise to seek me out when you return? I don't care how long it is, if I'm still alive I want you to call me as soon as you remember.'

'You'll be on standby for a little five-year-old babbling what others think is nonsense, will you?'

'You bet. I'll even adopt you if I can.'

That made me laugh, then cry a little, which was what I needed. I didn't cry much anymore. The first few deaths had been the most upsetting because I'd still had hope. I'd come to see that Father's offense had been ridiculously minor – killing a sacred white hart with an ill-timed arrow – but the Fey King's vengeance had been major. I'm not sure what happened to my original family, to Wren and Finch, though I've heard rumors over the years. I do know that I, as the eldest, was the first to go. My decline from the day the curse began was dramatic and public, a rapid withering away in front of my father's people as a warning to others what would happen if they dared stand up to the Sidhe. Looking back with the benefit of twenty-first century hindsight, I'd say I probably contracted a disease that attacked the immune system. I passed away on the eve before my sixteenth birthday.

The next thing I remember was slowly coming to the realization of who I really was a generation later. I'd been born in a different part of England and, despite my attempts to return to my home, I hadn't been allowed. The arguments I'd had with my second set of parents were famous in our village but I could understand why they refused to let me go. Travel was so dangerous and difficult then. I hadn't known that time was short. I'd foolishly thought I'd been given a second chance. I imagined that, when I was an adult, I might get back to see my parents in their old age, or my sisters in their prime. Yeah well, like that was going to happen. I just don't get the breaks. Instead I was killed during a Viking raid, slaughtered on a beach much like the one beyond the wall. My last memory was of the cold sea washing against my fingers as the life drained from me.

And so, it happened again.

And again.

And again. After many attempts at breaking the curse using methods from the superstitious to the scientific, I eventually gave up. I had a spell in the twelfth and thirteenth centuries where I went wild, living each life in a spree of reckless behavior. Many of those deaths were the result of criminal executions or abandonment by my community. I wised up and realized that a wild life leading to a miserable end was not the way to go. I had to steel myself for a long haul. I spent the returns in the later centuries of the last millennium gathering skills, like languages, piano playing and juggling. That helped pass the time constructively. I discovered some talents stuck, some faded with that life – it was impossible to predict. Depression set in during the nineteenth century when I had several experiences of extreme poverty. I've not really recovered.

You know what my biggest problem is? I can't see the point to my chain of life sentences. The only reason I've not tried to end it prematurely is I know that I'll just come back. Yo-Yo girl – that's me. Why rush it?

And maybe, there is still a glimmer of hope, the merest ember, that this will be the last time. That's the hardest part of all, the biggest cheat I play on my own heart.

. . .

I HANDED in my English essay along with everyone else on Monday. I had a moment's regret, the kind you get when you send an insulting message and want to call it back. I was getting that reckless feeling I experience when I know my links to this time are loosening. I was beginning to expose my peculiarities without caring what people thought about me. I had even committed them to paper.

I kept my head down over my civil war poetry assignment as Miss King marked our essays. She was still for a very long time, no darts launched from her desk, no prowling of the room to check we were still on task.

Towards the end of the lesson, she got up and began returning the essays to each student, murmuring a few words of praise or pointers where to improve. We are the top form so her standards are high. She saved mine until last, putting it down on my desk without a word. I turned to the back page. A note in red was scrawled across the bottom. *Where did you copy this from? Plagiarism is not smart. See me.*

I did see her with twenty twenty vision, but did she see me at all? Another miscalculation of mine: she hadn't believed it was my own work.

The bell rang and Sian got up to go.

'Coming?'

I grimaced. 'Can't. She wants to see me about my essay.'

'You really don't want to spend what's left of term in detention with her. Make up an excuse,' Sian whispered. 'I'll get you a hot chocolate from the canteen. See you in our usual corner.'

I waited for the room to empty. Here we are again, just the two of us, I was tempted to quip, but restrained myself.

'Linny, where did you get that material from?' Miss King asked, cutting straight to the chase. 'I can do an internet search with plagiarism software so you might as well come clean now.'

'It's not copied.'

'Nonsense. You write like you were there. You must've got it from a biography, or a diary. If it's original research, then I applaud you, but it reads so fluently I can't help but think you've copied a historian's account of the period, or a historical novel.'

'It's all my own work. Feel free to run whatever checks you like.'

She slammed the pile of books she was holding on the desk in front of me. 'That's exactly the kind of attitude that gets you into trouble. You bait us time and time again with your arrogance. Well, Linnet Grace, I am decades older than you and I know every trick in the book. If – when – I find out from where you've stolen your essay, you'll be on report as fast as you can say "Mary Shelley".'

'Or alternatively you could give me a merit for original work?'

She snatched the books up and stormed out.

'No merit then.' I gathered my files and followed her out into the corridor.

'Here, Linny, catch!'

A pencil case winged in from my left and struck me on the cheek.

'You're supposed to juggle it, you moron!' called Raymond, an Eaglestone boy from the baseball team who had bowled it at me underarm. His friends were laughing. 'Try again.' He lobbed a sneaker in my direction and I found myself under a barrage of hand-sized objects from all directions. I held my files up to shield my face.

'Stop it!' Some of the impacts were bruising.

'Come on, show us what you can do!' jeered Raymond.

Just when I thought it couldn't get any worse, that they'd have to give up, Jack came running down the corridor. 'What the hell do you think you're doing?' He pushed the ringleader in the chest, rapping him against the wall.

'I want to see her juggle,' Raymond said weakly, more shocked I think by seeing Jack go into Avenger mode than by the force of the shove.

'Say sorry to Linny.' Jack got right up in the kid's grid.

Raymond was recovering. 'Push off, dork.'

'Apologize!'

'Jack, it doesn't matter,' I said, scared now for my friend who was taking on the school jocks.

'It does.'

Swiftly, Raymond reversed their positions, pushing Jack up against the wall, forearm at his throat. 'I say she juggles or we'll have this out right here, right now.'

'Don't you dare, Linny! I can take him!' shouted Jack, seeing me hesitate over the things lying at my feet.

'What's going on?' The lazily amused voice wasn't the member of staff I had prayed for but Quinn, sauntering along the corridor with two of his new groupies, Charlie and Genny.

Raymond dropped his grip on Jack's neck. 'Nothing, Quinn.'

Quinn stopped in the space between the baseball team boys and me. 'It doesn't look like nothing. Are you all right?'

I nodded, not meeting his gaze.

'You'd better pick up those things,' said Quinn coolly to my assailants. 'Playtime is over.'

'Yes, Quinn.' Obediently the boys scooped up their belongings and ran off, leaving Jack and me. Jack crossed the corridor and put his arms around me, letting my head rest on his shoulder.

'What got into them?' he asked. 'You? Juggle? Have they gone crazy?'

Quinn rolled his eyes. 'Jay-sus. So, they wanted her to do her act? Then this is partly my fault. Linny, I'll have a word with them. It won't happen again.' He held out his hand to Jack. 'We've not met. I'm Quinn.'

Jack shook it reluctantly. 'Jack Burne.'

Quinn moved on. 'Like the scarf, Jack.'

My friend flushed and tucked his Crowthorne scarf under his jacket. 'Was he being ironic?'

'No, I don't think so.'

'*Do* you juggle?'

'What do you think?'

Jack took my arm. 'With you, I never know what to expect.'

'QUINN DEFENDED YOU?' asked Sian at lunch. Jack had retold our tale, adding a grudging admission that his own intervention hadn't been enough to save me from ritual humiliation in the corridor.

'He's not as bad as I thought,' Jack reflected.

'Just because he's good-looking and admired your scarf,' I said darkly. 'The Mighty Quinn strikes again.'

Jack was gazing with something like longing at the crowd of 'in' people surrounding Quinn. 'He seemed...okay to me. Maybe you got the wrong idea when he took you for a walk? He was just teasing.' Catching his tone, I had the unwanted premonition that next term, when I was gone, that Jack would also be sucked into the vortex around the newcomer.

Sian stuck her fork in the back of his hand.

'Ouch! What was that for?' He glared at her and rubbed the offended spot.

'That boy has charisma.'

'I know.' Jack sighed.

'It's a kind of charm.' Jack narrowed his eyes so Sian shifted her terminology. 'An act, deliberate, like a snake hypnotizing prey. You are not looking at a nice new boy attracting friends but a spider luring people into his web.'

Jack crumpled up his juice carton. 'I thought you said he was a snake?'

'Snake, spider? Same difference. He is dangerous, Jack. Steer clear.'

I pushed aside another uneaten meal. A headache pounded at my temples. 'He's staying at school over Christmas.'

Sian went pale. 'You didn't mention that last night! You can't be here alone with him.'

'I'll stay,' said Jack swiftly.

'You're going skiing,' I reminded him.

'Oh, yeah.'

'Sian, don't worry. It won't matter, not in the end.'

She met my eyes, misery in her expression, but she probably read the resignation in mine. 'Okay, if you say so.'

'He will hardly know I'm here,' I promised her. 'I'm thinking of spending the time catching up on my reading.' I'd taught myself Estonian on this visit and had some poetry in that language I wanted to read. Languages were another talent that stayed with me, the most useful one.

'You make it very difficult to be a good friend to you.' She stacked my things on her tray.

'No, I don't, because you two are the best friends I've ever had.'

9

GOODBYES ARE THE WORST

Over the next week of Christmas parties and concerts, I deliberately withdrew into myself. Miss King had not been able to prove I'd cheated (I hadn't) so we maintained a frosty politeness in lessons and I gave no more betraying flourishes of my knowledge of the past in English or anywhere else. In fact, I barely spoke. Sian gave me lots of hugs but respected that I needed to, well, disengage, I suppose you'd say. Jack was furious, telling me to snap out of it, saying he was going to rip up 'Linnet's theme' if I didn't take more interest in what was going on around me. I could see I was hurting him but didn't know how I could make it better. This whole situation really was hopeless and I was sliding into a deeper and deeper depression. Maybe it was better that he left for his skiing trip annoyed with me?

And if he did rip up his song, I mused, he'd probably only have to dig it out of the trashcan again for my funeral.

My brain was full of morbid thoughts like that.

The staff concern about my mood grew to the point where I was summoned to have a coffee with Mr Huntsman.

Pastoral care was not his strong suit and they only resorted to this in extremis; but no other teacher had got close to me, so as the housemaster, he was in the crosshairs.

'Linny, we're worried about you.' This was the first thing he said after handing me a cup of coffee that I didn't even like.

'No need to be, sir.'

'We all understand that being left behind by your parents over Christmas must have a depressing effect on anyone's spirits.'

'I'm over it.'

'Hmm.' He played with the spoon on his saucer. 'Cookie?' He waved at the tin, which was decorated with blue and red tessellated butterflies, a pattern that made my eyes ache.

'No thank you.'

'We've noticed that you're not eating – not enough. Many girls – not just girls – but mostly girls of your age go through a stage when they have an eating disorder. I've got some reading material here for you.' He awkwardly pushed some information leaflets towards me.

I picked them up and put them on my lap. 'Thanks.'

'So do you think that might be part of your problem?'

My problem was that I would be dead in two weeks' time. 'No.'

'If there are any, er, female concerns that you want to discuss with anyone, the nurse's door is always open.' If his gaunt face could blush it would be doing so now. 'And I've had a message from the school counselor. She wants you to go to see her in January for some sessions, to help with all that.'

'Fine.'

The teaspoon dropped with a clink. 'You agree?'

'Yes.'

'But your mother said you refused any help before.'

'Yes.'

'So what changed?'

I shrugged. I couldn't tell him nothing had changed. 'Is that a fritillary butterfly you've got there?' I gestured to the fragile creature lying under a glass dome on his desk.

'Oh, oh you know your butterflies, I see?' He beamed at me, all talk of eating disorders forgotten. 'I hadn't realized you take an interest.'

'I had a very good teacher.' A governess in the early nineteenth century in London, which was why I met Mary Shelley in the graveyard. We had been moth collecting.

'This is a rare species. I didn't catch this myself but a colleague of mine spotted it for sale and knew my collection was missing one. Would you like to watch me mount it with the others?'

It was cute I suppose that he thought observing him stick a pin through the dead body of a beautiful creature would cheer me up.

'I think I'll leave you to it. It looks like delicate work and I've homework to do.'

'All right then.' He sounded relieved. It was clearly a special moment for him and I was touched he had been prepared to make the sacrifice and share it with me. 'I'll let you see it when I've finished.' He got up to show me out. 'My daughter, Rowena, arrives tomorrow night. I've already told her that you and that new boy will be staying for the holidays and she's eager to meet you. Dinner after everyone leaves on Friday? We'll all need the boost I would think.'

I smiled my agreement. I hadn't realized that Mr Huntsman actually missed the hubbub in the house when we weren't there.

'We'll see you up in my private quarters at seven then.'
He shut the door before I could think of a polite refusal.

THERE WAS a special quality to the noise in the school on the
last day of term. With parents arriving to collect their kids,
voices rose to a high pitch, like seagulls. The snow was still
lying on the grounds, topped up by another fall, so the
driveways were scored with the passages of many sets of
wheels, sports fields pocked with footprints. Snowmen
slumped with neglect as their makers headed off home.

Sian brought her mom to find me to say goodbye. I was
sitting on the window seat in the corner of the study, hidden
behind the curtain like Jane Eyre in the first chapter of the
book. My soul lay in jagged pieces, feeling as if it were a
shattered mirror only just held by its frame.

'Oh, Linny, sweetie!' said Mrs Willowbrook, 'Sian broke
the news to me. I'm so sorry, my dear.' She pulled me to her
chest, my cheek rubbing up against her strings of beads and
knitted scarf ends. Her hair, once as red as her daughter's,
was now a shocking white like a puff of cloud around her
head. Sian had said that was a result of a close encounter
with the Sidhe, but refused to give the details.

My friend looked like she had been crying. 'Mom, there
has to be something we can do for her?'

Ah, so Sian hadn't entirely avoided the unrealistic hope
train I had traveled on board so many times.

'It's okay, Mrs Willowbrook, I know there isn't. Believe
me, I've tried everything.'

She ran through many of the wise woman methods of
dealing with curses and I ticked off every item on her list.

'You *have* tried everything I see.' She kissed her daughter
on the top of the head. 'I'm sorry, but I can't think of

anything else to say. I have heard that these kinds of curses can only be taken back by the original maker or their descendants. A fragment of their life force is bound up in it so as long as people of their blood survive the curse will survive.'

'I know. I had hoped during the Black Death – you know the one which killed half of Europe including myself, twice? – I had hoped then that maybe the plague would get them all, but some of them must've escaped.'

'The Sidhe don't get killed by human catastrophes like that. They wipe each other out in their interminable wars, but nothing we can do usually harms them. I'd say that you have had very bad luck.' She framed my face with her hand. 'But you'll be back?'

'Yes.'

'It's a kind of immortality, isn't it? Many would kill to be in your shoes.'

'And then kill to get out of them. Believe me, it rapidly gets old not getting old.'

'Sian wants to stay with you.'

'But you mustn't let her. Sometimes the curse takes out those around me. And there's a boy here, Quinn Ramsay. He mustn't notice her. He's already run across me a couple of times.'

'The Sidhe. Yes, she told me about him.' Mrs Willowbrook gave me a wicked little smile. 'Well then, maybe you could do us all a favor and take him out with you?'

'Mom!' said Sian.

'Ah yes, the protective spell on the boundary.'

'That's not what I meant. Quinn might be Sidhe but he's not done anything so bad as to die for it.'

'Neither has Linny. Sorry, darlings, but I find any discussion of that kind brings out my worst side. Don't fool yourselves, girls: no Sidhe has a heart. He might seem pleasant but he is pure ice and snow. It's the price they pay for their magic.' Mrs Willowbrook hugged me again, this time with solemn finality. 'I'm sorry I can't help you this time. When you come back, find us. Sian and I will spend the intervening years researching, looking for ways to help you. This wheel you're on must be stopped somehow, some day.'

'Thank you. But it's not your responsibility.'

'No, but it is what we do for those we love.'

Sian squeezed me tightly. 'I'll call.'

'Maybe you'd better not?' I suggested with a lump in my throat.

'Shut up. I'm calling you every day and you will pick up!'

'Or what?'

'Or I'll kill you.' We both laughed grimly at that. Tears pouring down her face, she pressed a squashy package in my hand. 'Your present. For now – and for afterwards. Wait until I'm gone though. You can open it Christmas morning.'

MY FAREWELL to Jack was much harder because he did not know. Trying to be normal with him was excruciating.

'Do you think I'm going to suck at skiing?' he asked me as I helped him carry his bags out to the car.

Yes. 'No, of course not.'

'I think I am. But you've got to try everything once, right? Just in case you turn out to be a master at it.'

'That's my philosophy.'

His dad waved at me from the front seat. Jack comes from a family of men with the build of NFL players. Genetics played a funny kind of trick on him giving him the stature of a flyweight boxer.

'You'd better cheer up over the holiday, Linnet Grace, or I'm going to do something drastic in January.'

I dredged up a smile. 'Like what?'

'Release a flock of sheep during the next school football match, or dye the swimming pool red.'

'Go for it.' I smiled again thinking that these could be a couple of harmless gestures done in my memory.

'Love you, Linny.'

'Love you too, Jack. Don't forget that. Stick with Sian, won't you?'

'Don't talk like that – like you won't be here. We'll stick together, the three musketeers.' He thumped his chest.

I didn't have the heart to copy the gesture. Tears were perilously close. 'Stay safe. Goodbye.'

'See you soon. I'll send pictures of my triumph on the slopes!' He drove off with much enthusiastic waving from the window.

I hugged my arms to myself. Jack was one of the last to go. Crowthorne was quiet now. I went back up to my bedroom so I could cry with no one watching. I hadn't lied when I'd said they were the best friends I'd ever made. I'd taken the decision not to avoid friendships this time. I'd avoided them on other visits and the entire life had been miserable and the end no easier.

IN THE HOLLY FORTRESS

Rowena Huntsman opened the door to my soft knock on the dot of seven.

'You must be Linny – welcome!' She wasn't what I expected. Her father always reminded me of a monk of old, one of the scholarly, earnest sort, lost in a library of moldering leather books. Somehow he had produced a daughter with sardonically arched eyebrows over doe brown eyes and swatch of brunette hair. She was dressed in tight grey jeans and a sparkly knit top, probably both designer from their quality. The Huntsman father and daughter were an example of a wizened old nut tree yielding a golden pear, like in the nursery rhyme I used to sing.

'Thanks. Am I the first?' I looked past her, fearful of meeting Quinn again now we were the only student occupants of Crowthorne House.

She moved back, waving me in with an elegant waft of her hand. Now I looked at her harder, she had prominent cheekbones like her father, but built on a smaller feminine scale. 'Just you so far. The new boy – Quinn something? – said he had another engagement. Local friends visiting.'

That was good. If he had people he knew near the school, maybe he'd spend the time with them rather than tripping over me? I relaxed a little as she conducted me into the living room.

I hadn't been in Mr Huntsman's apartment before but I wasn't surprised to find the butterfly theme from his study continued up here. The furnishings had been chosen as a neutral bronze background to his pictures and display cases. Many amazingly detailed photographs had been mounted in charcoal frames so there was barely a patch of wall free.

'Oh wow! These are lovely,' I said. 'I think I prefer these images of the living creatures to the dead ones in the cases.'

'Don't let my father hear you saying that, but thank you.' Rowena handed me a glass of warmed, spiced apple juice. She straightened one photo of a clouded yellow butterfly proprietorially.

'You took these?'

'That's my job, wildlife photographer, so I'm never without an idea for a present for my father.' She grinned at me, looking for a brief moment so much younger and less sophisticated. 'All I need do is go to the nearest patch of wild flowers and wait.'

I wondered where Mrs Huntsman lived, that was if there still was such a person. I couldn't see any sign of a wedding photo and the only family groups were fairly recent ones of just Rowena and her father. If I were a detective I'd probably deduce a painful divorce making older images unpleasant reminders. Sipping my drink, I pondered how to phrase the question that would satisfy my curiosity.

Mr Huntsman came in from the kitchen, wearing – rather surprisingly considering his sober image around the school – a flowered apron. 'Excellent, you're here on time, Linny. I was concerned that the glazed salmon would be overcooked.'

Rowena steered me to the table. 'My father is a secret foodie. You haven't lived until you've tasted one of his home cooked dinners.'

'Oh, I've lived all right,' I murmured.

Still, she was right about one thing. Her father served one of the most delicious meals I'd eaten in many lifetimes: the fish was perfect, accompanied by green beans steamed to just the right tenderness. This was followed by raspberry, white chocolate and pistachio profiteroles built up into a pyramid, almost too pretty to eat. But, don't worry, we sacrificed beauty for our appetites.

My housemaster seemed satisfied his part was done by providing the food, leaving Rowena to make the conversation. She was easy to talk to with lots of stories about the places she had gone as part of her job. Of course, she asked me questions about my ambitions, what I wanted to do after leaving school, all of which I tried to fend off. I didn't think saying I had no need to worry about that kind of thing would go down well. She had a very insistent manner though, so I had to come up with some kind of an answer. What would I do if I could live beyond sixteen? I asked myself. My mouth answered before my brain. I sketched out a future studying History at college – after all, I had a head start there – and possibly having a career making movies about the past to convey what it really was like, not the blinkered account most manage which leaves you with no idea what it was like for most of us to put on damp clothes and trudge to work in fields and factory, belly aching with hunger.

Hearing my enthusiasm for my imaginary future,

Rowena smiled. 'I'm glad I've met someone with her own passion – makes people so much more interesting, don't you think? You need to become a college lecturer then and write some popular history books, make your name.' Rowena offered me the cheese board.

Suddenly, it all seemed so absurd and so very sad. None of this would happen. 'Oh right, I'll do that then.'

She must have heard my bitterness. She patted my wrist. 'Don't be like that, Linny. Someone has to be the next TV documentary maker. Why not you?'

I smiled but hoped she'd change the subject. This was like walking over broken glass in bare feet.

'Tea, coffee?' asked Mr Huntsman, unfolding from his chair in the manner of a music stand, limb by long limb.

'Tea please,' I said quickly.

He nodded and went into the kitchen. Rowena followed with the plates. I could hear snatches of their conversation. He was telling his daughter about my eye for butterflies.

'You've won my father over,' she said on return with some handmade chocolate in a little silver dish. 'He thinks you should go into science, not history.'

'I'll see what happens. I like to keep my options open.'

'Very wise. So, what do you know about the new boy? Father says he's made quite a stir in the house. Must be extreme if he has noticed.'

'Quinn?' He's a Sidhe and casts spells – so tempting to blurt that out but I had to be sensible. 'He's okay, I suppose. Quickly made lots of friends. I'm not one of them.'

She nodded sagely. 'Ah yes, a natural born leader, according to my father, Crowthorne's own Pied Piper. All the teaching staff have noticed. I was hoping to meet this phenomenon tonight.'

'I expect you will soon. There's so few of us in the house now.'

'Maybe I'll catch him tomorrow then.' She smiled with a speculative glint in her eye. I wondered if her father had also mentioned that Quinn was a magnet for the girls in Crowthorne. That didn't seem the kind of thing Mr Huntsman would drop into casual conversation. They must be slightly concerned what we might do with no one else around. It would potentially be rather intense for just the two of us if I hadn't already vowed to avoid Quinn like the plague.

Actually, not like the plague, I amended silently, you couldn't avoid that.

Tea drunk, chocolates squeezed into a very full stomach, I got up to go. 'Thank you so much for having me, sir.'

'Our pleasure, Linny,' said Mr Huntsman. 'Do come by whenever you feel lonely. We plan to be here most of the time. Rowena is taking a sabbatical and helping me catalog my collection. You could help.' He looked hopeful.

'Father is donating it to the Museum of Science in Boston.' Rowena was obviously very proud of him.

'Oh, that's great, isn't it?' I said tentatively.

'It certainly is. You've probably noticed but it's got too big for him to keep here so he's listened to me and agreed to let others share it.'

Mr Huntsman shook his head in bemusement. 'Your mother never managed to persuade me to part with a single antenna.'

Rowena laughed. 'Well, you know what they say about fathers and their daughters.' She mimed wrapping something around her little finger.

'Quite so. I'm hopeless at saying no to you.' His gaunt face took on as adoring an expression as it was capable.

'Thanks for the offer of helping out. If I find myself at a loose end, I'll come by.' I thought that kinder than a blunt refusal.

'You can't say fairer than that. Goodnight,' said Rowena, showing me out. When we got to the door, she leaned a little closer. 'You can come back without helping with the butterfly count by the way. I'm very good at managing my father's enthusiasm.'

I murmured my thanks, but on my way back to my room, I found myself wondering about her. I kept away from Quinn because he took over other people's lives without so much as a 'by your leave'; Rowena was oddly similar without the magic. She was a little bit too much in control of her father, knowing which buttons to push. I didn't need her to manage how I spent my last few weeks. My resolution to keep myself apart, even from the Huntsmans, held firm.

THE NEXT FEW days passed very quietly. Sian kept her promise and called every day and I had hilarious photos from the slopes in the Rockies of Jack upside down in various snow banks or on his butt on the bottom of a beginner's run. *I do not suck at skiing,* he assured me. *I'm just waiting to hit my groove.*

Dear Jack.

On the Wednesday following the end of term, Sian rang again, but this time she didn't embark on a gentle chitchat.

'I've been thinking, Linny.'

'Uh-oh.'

'I just can't, *can't*, sit here knowing you are dying.'

'I'm not actually dying in the sense that I feel ill or anything.'

'But you know your days are limited. What kind of

friend am I to you to sit here surrounded by Christmas trees and presents and all of my six sisters, who by the way are driving me crazy, when you're on your own? I've decided: either you come here or I come to you.'

I should've foreseen this happening, but I have no magic of my own for fortune telling. I'm just the victim of it.

'I can't come to you. What if one of your family gets hurt in whatever takes me out in the end?'

'Okay, so I'm coming to the school.'

'Please, don't.'

'I am.' I could hear that her mind was made up but I didn't think she really understood the risk.

'Look, Sian, this is nothing new for me. I come back. But what if you die as well? You don't get another chance and I'll have that on my conscience for the rest of my many lives.'

'Stop thinking about yourself like some kind of library book that is taken out and put back on the shelf. You, Linnet Grace, in this life, are precious to me. I'll be with you.'

I thumped my forehead on a cushion. There was no stopping her by words. 'Stay with your family for Christmas. Don't come back until New Year's Eve, okay?' I would have to make sure I was gone before she did.

'That's when the curse falls, right?'

'Yes.'

'Always?'

'Yes.' That was a partial lie. Sometimes I fade a few days or weeks earlier, like that first time, losing consciousness before finally clinically dying on the last day of the year. It all depends what the curse has in store for me. I don't suppose there was a rule stopping me anticipating it. Well, whatever: I'd find out, wouldn't I?

'Okay. I'll tell Mom after Christmas too. No point having her and all my sisters nagging me about this.'

'Bring all the protective charms you can dream up, all right?'

'I'm all over that. Maybe this time I'll find the right combination to save you?'

'Maybe, but please don't hold out any hope. I know what that feels like.'

'You know what I'm always telling you: *Hope is the thing with feathers, that perches in the soul.*' Sian was into Emily Dickinson's poetry, going so far as to embroider it into her patchwork.

'Just bear in mind my hope flew off centuries ago. I wouldn't want to be responsible for that happening to yours.'

Following that disturbing call, I had to get out. I had to think of a way of stopping Sian putting herself in danger for me who was so not worth it. I took advantage of a break in the weather to put on my boots, wrap up in Sian's scarf and go for a walk. One thing I would say about my multiple lifetimes is that the world never fails to astonish me at how beautiful it is. On the last few visits I've noticed that we are spoiling many natural spots. There are, however, still places like Green Drake where you can feel in touch with the old days. I had scouted out a favorite bolthole in the school grounds a few years ago when I first arrived. A huge holly bush, several bushes really, had formed a natural rampart with a clear space in the middle. If you shouldered your way inside, protecting hands and face as best you could, you were left in your own hideaway. The old holly leaves made for a prickly rug so I had long since rolled in a circular log cut from a fallen tree to give me a comfortable place to sit. The enclosure was private and comforting. There was no sign that anything had changed since my first life once I was in the middle of the dark green fort with its flares of red berries.

I sat cross-legged on the log seat, closed my eyes, rested my hands palm upwards on my knees, and attempted to clear my thoughts. I couldn't have survived so many life-times without some idea of how to steady the ship when I felt rocked by wild waters. Time in prison at the end of the thirteenth century with a mystic who later was named a saint had taught me meditation. Schools now call it mind-fulness, but the idea is the same. It's a way of stopping the howl of confusion and fear that can rack any of us at any time.

Life is scary. Believe me, I know this from many first-hand experiences.

Slow breathing. Openness to the sounds around me – the quiet of snow, everything wearing a white muffler. A pause in the busy-ness of the world. I was reaching the point where my inner voice settled and I felt something like peace steal over me.

Listen.

'She's at the school?' A boy's voice.

'Yes, that's what I've been telling you. Dad's had people keeping tabs on her, knowing what she's like. Finally, after all these years our paths have crossed.'

My eyes flicked open. Quinn and a stranger, a boy of his age, were pacing the boundary. By some lucky (or was it unlucky?) chance they stopped within earshot of my retreat.

'On her own? No others show the touch of dark magic?'

'I tested the ones in my house for magical skills but nothing came up. A few had remarkable gifts but I didn't discover anything to worry about. No, I think she dared to come here alone. People know that Green Drake is a key site of the old magic. She must want it too. It's strategic.'

His companion laughed in disbelief. Through the grill of leaves I glimpsed a cheek, dark to Quinn's white pallor. He had a head of tightly curled black hair arranged in tiny spikes like a sea anemone. This was now dotted with snowflakes. The boy was a fool not wearing a hat in this bitter weather. 'Doesn't she know what she's up against?'

'I'm not sure she realizes yet. The deadly nightshade boundary charm is a strong one. We've got a few weeks to get dug in before everyone comes back.' Were they talking about me? Or did they mean Sian and her counter-charms?

The other boy held up his hands, like someone standing before a fire wanting to absorb the heat. 'Yeah, I can sense it. Very strong. Good one.'

'I'm not bad at that stuff. You shouldn't listen to my brothers. They make me sound like the worst hedge wizard.'

'That reminds me. Artair wanted you to know he'll be here by New Year's Eve.'

'Really?' Quinn groaned. 'Big brother doesn't think I can handle this myself?'

'It might not be such a walk in the park as you expect.'

'It's never a walk in the park with her cursed kind, but I'm ready. I won't fail you. Come on, let's see how the others are finding the accommodation I arranged for them.'

The stranger hooted. 'Accommodation? A couple of tents in the woods! They aren't pleased, I can tell you that now. *I'm* not pleased. We're draining our powers just so we can keep warm.'

Quinn batted the boy in the stomach. 'You're softening up, Conall. It'll do you good. Build a fire like normal people would.'

'Says the guy staying under a roof with hot water.'

'I am your commander on this mission.'

'Yeah, yeah, you tell yourself that if it makes you feel less guilty.'

'We can't risk moving you into the school buildings. There are still people around and the shielding doesn't work so well on four walls.'

'I know – I get it. And we have to be careful about trans- formations – I got the memo.'

'Not just careful – they're banned. I expect she'll be on the watch for them, knowing we're at our weakest. It's an interesting standoff, light against dark magic.' He clapped his friend on the shoulder. 'Don't worry, I won't let anything happen. I'll destroy her before she lays a finger on any of us.'

I held my breath and waited for the sound of their foot- steps and voices to fade. My hands were now clenched, trembling with shock at hearing such deadly threats. I couldn't decide if they were talking about Sian or me. The talk of curses suggested I was the one they had in their sights. But what did they mean about Green Drake having old magic? Was there a secret here of how to break the curse?

If only I had more time to look into that but my days were numbered. Literally.

Even so, I couldn't be sure that they were talking about me and that Sian was safe. Mrs Willowbrook had warned me that the Sidhe were enemies of her kind and the conver- sation could also mean that Quinn had detected Sian and was setting an ambush for her on her return. My vow to stop her coming back early was more important than ever, and, if I could get Quinn expelled or arrested for being part of my end, then all the better. At least that answered that question that haunted my lifetimes. I now knew how I was likely to die this time. Not content for the curse to take its usual course, I was going to provoke the Sidhe to assassinate me early.

11

FROZEN FALLS

It was a strange reversal of my previous strategy of avoiding Quinn; now I dogged his every move. He had a secret he wanted to keep. If he discovered that I knew what he was up to, maybe he would be hurried into silencing me? Mrs Willowbrook had said the Sidhe had no heart so I wasn't working on a normal boy with a conscience; I had to think of it more like baiting a wolf so it would lash out.

Ignoring the jellylike feeling in my stomach, I put my tray down next to his at breakfast. We were alone in the echoing dining hall, stone trees branching beautifully but fruitlessly overhead.

'Hi, Quinn.'

'Linny, not seen you around. How's your vacation so far?' He gave me one of his lazy smiles. His blue eyes were ringed with a darker circle, a startling effect when they were turned on you. No wonder so many swam into his net. It was hard to reconcile the outer package with what I knew was inside.

'Fine thanks. Been feeling a bit lonely, to be honest.'

'Oh?'

'Yeah. Mr Huntsman invited me to help catalog his butterflies but, well...'

He grinned, dimples appearing in his cheeks, which made him look more boyish, more charming, if that was possible. 'That does sound boring. He's got his daughter staying, hasn't he?'

'Rowena. Yes. She seems nice. Wildlife photographer. Don't be surprised if you see her out and about looking for animals. So what have you been doing?' Besides plotting death and destruction for mere mortals.

'Not much. I'm behind on my coursework having only just arrived so I've been catching up in the library.'

'That's odd. I haven't seen you in there.'

'That would be due to my ninja skills of coming and going undetected.' He said it lightly so I wouldn't take it seriously. He didn't know that I remembered his ability to pass through locked doors.

I played along. 'Learned that at the same time as you learned juggling, did you?'

'I have four brothers, which explains why my parents settled on the name Quinn – number five. It's amazing what the older ones can teach you. How about you? Brothers and sisters?'

'Two – one of each – twins. I'm the eldest.'

'Where are they?'

'Australia, I think.'

'You don't know?'

'My parents decided to go without me so I'm not really talking to them right now.'

'That's harsh, being left.'

'I thought so.'

He stretched his arms above his head, searching for something appropriate to say in response. 'I've been left behind too as Dad's on tour.' Royal progress he probably meant, like Tudor monarchs used to do, visiting his Sidhe minions. I had a horrible recollection of the black eyes, curved sword pointing at me. *Stay far away, Fey King.*

'Linny, are you okay? You've gone pale.'

'I'm fine.'

'So, do you want to do something together later? I have a free afternoon.'

Interesting. 'Do you want to go for a walk?'

'In this weather? I was thinking more along the lines of a game of badminton. They've left the nets up for me.' No doubt he had turned his charisma on the caretaker.

'Okay. I'll meet you in the gym at three.' I got up and cleared my tray. 'See you later.'

'Are you as good at badminton as you are at juggling?'

'You'll see.'

THE ANSWER WAS NO. Quinn had me running around the court until he decided to take it easy on me. It was odd playing with the boy I'd picked as my killer. I had to keep reminding myself that this guy, who seemed perfectly ordinary when bantering about my lack of skills, hid a dark side.

'Aw, come on, Miss Grace, that was an easy one!'

'You have a much longer reach than me, Mister Ramsay.'

'I was expecting great things after juggling. Where did you learn that, by the way?' He tapped the shuttlecock over the net.

'At the circus, of course.' I hit it back.

'You went to what, a Saturday circus school?' He was taking the rally gently this time.

'No, full time. It was my life.'

'Not heard of anyone doing that before, except for guys who join the Cirque du Soleil. You weren't with them?'

'No, another company. You wouldn't know them.'

'Shame you couldn't carry on with it. I can't see the PE staff offering those skills here – they're far too traditional.' He swiped the shuttlecock into the back right-hand corner. 'Sorry, forgot.'

I picked it up. 'My serve?'

'What else did you learn at the circus school then?'

'Not racket sports.'

He laughed. 'I can see that.'

'I can tumble.' That's what we used to call it. They now call it gymnastics.

He caught the shuttlecock rather than return it. 'Care to demonstrate?'

Why not? I felt an absurd desire to show him what I was and stop this stupid pretense. I put down my racket, rolling my shoulders to check I was properly warmed up. 'It's a while since I did this.' I took a run up and went through routine of flips and somersaults ending with a back three and a half twist.

It must've impressed because Quinn applauded. 'You weren't joking when you said you tumbled. What've you got in your legs? Springs? You could give Simone Biles a run for her money.'

'It helps being small. I'd normally finish that move on my father's shoulders.' I felt a twist of homesickness for my dad at the turn of that century. Bill Valdifiori had a wonderful walrus mustache and a rumbling laugh. He'd been one of the best.

'Your dad's an acrobat?'

'Was. He was. Sorry, I'd better go. I've…er…stuff I need to

do.' I swiped a towel over my face to hide the fact that I was crying.

'Hey, hey.' To my complete shock, an arm surrounded my shoulders. 'I didn't mean to upset you with my questions. I thought you'd enjoy showing me your talents.'

'Not your fault.' I didn't want to emerge from the towel – ever.

He rubbed my upper arm, a friendly gesture, commiserating. 'You should tell your parents how upset you are being left behind.'

It was no good: I had to face him. 'They know.' What was I doing, accepting comfort from my enemy? He had mastered the act of seeming a reasonable human being and I was at the point where I would accept any crumb of sympathy.

'Tell them you want to join them. If money's the problem...' He stopped. What had he been about to offer?

'Money isn't the problem.'

'It's just that the school over the holidays isn't a place you should be.' Was he trying to get rid of me? That didn't make much sense with the conversation I had overheard. Or was it just a pretense as he was already aware I had no choice but stay? At least that fitted better with what I knew about him. I wouldn't like to think he could actually be kind.

'Yeah, well, it looks like we're both stuck here, doesn't it?'

Handing him the racket, I took off for the girls' changing rooms. I passed the three Chinese students, two girls and a boy, on their way to the next fixture in Quinn's busy afternoon. From the evidence of their matching kit and deft warm-up swipes in the air with their rackets, it definitely looked like he'd get more of a game from them. They smiled and nodded politely. Mandarin was at the top of my list of languages to learn in my next life. I made do with the couple of phrases I'd picked up which were answered with much wider grins.

With them occupying Quinn, it looked like the coast was clear for me to scout out his encampment to see exactly what I was up against. Quinn and his friend had talked about shielding so it was possible I wouldn't be able to detect them but I could work out a likely location if I went by footprints – they might not have thought to disguise those.

It was getting dark as I began my slow walk around the grounds, walking anti-clockwise to the clockwise I had taken with Quinn. Widdershins we used to call it – such a lovely word though it was regarded as an unlucky direction by the superstitious back in the day. So many of my favorite words had dropped out of usage. I scooped a handful of snow off a wall and threw a ball at a statue in the rose garden by the library. It was cast in concrete to look like a prune-faced maiden in a bonnet. She gave the impression of being the sort who would drive past you in her carriage and not spare a thought for the flower seller she'd just splashed in the gutter muck. I'd sold violets – picking them as soon as they appeared in spring and walking all the way into London to hawk them on street corners. There had been lots of rich girls like her who had ignored me. Even with my best efforts crying my wares, I hadn't been able to stop my family's slide into the workhouse.

Don't think about that. I hugged my arms to myself.

Were there voices on the wind? I stopped, trying to quieten my breathing. I could hear laughter, singing, raucous, like the football team winding down in the showers after a match. I tried to sense which direction it was coming from – deeper in the woods that was certain. I started walking again and the singing cut off abruptly.

Had they spotted me?

I followed the wall. Here the wooded path went through a dell, the lowest point of the grounds. Quinn had been very interested in it when we did our walk together, stopping to check the little bridge over the stream and the natural waterfall that trickled over a rocky outcrop. The waterfall had frozen, forming an architectural fantasy of columns and cauliflower florets. Were the Sidhe here? It made sense. A camp down among the trees would be hard to see, even if there were no protections; and the path did seem very well trodden, considering how few students were left in the school.

I was debating whether or not to leave the path to explore further when I saw someone in a red padded jacket approaching. Red Riding Hood in the forest. She waved her hand. If I hadn't already noticed that she was carrying a camera, I could've worked out who it was from her energetic walk.

'Linny, have you come to admire the waterfall too?' she called.

'Yes, Miss Huntsman.'

She arrived at my side. 'Call me Rowena.' She took out a little black device and held it out. 'Damn, the light is already failing. I've left it too late. Still, I might as well see what a long exposure produces.' She deftly set up her tripod and camera.

'Can I help?'

'I'm fine. I'm used to doing this in far worse conditions.'

'I bet.'

She took a couple of shots, looked at the viewing screen and gave a hum of content. 'Not too bad, quite atmospheric. How about I take a picture of you?'

I held my mittened hands up in front of my face. 'No, no, I'm fine.'

'You can send it to your parents.'

'Really not.'

'Send it to your friends then. We'll make it as painless as possible. Lean on the bridge there.' She took the camera off the tripod and pointed it at me. I remembered how hard she was to refuse and decided just to get it over with. 'Don't grimace. I prefer you looking sad than that ghastly smile.'

I let my features drop into the expression that truly reflected my mood.

'That's good. Yeah, stay like that.' She took a burst. 'One more.'

I wondered what she had seen that she would call good. 'Can I see the image?'

'I'll email it to you if it comes out okay.' She put the camera back in its case. 'Carry the tripod for me?'

We walked back towards Crowthorne house. I'm not usually a sensitive person but I had the impression that the wood – or something in the wood – sighed with relief once we left the dell. I didn't hear the football chants again.

12

JUST KILL ME NOW

Christmas Eve arrived with a temporary break in the weather. The snow had begun to melt thanks to a messy splurge of rain, green patches emerging on the lawns like an outbreak of a dire rash. I preferred the whited-out world to this. I checked the weather forecast. The cold would take a grip by evening, more snow promised.

Would today be a good day to die? I looked at myself in the mirror. My features were so familiar, repeating again and again over the centuries – always the brown hair and grey-blue eyes, the color of slate. I was tired of seeing them. I traced the curve of my cheek, the arch of my eyebrow.

Ready to give this up now? I asked myself.

Yes, if it saved Sian. At least this death would have a point.

But how to provoke the Sidhe boy to kill me? I pondered my options and decided following him to his camp was the best move. If I marched in among them, I'd be challenging them all. Which one actually did the deed wasn't important and I still had killing myself as an absolute last resort. The key thing was making sure people knew who I had been with at the time of my death. I wanted Quinn under suspicion, or chucked out, so that he couldn't risk doing anything to Sian.

I sent a message to Jack – safer than involving her. *Things are looking up. Going for a walk with Quinn.*

I thought he'd be out on the slopes but I got a message back immediately. *Wow! I thought you didn't like him?*

We're the only ones here. Of course we have to get along.

Tell me all the details when you get back.

It's not a date.

Not yet!

I had known the ever-optimistic Jack would leap to conclusions. At least one of my snares was now set. I just had to follow Quinn without being spotted too soon.

The rain helped. Waiting in the common room with the door ajar, I saw Quinn hurry out at eleven. He was carrying a box from the school kitchen – Danish pastries from the sweet odor. With hood pulled up, he had his thoughts on his friends that he had made camp in the open, not on who might trail him. Keeping back, I made my way to the dell. I was just in time to spot Quinn jumping off the side of the path into a gully and splashing along a muddy rivulet that had been cleared of brambles. I hadn't noticed that the day before but it was a sign that I was right in my guess that they'd picked the dell for their tents. Slipping down the bank, I ripped a hole in my jeans and got badly scratched. I ignored the pain. I wouldn't be around long enough for the hurts to matter.

Oh lord. My stomach was squirming like I'd swallowed a bucket of live eels. I felt sick. Was I really going to do this? I hadn't been executed for centuries. It is the worst feeling in the world walking to the scaffold. You get light-headed, overcome by a sensation of not being quite there. It's like stumbling into a nightmare but your rational part knows it is for real.

A cheer shook me out of my terror. *You can do this, Linny.* I picked myself up and waded after my quarry, cold mud squelching up to my ankles. I fell over several times. Where were they?

And then I was through. The only sign of the protection I could see was a natural screen of laurel bushes, thick shiny leaves blocking the view of the camp from the path. In the clearing beyond, a circle of five tents surrounded a campfire, which had been built so it was partially sheltered by a small square of corrugated iron roof. They were using the hot iron as a rack to dry clothes in the wet. Smoke curled up, defying the rain. A group of boys sat on log-seats drinking from tin cups and eating pastries, looking bedraggled but cheerful. It could almost be an innocent scout camp until you noticed that they were armed with a motley selection of knives and bows and arrows. I had a sudden flashback to the outlaws I'd once lived with in the middle of the twelfth century.

'What the hell is she doing here?' The one called Conall got to his feet and pointed at me. All the boys set aside their breakfast and followed his lead. I found myself a target of their weapons. Quinn who had been sitting with his back to me, turned and groaned. He gave the order to stand down with a flick of his wrist.

'Linny, so...er...welcome to our camp.' He came towards me, trying to look at ease with the situation. 'I invited a couple of friends for Christmas – completely against school rules of course but, well, you don't look the kind to tell.'

I'd made a count already. There were ten of them, all Sidhe no doubt. 'Friends? With weapons?'

'These are just for playacting, you know? We...er...war

game for fun.' He moved closer, that 'trust me' smile now
back in place.

'How did she get through the protection?' asked one boy,
notable for his shock of white-blond hair.

'Not sure, Liam. How did you find us, Linny?' He was
pushing his power at me again but I found it had no more
effect than seeing a wind blowing from behind glass.

'I followed you. Look, I know why you're here.'

The smile vanished. 'You do?'

'This is about the curse.'

A threatening murmur went around the circle of boys.
Quinn held up his hand. 'What do you know?'

'I know you're Sidhe. I know you've put a protective spell
on the boundary – that you're here for a purpose. Quite why
you've bothered when the curse was doing fine by itself, I
don't know.' I gave a bleak laugh and rubbed my face with the
back of a mitten. 'You thought you wiped my memory but I
think I must've learned to resist mind tricks many lives ago.'

'What are you talking about?' Quinn's eyes were blazing.
The power he normally kept leashed was so close to the
surface. Yes, this would be a quick, clean death. I turned my
face to the sky, letting the rain wash away the fear.

'Just kill me now.' I closed my eyes.

A terrible silence followed. Please make it quick before I
lost my courage.

'What the hell is this?' A hand gripped my arm and gave
me a rough shake. Oh no, he was going to string this out.
Make me wait for New Year.

'Please, I want it to be now. You put the curse on me. For
once, let me die when I choose.'

'Is this girl crazy?' asked Conall.

'I'm not sure. I barely know her.' Quinn sounded

perplexed rather than murderous. This was going horribly wrong.

'But your forgetting charm doesn't work on her?'

'So it would seem. Maybe she's resistant to magic? There are always exceptions.'

I laughed, or was it a sob? 'If only. Your kind put a curse on me about fifteen hundred years ago, give or take a century or two. I always die just before my sixteenth birthday on New Year's Eve but, guess what? I then come back a generation later and the whole cycle starts over. I must've lived about fifty short lives by now and I'm ready to give up this one, so, please, just do it.'

The grip on my arm dropped.

'She's one of them,' said Conall. 'Hunter's moon, I never thought...'

'Yeah, what are the odds?' Quinn sounded repulsed. 'At least, it explains why she's resistant to my powers. A major curse like that blocks everything else.'

'So she knows we're here and she's a threat? What do we do?'

'Nothing.' Quinn's tone was cold. 'The curse will take her. When did you say? New Year's Eve? The protective barrier will hold others off and who's going to take any notice of a mad girl talking about Sidhe in the woods?'

He had no mercy. He wasn't going to do it. I dropped to my knees, head bowed. I'd steeled myself for this moment but to find it refused was worse. 'Please.'

'Keep back from her.' There was a snap in Quinn's voice that hadn't been there before. 'Nobody touch her. She's full of dark magic. Don't risk it.'

'Isn't it enough? All my father did was kill a deer.'

'You think this is about hunting an animal?'

'Isn't it?' The rain was dripping off my face, falling on my jeans. Or was it tears?

'Your father killed the light – he murdered our hope, our balance. It will never be enough.' He turned his back on me. 'Strike camp. We're moving.'

I stayed on my knees, too exhausted to do anything. I could hear the sounds of tents being taken down, subdued voices around me.

'What are you going to do about her? She doesn't look in a good way,' asked Conall.

'She'll survive. Whatever she tries, she can't die before the curse is due to take effect. Regard her as *maledicta*.'

'Quinn.'

'She doesn't exist for us, okay?

'All right. You're the boss.'

They left. My legs were numb, my whole body shaken to the core. I curled up on my side and wept.

13

ZERO GRAVITY

It was getting dark when Rowena found me.

'Oh Linny, are you all right? Have you had a fall?' She covered me with her red jacket. 'Oh, dear lord, you're freezing!'

It was beginning to snow again, I saw. According to Quinn I had another week of this to endure.

'Do you need to go to hospital?'

'I'm all right.'

'Don't give me that. You're not all right. Can you walk?' She pulled me to my feet. 'Let's get you inside. A warm bath and some soup – that's what you need.' She made a call. 'Yes, she was where Quinn said he last saw her. Doesn't look like anything too serious but she's very cold. I'm bringing her back now. Get your chicken broth on the stove.'

I took a stumbling step forward. This must've been what Mary Shelley imagined it was like to be Frankenstein's creature just coming to life, limbs too heavy, nerves misfiring.

'What happened, Linny? Did someone do something to you?' I could see that she was checking me for injury.

'No, no one did anything. That was the problem.'

'Sorry, what?'

'I can't explain. Please don't ask.'

I let her guide me back to Crowthorne and run a shower for me.

'Don't lock the door while you're under the water in case you faint. I'll stay outside. Just shout if you need help.'

I nodded wearily, went into the bathroom and stripped off my clothes. The scratches I'd picked up earlier were now making themselves felt. I was a mess.

Come on, Linny, think! My brain was kicking back in now I was warming up. *Quinn hadn't known about you. He isn't here to kill you. This has to be about Sian and her hedge witch family.*

Nothing mattered now but keeping her safe. That was the last thing I could do in this life. I hauled myself into the shower cubicle, swaying dangerously as I negotiated stepping in. I was close to passing out with the combination of cold and not having eaten, but I couldn't do anything so idiotic as lose consciousness now. There was so little time left. After standing numbly under the spray, I roughly dried off and put on some pajamas, covering the top with my favorite sweater. A quick comb through my tangled hair and I exited the bathroom.

Rowena looked up from the book she was reading. 'Feeling better? You look more yourself. You had me worried for a moment.'

'Thanks for finding me.'

'You should've taken a phone with you.'

I'd had it in my pocket all along. 'I will next time.'

'Right, well, let's get some food inside you. My father has soup ready waiting.'

'I just need to send a message. I'll join you in a moment.'

'Okay, but don't be long.'

Once she had left, I got out my phone, noticing that it

was almost out of battery. *Sian, I have a dying wish. Will you grant it?*

Her reply winged back immediately. *Where have you been all day?*

Will you grant it?

What is it?

Stay away from Green Drake. Quinn has summoned his friends and they don't look like they are fans of your family. I couldn't spell out the threat to her hedge witch family in case this was found after my death.

There was a pause before she replied. *How many?*

Ten.

A whole squad. That's pretty serious.

So will you promise? It's the last thing I'm going to ask of you.

I'll think about it.

No, I need a promise. They're not here for me. They're leaving me alone. If you love me you'll do this.

Emotional blackmail?

Too right.

There was a long pause. *Yes, I promise but I don't like it.*

I'm not keen on it myself.

I'll be with you through it all. We'll speak as you go to sleep that night.

I felt a huge wave of relief, both for the promise of company and the fact that I'd stopped her walking into the trap. *Yes, we'll do that. By the way what does maledicta mean?*

It means someone – a female someone with the feminine ending – is cursed. You are supposed to ignore her, pretend she isn't there.

You've never done that even though you've known.

That's because you're my friend and Quinn's kind don't set the rules for me. Who said it to you?

Our friendly neighborhood royal of course. Thank you for

ignoring the rules. Must go. Having dinner with Mr Huntsman and Rowena. I didn't think she needed to know about the whole woods episode. It might change her mind about staying away.

Be careful.

Hardly need to worry about that kind of thing now. I put the phone on charge and went up to the Huntsmans' flat. Inviting me in, my house master mumbled something about I shouldn't go rambling in the thaw, far too dangerous underfoot, and put a bowl of steaming soup in front of me. It smelt of lemon and thyme. Despite all that had happened, I discovered that I did have an appetite.

I looked around. 'Where's Rowena? I thought she was going to be here?'

'She didn't think any of us should spend Christmas Eve alone. She's gone to find the other boarder,' he said, nudging the basket of fresh baked rolls towards me.

This would be interesting. I had passed beyond fear and entered the weightless zone of recklessness. I was floating in that zero gravity, uncaring of what I said and to whom I said it. From feeling helpless earlier, I suddenly felt powerful. No one is stronger than the one who has nothing left to lose.

I'd finished my first bowl and had accepted a refill when Rowena arrived with Quinn. He was following her in his usual 'just behind your shoulder' position, like she was carrying a ticking bomb and he was waiting for the signal to dive for cover. He avoided contact with any of us, saying the merest hello to Mr Huntsman and dropping in a chair as far from me as possible.

Rowena took a place at the head of the table. 'How's the broth?'

'Phenomenal. Good enough to wake the dead,' I

quipped, giving Quinn a hard smile. His eyes slid by me. 'So, Quinn, how was your day?'

'Mr Huntsman, I've heard you are cataloguing your collection. How many specimens do you have?' Quinn asked, leaning back so the teacher could put a bowl of soup in front of him.

'Oh, I didn't know you were interested.' Mr Huntsman beamed at him, quite oblivious to the undercurrents in the room, me dancing on a knife-edge, Quinn trying to ignore me, Rowena watching us with a puzzled expression.

'Yes, Quinn is absolutely fascinated by the wildlife in the woods. You'll see him out there in all weathers, looking for his little friends,' I said blithely.

'Not a good time of year to search for butterflies, or moths,' said Mr Huntsman regretfully. 'Now's the time for organizing research and reading up on new species.'

'Oh, I don't know. It seems to me like there's a lot happening in the woods if you know where to look.'

'That's true, if your interests go beyond butterflies. You can see the birds in residence for the cold season with so little leaf canopy. Rowena has taken some wonderful shots already, thanks to the snow.'

'I'm sure if she looks hard she'll be able to see quite a few winter visitors.'

'I've been staking out the beach. That's where most of the migrating birds arrive,' Rowena remarked, tearing her roll in half. 'Could you pass the butter?'

Quinn pushed the dish in her direction. 'I'm sure that's a fascinating study. How do you find making your living as a photographer?'

'Up and down like most creative careers, but I make enough to keep body and soul together.'

'I imagine you do.' He bit into a seeded roll. 'This is delicious. Do you bake, sir?'

'One of my passions.' Mr Huntsman smiled shyly.

'Will you be staying long, Miss Huntsman?' Quinn asked.

'Rowena, please. Not sure. I'll see how this assignment goes,' she replied.

'Assignment?'

'The cataloguing of my father's collection.'

'Sorry, yes, I should've realized. Too big a job for one person.'

'I understood that that's your philosophy,' I cut in. 'You need about ten friends to do anything.'

Mr Huntsman peered at me. 'That doesn't sound very kind of you, Linny. I'm surprised. Quinn can't help being popular. No need to be jealous.'

'Oh, I'm not jealous. I have the perfect life. I'm eternally grateful for the gift.' I dared Quinn to meet my gaze but he continued to act as if I weren't in the room.

'Can I have seconds?' he asked.

'I must be on about my fiftieth – it's that good, I keep on coming back for more,' I said.

Mr Huntsman fetched the pot and served us both refills. 'A slight exaggeration as that will be your third bowl, Linny, but I'm pleased you both like it.'

'You can certainly put the food away, Linny. I have to watch my waistline.' Rowena shook her head when her dad offered her more.

'I don't have to worry about my weight. What would be the point? Quinn, do you have a magic gift for burning through the calories quickly?'

He took a mouthful to avoid answering.

'I'd say a tall young man like him can probably eat what

he likes and not worry about it either. Isn't that right?' asked Rowena.

He nodded at her and swallowed. 'Never been a problem.'

I wondered if I could force him to acknowledge me in some way. 'Quinn, you told me earlier you had brothers. What are their names?'

He got up from the table. 'Sorry, I've just remembered. Dad was going to ring me to wish me "Happy Christmas" and I've left my phone in my bedroom. Thanks so much for supper.'

'But there's dessert!' protested Mr Huntsman.

'And believe me his desserts are as good as his other courses.' I smiled ferociously at Quinn. I decided that forcing him into retreat was something of a victory if he wasn't going to talk to me.

'That's so kind of you, sir, but Dad only has a short window of opportunity to ring between catching flights.'

'You'll be here for lunch tomorrow I hope?' asked Mr Huntsman.

But Quinn had gone without replying.

'He's an odd young man, isn't he?' remarked the housemaster.

'Father, not everyone thinks spending the evening with their teacher is the definition of a good time,' said Rowena.

'Not even if the food is phenomenal?' I asked.

Rowena smiled. 'Not even then. Still, despite the fact that he's being less than forthcoming with us tonight, he did tell us earlier where we might find you when we were about to send out an alert.'

'How did you know I was missing?'

'Swipe card. Showed you'd gone out and not come back. No one saw you at lunch, you'd not left by any of the gates, so we worked out you must've twisted your ankle or had some kind of fall. That was it, wasn't it?'

'Yes, I think something twisted.' I certainly had screwed up my attempt at being killed.

Mr Huntsman returned from the kitchen bearing a beautifully sculpted chocolate cake decorated with holly. 'Yule log, anyone?'

14

UNHAPPY CHRISTMAS

I had planned to stay in bed for most of Christmas Day
but I hadn't bargained on my little brother's eagerness
to speak to me. My phone, left on vibrate, began a
mad jig at six in the morning. Blearily I accepted the call.

'Hey, Linny, Merry Christmas!' Paul's freckled face
grinned at me. He so often reminded me of Finch.

I shoved my hair out of my eyes. 'Thanks – and to you.'

'So what did you get? Mom said they'd sent you a great
present.'

'She won't've opened them yet, silly,' says Claire,
squeezing her face next to her twin's, hers a little sunburned
across the nose. 'It's early morning there.'

I yawned. 'Having fun?'

'This place is amazing. Check this out.' Paul did a three-
sixty scan of their apartment giving me a glimpse of a night-
dark sea and white sand beach and my parents sitting at a
dinner table finishing their meal. 'Wave to Linny.'

Rather sheepishly they both did so. I didn't say anything,
nor did I wave.

'We're really annoyed at you not wanting to come with

us,' said Claire, angling the phone back to her face. 'I've had to share a bedroom with him!' She elbowed our brother. 'I mean I know you have exams and friends and stuff, but we miss you!'

'Is that what Mom told you? That I didn't want to come?'

The phone was whisked out of Paul's hands and my mom came on the screen. 'Happy Christmas, Linny.' She was walking out onto the balcony.

'Mom, you lied.'

'I thought it best that they didn't feel to blame for you being left behind. You can see how relaxed they are. It was a good decision.'

'You know something? Right now, I think I hate you.'

'I didn't expect any other reaction, but this wasn't about you. It was about making the twins happy and stable. I promise we'll bring you here when you're better. I have to say I'm pleased you've agreed to see a counselor. If you get over all of this...this fatalism, then the family can be back together again without hurting each other.'

I didn't want to speak to her. 'Pass me back to the twins please.'

'Your dad wants to say hello.' The phone ended up in my father's possession.

'Linny, I hope you're enjoying the holidays?' He had gone grey since I'd last seen them in the summer, hairline retreating further up his forehead. He looked old and stressed. I quelled a twinge of pity. I was the one left behind, not him.

'What do you think?'

'The school said they'd make sure you didn't miss out.'

'And that's complete nonsense, as you well know. I'm here pretty much on my own, apart from an older boy who doesn't talk to me and three Chinese students who *can't* talk to me.'

His eyes skittered away from mine. 'Have you opened your present yet? We hope it'll partly make up for you missing out on this trip.'

'No, I haven't. Can I say goodbye to the twins?'

'Your mother's sent them to bed. It's late here. I'll pass your message on.'

'I don't think I'll ever forgive you and Mom for this.'

'Now, young lady, don't take that tone with me. You have much to be grateful for – good school, roof over your head, you've never wanted for anything.'

'Just your love – and that's everything. I'd take a work-house and real affection over this. No need to call again. Bye, Dad.' I cut him off before he could deliver another lecture.

I set the phone back on the bedside table. Better luck next time in the parent department.

A couple of hours later I made myself get up. I discovered someone had stacked the presents I'd been sent outside my door. Mr Huntsman playing Santa Claus? The idea made me smile bleakly. He fitted the grim tone of my last Christmas. I opened my parents' present and discovered a top of the range phone with the maximum memory. Pointless. I didn't bother to open the little white box. If I left it untouched they might be able to get a refund. The twins had done better though. They'd sent me a book of fairy tales. That was more like it. They knew I collected old books – it kept me in touch with my previous childhoods – and I'd long wanted this edition from 1909 with pictures by Arthur Rackham. They must've scoured eBay. The illustrations were scary, but then so were fairy tales, full of malevolent cats and gathering crows, the stuff of the twilight world. I would enjoy reading that later.

Jack hadn't got me a present, saying his theme, when he finished it, was my gift. I hope he hurried up or I'd never hear the whole piece. The last present I opened was from Sian. I wasn't surprised to see the rug fall out. It came with a note.

This has been woven with charms for peace and hope.

I wrapped it around my shoulders, feeling a little like Joseph in his technicolored dream coat. Maybe the gloom did lift slightly – or it might have been the thought of my friend putting so much loving care into the gift. When she left, she had said it was for now and for after. She intended me to cocoon myself in it on my last night.

Oh Sian, you might not be here in person, but you've found an excellent substitute.

As THERE WAS no food service in hall, I wandered downstairs and fixed myself breakfast from the croissants and cereals left for me in the kitchenette just off the common room. I wondered where Quinn was – out with his troops? He'd certainly surrendered the field to me as far as Crowthorne was concerned with no sign he had eaten here.

'I'm lonely.' To my embarrassment, I realized I'd said it out loud. I was looking for my mortal enemy because I was so desperate. This wouldn't do. I don't ever mope. I try not to feel sorry for myself and don't cling to others.

I turned on the TV to find they were playing some decent movies. Settling down with my rug around me, I prepared for a marathon session of mind-numbing Hollywood.

The second film that ended with a family reuniting

against the odds, lessons learned, apologies made, had me reaching for the controller. Enough. I picked up the twins' present and slowly leafed through the book. A glimpse into the dark world of the Grimm Brothers would pep me up.

When I looked away from the page, I found Quinn sitting in the armchair opposite me.

'Jeez! Cough before coming in, won't you?' He was not joking when he said he could move about the place silently. 'Ah, but you're not allowed to talk to me – I forgot. Unhappy Christmas by the way.' I closed the book and tucked it under Sian's rug. 'I thought you'd be out playing war games with your friends, not sitting with the losers inside?'

His eyes were impossibly intense – a kind of icy blue like the skies on a cold clear day. 'I came to say I'm sorry for the way I reacted yesterday.'

I pulled the rug up over my chest. 'Which part? The refusal to kill me or the leaving me in the snow?'

'Pushing the maledicta order on my men. Conall has been giving me grief about that.'

'I thought them were the rules.' My tone was mocking.

'Technically, they are, but we have latitude to interpret them more liberally when it isn't the original offender.'

Who put that stick up his butt? He sounded so formal. 'So you admit I'm not to blame?'

'Blood bears responsibility.'

'Tell that to a judge – oh, but I remember now: the Fey King didn't bother with due process.'

'It's not a human term, not a matter of choice. In our world it's a fact.'

'Your world being?'

'You know what I am.'

'Not really. Enlighten me.'

'We are the Sidhe, people with magic.'

'Human?'

'That's debatable. Our origins are...disputed.'

'Lost in the mists of time, hey? I know all about that.' I rested my head on the chair back, eyes half closed. 'I never really have understood what you are all for, though. I don't get why your lot cursed my family. I get revenge – I'm feeling pretty vengeful myself with you sitting here with your half-baked apology — but surely even a Sidhe vengeance has limits?'

'What your father did still affects those of my family through all generations.'

Mrs Willowbrook had warned me: the Sidhe were snow and ice, no heart. 'Okay, so it's not me, it's you. Fine. I don't want to waste the little time left protesting that your system is stupid. I can't see the point.'

'Do you know how...how inconvenient you are?' I was pleased to see that he looked exasperated, pushing his fingers through his hair like he'd prefer to give it a good tug.

'Aw, that's so sweet of you.'

'It's hard for you to understand, I get that.'

'Understand why you all marched out on me leaving me to freeze in the snow? Um, yep, I am struggling with that one. It kinda lacked humanity, don't you think?'

'I was in shock – not at my best.'

'Poor you.'

'Think of it like this: what if you met someone who suddenly announced they were the child of the one who was responsible for the biggest catastrophe known to humankind, worse than the slaughter of innocents by all the dictators of the twentieth century put together?'

'I'd say, hey Miss Stalin-Hitler-Mussolini, nice to meet you. Must suck coming from that background but I judge people by who they are, not who their parents were.'

'I knew this was useless.' Quinn was talking to himself now.

'Can you fault my logic?'

'It's odd talking to you. Sometimes you seem like a much older person yet you look so young for your age.'

'I have your lot to thank for that.' I hugged my knees to my chest. 'You know what I miss, Fey boy? Growing up. Knowing what it's like to see my own children, grandchildren, having a career. I'm stuck with lots of starts and no finishes.'

'I get that you might be resentful—'

'Ya think?'

'But the curse is about balance. Your father took something vital away from us so the curse extracts the same from him and his blood. That's how magic works. It's not really anything personal.'

'Did you really just say that?' I shook my head in disbelief. 'Not personal? Don't you have feelings like a real person? Or imagination? Can't you see how it is intensely personal for me? I'm going to die in six days' time. I can't say I'm feeling philosophical about the prospect – or balanced.' I closed my eyes, familiar wave of tiredness swamping me. 'Just go away, Quinn.'

When I opened them a few minutes later, he had gone.

15

COUNTDOWN

And so began the countdown. I woke each morning trying to savor these last few days of being fifteen in this era. It hadn't been so bad: life was comfortable; girls got more respect than in any previous era; the technology was amazing, almost as impressive as seeing my first steam train. I wrote a list of all the things I liked and sent upbeat messages to all my contacts. I didn't want family or friends to mistake my death as a suicide. If the Sidhe curse was going to kill me, I wanted that to get the blame, however indirectly.

I smiled and chatted to Rowena when our paths crossed.

I complimented Mr Huntsman on the spectacular Christmas dinner he had cooked for the three of us.

I read my Estonian poetry and made a start on Mandarin, hoping some of it would stick for next time.

And above all, I ignored the deep yawning depression that was there when I stopped to think.

31ST DECEMBER. The last square to cross off on my calendar.

I had a long shower, went for a walk, ate far too much chocolate. I had no sign of what it was that was going to kill me as I was feeling well in myself, no headache, no temperature. Mrs Bailey tried to persuade me to go to the circus with the Chinese students but I refused for all our sakes. A minivan crash was not something I wanted to bring upon the others and besides, who wants to spend their last hours watching clowns?

My nails were bitten to the quick. How was it going to happen?

By evening I was feeling sick and close to tears, courage at a low ebb. I paced my bedroom. At ten-thirty I heard a knock on the door. Thinking it was Rowena, I opened it, prepared to make some excuse for not coming up for supper and to see in the New Year as she had suggested.

It was Quinn.

I swore and closed the door.

'Look, I've tried to imagine and I'm sorry it's like this, okay?' he shouted, then stomped away.

I opened the door to check he was gone and found a posy of winter greenery. I threw it in the trash, then that not being good enough, chucked it out of the window.

Please, please, please.

Prayers had never worked. Have some dignity.

I got off my knees and wrapped myself in Sian's rug. Okay, face facts: the time had come for a goodbye call.

'Sian, it's me.'

I heard her gulp. 'How are you holding up?'

'Nervous but it's not like I haven't done this before.'

'I've got a list of things I want to say to you.' I could hear crackling on the other end as she unfolded it. 'I knew I'd completely forget everything. Do you want to hear them?'

'Please.'

'You are the best friend I'll ever have and I love you.'

'Oh, oh, well, that's good. Same here.' She was killing me in other ways.

'Mom and I, we really will work hard to find a way out for you next time round so search for us. We'll make sure we are on whatever Internet thing is the main way of communicating and I'll leave my current address at the school. We will've had years to figure out a solution for you.'

'Quinn told me it was "nothing personal", something to do with the balance.'

'And what did you say?'

'I think I laughed – or maybe I cried. Both feel kind of similar right now.' I had that itchy feeling again and began pacing. 'Tell me something else.'

'You play the piano beautifully.'

'Thanks.'

'But I'm really cross you hid your juggling skills. Next time don't hide.'

'But people find it strange that a little kid can do these things, speak ten languages and so on.'

'And they don't find you strange for other reasons?'

'You have a point.'

'Here's another one: I think you are very brave.'

'Not much choice when you're me.'

'No, that's where you're wrong. Courage is facing what you know you have to do, like people going over the top in the trenches.'

'That was a terrible war. I'm pleased I missed that. Died a few years before. Came back in time for the second round though. That was also rough.'

'There's so much you haven't told me.'

'I can be a bit of a history bore so I tend not to say a lot.'

'People wouldn't be bored: they'd be fascinated.'

'It's kind of hard to explain though.' I checked the clock. It was already eleven. 'Oh lord.'

She could hear I was cracking up. 'Linny, how do you want to do this? What can I do to help?'

'I think…I think I want to sleep through it, not know how it's done.'

'Can you sleep?'

'I don't know.'

'I could read you my Chemistry notes. That should do the trick.'

Even at this late stage, that made me laugh. 'Yeah, you could.'

'But I did put a relaxation charm into the rug. It might work better.'

'Quinn said little magics didn't work on someone with a curse.'

'I doubt he knows the first thing about hedge witch charms so I wouldn't take any notice of a Sidhe. This is not magic aimed against him so the boundary spell shouldn't affect it.'

'Okay, I'll try it. Keep on talking, will you?'

'I will. I've got all my sisters here, and my mom. They're all helping me work the charm.'

I closed my eyes briefly and blinked away a tear. 'Thank them for me?'

'No need. Just lie down.'

'I love you too, you know? And Jack? Don't tell him he sucks at skiing, which he so totally does.'

'I won't, though he knows, of course. Now pull the rug over yourself – that's all of us sending you the most peaceful, most relaxing energy we can.'

I held on to a silver patch near my chin, willing this to work. 'It hasn't been so bad this time, you know?'

She paused, taking a moment to control her emotions. 'It's been a privilege being your friend, Linny. Remember me, won't you?'

'I will, eventually.'

'Now close your eyes and listen to our voices.' I could now hear a soft murmuring coming across the airwaves, like the rustle of leaves on a summer's day. I thought of willows bending over a river, washing their tendrils in the currents. Starlit nights and a fox crossing a snowy field. A rainbow I'd seen over the nearby lighthouse. Seals beached on the rocky inlets of the islands and puffins playing in the water, only a short boat trip away. Green Drake itself, majestic buildings and extensive grounds, waterspout gutters in the shape of dragons. My holly fortress. This had not been a bad place to spend the last year and a half.

I slipped into sleep as easily as one of those seals sliding into the water and vanishing below the surface.

16

IN-BETWEEN

17

THIS CAN'T BE RIGHT

I woke up.

No, this can't be right. I must be dreaming.

I grabbed my phone and stared at the screen. 07:06 Sunday, 1st January.

I threw back the covers and ran to the window. It was still dark outside but it was the early morning sort, where the light is just beginning to win on the eastern horizon.

I rang Sian's number.

'Hello?' She sounded terrified. She probably thought it was the police checking up on the content of my last call.

'Sian, I'm not dead.'

'Linny!' I could hear her squealing. 'Mom, Mom, Linny's alive!'

'I don't understand. Tell me, is it New Year's Day? Really, truly?'

'Oh my word, happy birthday. You're sixteen. Linny, you're sixteen!'

A great wrenching howl burst from inside me. After so long, after so much suffering. Please, please let this be real!

I heard thumping on the door. 'What's going on?'

I banged it open and stared defiantly at Quinn. 'Up yours and your whole Sidhe family, Quinn Ramsay, I'm damn well alive!' I danced on the spot. 'Take that, you stupid curse. I've broken it – I'm free. I'll get old and die properly and never ever come back!' I began laughing, hiccupping, jumping.

'No, it can't be.' He looked ashen – struck dumb.

'Trust you to rain on my parade with your long face. But hey, tell you something, I don't care if you don't approve of the fact I've NOT DIED. Whatever it was has been paid, cancelled, gone. Scram, Sidhe boy, I'm going to have a sixteenth birthday party like no other.' I shut the door in his face. 'Did you hear that?' I asked Sian.

'Yeah, you go, girl. Who are you going to party with?'

'I don't know yet. Rowena Huntsman, maybe, and three very confused Chinese students.'

'Just take it easy, okay? Mom's saying you've had a shock.'

'The shock of waking up alive. Most people do that every day.'

'But in your case, that's major. Don't assume too much, okay?'

'You're saying it's not over?'

'I'm saying be careful. Mom and I will try and work out why it changed for you this time. I still can't quite believe it. Oh, Linny, I'm so thrilled for you. So relieved.'

I was grinning like the recipient of an unexpected Oscar. 'So am I, fifty times over. Every single one of the past me's are cheering.' One thought made me sober. 'But what do I tell my parents? They are going to be insufferable. "I told you so" will start every sentence.'

Even seeing sixteen has its drawbacks.

. . .

LIFE WAS TOO wonderful to spend it inside. I dressed quickly and ran out into the snow. A fresh covering had fallen, hiding the marks made by others over the last few days. It was visible sign of what I was feeling inside – a new start, fresh page. And what did sixteen feel like? Like fifteen to be honest but without the specter of death to spoil it.

I jogged around the hockey pitch and once warmed up did a tumble routine, ending with a round of applause for myself.

'Right, snow time!' Setting to work, I rolled a big snow-ball for the base of my snowman and a second smaller one for his head. I made him six feet, donated to him my Crowthorne scarf and a black woolly hat from lost property, and named him Quinn Ramsay. Next I lined up a row of snowballs and let rip in a therapeutic barrage, singing 'Ding dong merrily on high' at full volume.

'Linny?' Quinn was approaching me, hands dug in the pocket of his black coat.

'Quinn, meet Quinn, your snow brother.'

He stood in front of the much-pelted target and cocked his head. 'He's been in the wars.'

'Yeah, well, I had some issues to work through this morning.' I packed the snow into another ball in my hands, so tempted by the real thing.

'I need you to come with me.'

'Uh-uh, not again. Nope. Not having anything to do with the Sidhe. Not hunting near them, not casting charms or having midnight chats. Buzz off, Quinn.'

He gazed up to the skies. 'If only you knew who you were talking to.'

'I get it; you're some kind of princeling, but not of my royal family. The Buckingham Palace ones were mine as I was once English, and guess what? They don't go around putting curses on their subjects.'

He smiled slightly at that. 'Are you so sure? Every family has their secrets.'

'Doesn't matter if the queen does cast spells in the basement of the palace as I'm American now. A republican. I don't take any notice of royals anymore.'

'Seriously, I need you to come to the camp.'

'Joking?'

'We need to–'

I started backing away, reminding myself that I now had so much to lose. 'You need nothing from me. You've extracted a penalty of blood, sweat and tears. That's enough. Stop.'

He held out a hand. 'Please.'

I told him succinctly where he could go.

'Okay, then. Sorry it has to be this way.' He gave a high-pitched whistle. Another boy, older and unfamiliar, approached from the wooded margin of the field. Six followers came behind.

'I thought you said the Maledicta would come quietly,' said the stranger.

'I was wrong, Artair. I always get her wrong. Don't frighten her.' This was to the little posse he had summoned to round me up.

I threw the snowball at Quinn's head and made a dash for the nearest building, which happened to be the gym. I only got halfway across the pitch when someone tackled, bringing me face down into the snow. I screamed and struggled but the same person pushed my head down so all I got was a mouthful of ice. My arms were yanked behind me and tied, the scarf from the snowman used to gag me, then I was dragged hurriedly away into the trees. I kicked out at the nearest shins but found that resulted in me being thrown over a shoulder.

'Stop it, you can't win!' warned Quinn, placing a hand on my hair.

I tried to head butt him but only succeeded in bashing my chin on the carrier's back. 'Squirmy little thing, isn't she?' said my abductor. I recognized Conall's voice. And I'd thought him the kind one.

Options temporarily exhausted, I lay still, watching for an opportunity. No way was I going to let them take this gift of a life away from me. To hell with their balance or whatever their issue was with me for actually surviving.

The Sidhe passed single file through a screen of bushes and I found myself in the middle of the new camp pitched among pines. The ground was covered with old needles so made a soft landing when I was dumped by the fire. I immediately jumped up but Conall was ready for me this time.

'Legs?'

'Yeah, we'll have to go the whole hog.' Quinn threw him a thin grey rope. My boots were removed and ankles tied.

The older boy circled me. He bore a strong family resemblance to Quinn though his eyes were green. He had to be the brother Quinn had mentioned who had been expected to arrive New Year's Eve. Another Sidhe prince when one was more than enough. I was tempted to spit at him but the gag prevented me. Maybe that was just as well as he didn't even pretend to look friendly. 'She's one of the three cursed sisters?'

'The eldest. The one who dies on the eve of her sixteenth birthday like Lihtan did – except Linny didn't this time.' Quinn crouched beside me. 'I'm going to take the scarf away. The magic protection stops noise escaping so there's no point in screaming, okay?' He gently tugged it down.

I was quick with my protests. 'It's not fair. It's not my fault I didn't die. You can't kill me. People will know it's you – they'll work it out.'

He brushed a leaf out of my hair. 'You've got this all wrong. We just want to know why the curse didn't work.'

'So you can fix it? No thank you. You can't do that to me. I've had enough!' The thought that I might have to die again after having so nearly escaped was worse than anything I'd faced to date. 'Please, Quinn, I know you hate me and everything, but not that. Not that.' I shuddered. 'I can't believe this. I was so...happy.'

He rested a hand on my shoulder then got up. 'Conall?'

His friend took his place. 'I'm just going to see what magic is going on inside you, okay, Linny?'

'Not okay,' I whispered.

'Sorry, but I have to – for your own good.' He held up his hands to me like he had to the wall. He paused at my wrist, finding the bracelet. 'Hedge witch magic but weak,' he reported. 'Not enough to stop it.' He closed his eyes, frown lines appearing on his forehead. 'I can sense the curse. It's in every bone, every cell. I've never felt this level of malevolence before. There's no way she should be alive this morning. It's...waiting.'

'Waiting for what? Did it get fooled by the Leap Year or something?' asked Quinn.

'No, that has no effect. The curse is much cleverer than that. Quinn, did you say you used her when you cast the boundary charm?'

'Yeah.' He looked embarrassed by the admission. 'I didn't know, obviously. I just thought she looked the sweet

easygoing kind of girl that normally makes it easy to manipulate her memories.'

'Remind me not to ask your advice on girls in future. I'm
sorry, Linny, but the curse is still there. I think it's being held
off by the boundary charm. Quinn, she's the feminine
balance to your male presence in the spell so it protects her
too. That was a powerful Sidhe incantation cast by one of
royal blood and done in one of the centers of old magic. The
strength of it was enough to reach stalemate with the curse.'

'Are you saying that as long as the nightshade boundary
charm remains, as long as she stays inside the school wall,
then she'll live?' asked Quinn.

'Yes. But as soon as she steps outside, then it'll take
immediate effect.'

This couldn't be true. 'No! No, I don't believe you. I
refuse to believe you! Untie me!'

Quinn gave Conall the nod. He slipped my ankles and
wrists free and I sprang to my feet, shoving my feet back in
the boots.

'I'm leaving, right now. I'm going to prove that you're
wrong.'

'If you do that, you'll die,' said Conall.

Artair gave a shrug. 'Who cares? Let the Maledicta kill
herself if she wishes. She's in the way.'

His scorn quashed my impulse to test their words. I
stood utterly gutted in the middle of my enemies. Most of
them looked sympathetic but a few like Quinn's brother
looked as if they couldn't care two hoots. 'Are you saying...
are you saying I can never leave school?'

Conall shuffled his feet awkwardly. 'I'm saying if you do
then you'll die. That's not quite the same thing.'

'But they won't let me stay. It's not an option.'

'You've got a reprieve, girl. Make the most of it,' said

Artair. 'Take her back, Quinn, we've got more important business here.'

'Okay. Won't be long. Come on, Linny.'

Artair caught his brother's elbow as Quinn moved past him. 'She won't tell anyone, will she? Your forgetting charms don't work, I guess, because the curse blocks any magic?'

'Yeah. I hadn't factored that in either.'

'So just tell her that we'll shove her over the wall if she breathes a word of our presence to anyone.'

'Artair, there's no need to be so cruel.'

'There's every need. Our kingdom is at stake, the balance of the whole world is on the edge of a precipice.'

'That's not Linny's fault.'

'I didn't say she was to blame but she's part of it, like it or not. Civilians don't ask to be caught up in a war but it affects them nonetheless.'

Quinn took my arm. I was so numb with this new shock that I didn't shake free. It might've been better to die last night when I was resigned to it. Who wants to stay at school for ever even if they could?

18

TRUCE

I got as far as the edge of the woods before I couldn't go any further. I stopped Quinn by the simple expedient of sitting down.

'Linny?'

'Go away.'

'I'm sorry.'

'You've said that before but have you actually done anything to show that you mean it? No, you just threw me under the cursed bus last night and, when it swerved, announced just now it was still waiting for me beyond the walls, motor running.'

Rather than haul me to my feet, Quinn sat down beside me. We watched a robin flutter out of a bush and inspect us hopefully before giving up when no crumbs were forthcoming.

'You confuse me – challenge me. You said I had no imagination, so I've been trying to imagine what it's like being you these last few days.' His voice was more conciliatory than usual.

'Don't bother. No one can know what it's like to be me. My experience is unique.'

'I was raised strictly as a Sidhe; we don't spend much time thinking about ordinary people.'

'Really? I would never've guessed.'

'It's a fault, I see that, but we don't usually stay long enough in one place for it to matter.'

'Charm them into cooperation and then you're gone?'

'Something like that. But I've been thinking about you, can't stop it really, and I don't like what my thoughts make me feel.'

'So it's all about you, is it?' I asked sourly. 'I thought this was my tragedy.'

He huffed. 'I'm just trying to explain.'

I sighed, but really, I was interested to hear what he had to say. 'So what does it make you feel?'

'Pity. Sadness. Sorrow.'

I gulped. I didn't want my enemy to feel sorry for me. 'Why are you here, Quinn? It's not to feel sad for me, is it? Come on, you can tell me. As your delightful brother said, you can always boot me over the wall for an instant death sentence if I tell anyone. Is it about my friend?'

'Which one? The hedge witch?'

'You...you know about her?'

'Of course. Even an infant Sidhe could sense her power. Hedge witches have a flashy, superficial kind of natural magic, skimmed off the surface of nature. Theirs is nothing like the deeper, hidden currents of Sidhe power which are much harder to detect. No, we're not in the least worried by her.'

I let the arrogance pass as I wanted the reassurance too much. 'Is that the truth?'

'Linny, hedge witches are like oxpecker birds perched on a black rhino – a helpful nuisance, clearing off the bugs. We tolerate them because we know they release some of the little magics into the world, which in the main are good spells. We're not bothered by them unless they try something too ambitious.' He gestured to my bracelet. 'That wouldn't've worked even without the deadly nightshade boundary charm.'

I rubbed my face with my hands. 'Your mistake in picking me for the spell has kind of saved me, or at least brought me a...what was it your brother said? A reprieve?'

He nodded. 'I've been thinking. There are ways we can hide you when we're done here. I could reinforce the boundary charm to survive when I'm gone and you could stay.'

'Live in the woods all my life? What kind of existence is that? It was fine for Thoreau but I'm a twenty-first century gal.'

'That's up to you. I'm just saying it's your choice if you want to go that route.'

'You still haven't told me why you're here.'

He blew on his fingers. I'd gone beyond feeling cold. 'I suppose as you can't leave you'd better know so you can protect yourself. A powerful dark force is threatening this place. Green Drake has been the center of light magic for centuries, vital to the world's balance. We want to keep it that way.'

'I still don't understand: what is this magic? Why is it so important?'

He sighed. 'I keep forgetting: you really don't know the basics.'

'Then you'd better be my Merlin.'

'Hah-hah. Okay, my apprentice, magic to the world is like breath to the body: we need it to live, even humans who don't know it's there. I guess another name for it is the earth's life force.'

'Got it.' I sketched a mocking tick in the air.

'Light and dark magic in balance are creative, full of potential, like male and female, but if the whole world goes dark, then our lives become twisted, ugly versions of that. Eventually we die as that way leads only to extinction.'

'You do light magic, not dark?'

'Can't you tell?'

I shook my head.

'I suppose I deserved that.' He smiled ruefully. 'We try to – we don't always succeed. Some of us get taken by the dark. There's always a Morgan La Faye to every Merlin. We mustn't let the dark dominate because it will crush the light.'

'And the curse is what? Light or dark?'

'Definitely dark. I told you that your father took the light. What I meant was that he killed one of us who was transformed into the shape of a hart.'

I remembered the human expression in the stag's eyes; some part of me had always known. 'I'm sorry for that.'

'It wasn't just any ordinary person but a son of the Fey King. His name was Lihtan, and he was appointed in that generation as our guardian of the light, a kind of channel or focus for it to spread into the world and into the Sidhe. He was only fifteen, but he was extraordinary.'

'You put too many eggs in one basket, huh?'

He grimaced. 'He was like our federal reserve, holding our light magic currency. He carried the hopes of all the Sidhe. If he lived, he would've been the next Fey King.'

'Okay, let's look at this another way. My father killed a boy who was running about as a stag? How was he to know? It was one big snafu.'

'I grant you that he didn't realize what he was doing. All the same, he blew up the whole way that magic had been channeled for centuries. The light magic fled Lihtan's body and now hides in places like this. These centers are its sanctuary. Without them the world would tumble completely into dark magic and we'd all be lost from the light.' 'He twisted a twig in his hand, a crude kind of wand.

It sounded a stupid way of organizing things if it was so vulnerable to a stray arrow. 'And what about the dark magic?'

'That stayed in the Sidhe. It clings to us. All of us have to struggle against that part of us, reminding ourselves that we also should've inherited a light balance. It's a constant act, I supposed you'd say, of *will* not to surrender. Some prefer power to goodness, kindness, love.' He snapped the twig, and threw away the pieces. 'I'm telling you too much. We must go.'

'No, it's helpful. I've never understood what this was all about and, if I still have this curse to contend with, maybe I should take the reprieve as my time of finding out?'

Quinn looked at me then, and I felt that maybe for the first time he was really seeing me, Linny, not just some random girl or even the Maledicta. Oddly, his conclusion was identical to Sian's.

'You're very brave.'

'I don't seem to have been given a choice in that. Do you know what happened to my sisters? They were also cursed.'

'No. We lost track of all of you. Curse magic is not good to be around.'

I laughed darkly. 'You're telling me?'

'Legend says you were hidden by a powerful Sidhe, put in quarantine for our safety, but that doesn't seem to be the case for you.'

'I'd say I was abandoned.'

He held out a hand. 'It's not exactly been plain sailing for us, has it? How about a truce?'

What did I have to lose? My life was already forfeit and my first father would want me to try diplomacy against such a powerful foe. I shook his hand. 'Truce.'

'I'll ask my father about curse magic. He's the most powerful of us. He might know a way to break it without harming the fragile balance.'

I shook my head. 'There's that word again, balance. I could grow to hate it.'

'It's more than a word. We shade towards the dark because we lost the light and have to go seek it in places similar to this. Start meddling with powerful magic like yours and then we could tip over into the dark completely, and believe me, the world does not want to see what we would become then.'

'So I was right. It's not about me, it's you.'

'Yes.' Quinn gave me a wry smile. We began walking again, awkward in the new skin of our truce. 'Tell me something, what about your other friend?'

'Who, Jack?'

'Not Jack – Mr Huntsman's daughter, Rowena.'

'What about her?'

'Has she done anything, said anything?'

It was suddenly so obvious. 'Is she why you're here?'

'I didn't say that. I'm here to protect this well of light magic.'

But he had dropped a heavy hint, hadn't he? 'No, she's

not said anything much. We're not exactly friends – something of an age gap.'

'Yeah, you're so much older than her.' He risked a smile at me.

'I can't believe you just joked about my situation.'

'What's the alternative? Cry?'

'Yeah, you're right, I've tried that. Joke away. She's interested in you, I think.'

'Thanks for pretty much exposing the whole camp to her on Christmas Eve.'

'Tough.'

'See, I was right: such a sweet, easygoing girl.'

'This exterior?' I pointed to myself, knowing he was seeing wavy long brown hair and wide grey eyes, a scattering of freckles. 'False advertising. I was an outlaw once. Thief on several occasions. Killed a few people, not on purpose, just because they were near me at the end, so consider yourself warned.'

'I get it: you can look after yourself.'

'Don't dismiss me like your brother does. My agenda is to break this curse. If it crosses what you're here to do, then don't expect me to back down.'

'Understood. And know that if you are in our way, we'll have to go through you.'

'Is that the end of our truce?'

'No, just stating our positions. Try to enjoy your birthday, Linny. I'm sorry I had to spoil it but if you hadn't known the truth you might've left the grounds and killed yourself by mistake.'

'Yeah, you're a real hero.'

'I wouldn't go that far. Many happy returns. Sincerely meant.' He left me at the door of Crowthorne and jogged back to the woods.

. . .

I CANCELLED my plans for a birthday party and settled for thinking as I stretched out on my bed. I'd learned a lot, not much of it good, but at least I had a more accurate picture of my situation. Quinn was right that his insistence that I get checked out by his magic detector friend had saved my life – or at least prolonged this temporary version I had.

If I managed to live here for a full span of years, would that mean I just died and came back again much later? Or would it short-circuit the curse? Conall had said it was in every cell of my body, making me think of a disease that no amount of treatment could cure. I sensed there was no real escape from it.

Did my sisters also suffer from the same curse? Weighing the evidence, I rather thought not. The rumors I'd heard suggested they each had had their own sad fate to manage. If that hadn't included coming back then they'd be long gone. Lucky them.

Or had they been hidden by a dark Sidhe? That was what Quinn had suggested. Could they also be somewhere then in this time? If that was the case, all the more reason to make this reprieve permanent and try to find them. We'd been good friends as well as sisters. I'd missed them for centuries.

So back to square one: how to break the curse?

I didn't trust Quinn or his father to tell me if it upset their balance obsession. I'd put my faith in the hedge witches the Sidhe dismissed. And at least, I'd found out from Quinn that Sian wasn't the target. That was one really good thing to come out of a car crash of a morning.

I had been warned about telling people about the Sidhe. I decided texting wasn't the same thing at all so Artair could go boil his own head for all I cared. Besides Sian already knew that they were here.

Do you want the good or the bad news?

Sian immediately responded. *Oh no.*

Good news is that I'm still alive. Bad news is that it is the boundary charm keeping me that way. I'm only here as long as it is and I stay on the school grounds.

WTF!

My thoughts exactly. Can you do something for me?

Yes.

Get all your family onto researching curses and how to break them. I have a reprieve and I'm intending to use it.

Could Quinn not just make you a bracelet or something that would allow you to carry the protection with you?

I'll ask him but his friend did say that part of the reason it worked was that Green Drake is a site of old magic.

I think that's probably right. It's why all in my family enroll in the school. We can all feel it. It's very special.

BTW they're not here for you. Hedge witches aren't on their radar. They're in some kind of standoff with Mr Huntsman's daughter.

I asked Mom about her when you said you'd met her. She doesn't remember Mr Huntsman ever mentioning a daughter before and all my sisters went to the school. The eldest is about the same age.

Curiouser and curiouser. Do you think she might be one of the dark Sidhe that Quinn claims to be fighting? Or is he pretending and he's the dark Sidhe and she's the nice one?

Don't know and to us hedge witches both dark and light ones are toxic. They both have too much power. Steer clear.

Sadly, I think that if I'm going to find any answers it is going to come from getting up close and personal with the magic squad.

Don't anger them.

I thought of the snowman and the fight in the snow. *You know me I'm sweetness and light.*

Linny!

I promise. Miss Congeniality signing off now. I've got a dark or possibly light Sidhe to spy upon.

19

STARRY SKIES

It was an odd day, a blend of normal and extraordinary, like I had a pair of rainbow spectacles that kept falling down over my eyes, weirding everything. I had to pinch myself several times as I caught sight of the date on my phone and the stream of birthday messages. The three Chinese students, Chao, Liling and Mei (we'd progressed to names), had found out that it was my birthday and baked me a cake. They brought this to lunch and sang 'Happy Birthday' to me while the member of staff on duty took a photo of us. My cheeks ached with the fake smile I assumed so as not to hurt their feelings.

'You want go with us?' Chao asked, showing me a map with a walk they intended to do to the lighthouse.

'Oh, thank you, that's very kind of you, but I've got...a cold and think I should stay inside.'

'Yes, we saw you playing in snow with Quinn and friends. Very funny.'

That was one word for it.

'You get cold in snow?' asked Mei, her pretty face looking most concerned for me.

'Yes, that's right. So wrap up warm for your walk.' I'm not sure they understood me but we parted with much nodding and smiling. Mandarin – I must crack that one on my quest to speak all major world languages.

As I walked back to Crowthorne, a SUV drew up beside me. Miss King was driving but it was Rowena in the passenger seat who opened the window.

'Linny, I'm pleased we caught you. I hear it's your special day – sixteen! Fancy a trip to the beach? I'm photographing seabirds.'

I had a mental image of getting in the rear of the car, driving as far as the gates and dropping dead. 'Um, no thanks, not today. Have a nice afternoon. Happy New Year.'

'And to you.'

The car sped away. It was hard to imagine in the full light of day that Rowena was up to anything sinister. I decided to research her on the internet to see where she had come from and what she was really doing here, but not on my birthday. Even if I was spending it alone, I should do something to mark the moment.

So I played the piano. I hadn't shown anyone my full repertoire as they might wonder how a girl had gathered so many songs, some of them no longer in anyone's music library. I started back in the eighteenth century when the instrument had been invented, then progressed through Victorian ballads, twentieth century jazz and finally modern songs. Musicality was something else that stayed with me in each lifetime.

Feeling cramp starting in my calf owing to the fact that I had sat at the piano far too long, I decided to go back outside. The stars were already out, the skies clear. I walked out into the middle of the biggest field – the football pitch. No one else had been there so mine were the only set of footprints. I fell on my back and made a snow angel.

'Don't get claustrophobic,' I told myself. 'Don't think of the boundary wall as a jail.' But it was: a beautiful snow-lined prison camp.

'Talking to yourself now?' Quinn had crept up on me again. He was lying in the snow with me, head to my head, like we were two spokes on a wheel, and I hadn't even noticed.

I went up on one elbow. 'It's rude to eavesdrop.' I wish I didn't get a little flip in my stomach when I saw him. Last thing I wanted to be was like every other girl who came into his orbit. *Remember, you don't know if you can trust him.*

'No eaves anywhere near us. What are you looking at?'

'You.'

'Before you realized I was here.'

I lay back. OK, so we'd talk like this, would we? 'The sky. It doesn't change.' A crescent moon was riding over the dark hem of treetops. Orion was striding across the darkness, sword hanging from his belt. It was one of those clear nights when you could feel yourself floating in the infinity of space with very little effort on your part.

'You're right. It's one of our few reliable things.' He let the silence fall between us, oddly comfortable considering how most of our exchanges had been bitter ones.

'What are you doing here with me? I thought I was bad to be around?'

'I feel a strange kind of...' he searched for a word, discarded a few, then went for, 'responsibility for you – first time I've felt that for someone who isn't a Sidhe. I can't seem to leave you alone. And Conall told me that it wasn't right that you spend your birthday alone.'

I held my hand up to the sky, blotting out a patch of stars. 'How old are you, Quinn?'

'Seventeen.'

'Is that a human seventeen or a Sidhe one?'

'It's the same thing. We age like you do.'

'Not like I do.'

'I meant like other humans do.'

'And they put you in charge of your posse?' I mimed shooting the moon.

'My what?'

'Your gang of desperadoes, outlaws, the magic squad, take your pick.'

'You're talking about my men?'

'Yep. Seems a big task for someone of your age.'

He rolled on to his side, head supported on his left hand. This put his face over mine but upside down. Our eyes met. 'But it has to be someone of my age. Until we turn eighteen we are closest to the light magic. We feel it in a way that older Sidhe can't.'

'Getting old gets in the way?' I felt vulnerable like this so rolled to mirror his pose, face to face across the little patch of compressed snow. I noticed the flakes weren't melting in his hair, but glimmering like a coronet. I tried not to be impressed.

'Only because our character is formed by then. It takes someone who is still growing, choosing their path, to talk to it.'

'You talk to magic?'

'It's more like communing with it but I thought that sounded weird.'

'Both sound weird, Quinn. The whole Sidhe thing is one world of weird.' Facing him suddenly became too much, so I flopped back up to look up at Orion. I could feel Quinn was still studying me. 'Why are you staring?'

'I was wondering.'

'Wondering what?'

'If you've ever been kissed?'

Oh, man. Make a joke, make a joke. 'Well, there was this boy in the sixteenth century who kissed me at one of the Thames Frost Fairs. He stole my purse too of course but I thought he was a very charming thief.' Actually, he'd had terrible bad breath and forced the kiss on me but I preferred a more romantic version.

'What's a Frost Fair?' He moved a little closer.

Concentrate, Linny. 'It...it happened when the Thames froze. The whole of London moved out onto the ice. There were food stalls, rides, things to buy, dancing. Everyone came, from the lords and ladies to the poor people like me.'

'That's awesome. You mean Shakespeare? Queen Elizabeth?'

'I suppose so but I was just one unimportant servant girl. I didn't know then that the man from the Globe would end up so famous and they didn't let me near royalty.'

He traced my lips with a cold fingertip, a feather touch like a snowflake falling on bare skin. 'You're near royalty now.'

I swatted at his hand as if it were a mosquito. 'I told you, you're not mine.'

'You're under one of our curses so you are at least half in our world.'

'Hardly a good way of recruiting subjects.'

'Terrible way, but I'm working with what I've got because I really, really want to give you a birthday kiss. It's a Sidhe tradition.' He smiled, expression full of mischief.

I screwed my eyes closed against his charisma. 'You've made that up!'

'Have I?'

I felt warmth along my left side. I turned my head, opened my eyes and found he had edged as close as he could. He now bent over me. Did I want to be kissed by him? I was afraid I did want that, partly because I was just so lonely and partly because...

I pressed my fingers lightly into his chest. His heart thudded just under their tips, a little fast. He wasn't as calm as he looked. 'All right then. As a "thank you" for stopping me killing myself today, we can kiss. And to seal our truce.'

He leaned over me and pressed his lips gently against mine. 'Happy Birthday.'

His kiss felt warm and incredibly sweet, skating the line between friendly and something more. 'Thank you,' I whispered.

'So, better or worse than the boy from the Frost Fair?' As he pulled away, he was looking too smug, so I told a lie.

'You have a lot to learn about human girls, Quinn Ramsay.' I got up and brushed the ice off as best I could. 'What are you doing lying about in the snow, you fool? Don't you realize you could catch cold? And someone might take advantage.' I threw a barely compacted snowball at him that disintegrated before impact.

He sprang up. 'That's fightin' talk, ma'am.' He scooped up a handful. His hit me in that awkward spot between scarf and chin.

'Urgh!' My answer was a much better made missile that hit his shoulder.

'Right, that's it: war!'

Laughing, running, scooping, we continued to pelt each

other for a good ten minutes until we were breathless and, in my case, exhausted. I was the first to sue for peace. 'Pax!'

He sent a last cheeky snowball winging my way before holding up his hands. "Okay, pax.'

'Want some cake? The Chinese students made me one. Chocolate – and you can't go wrong with that, can you?'

He glanced over towards the camp. 'I should really be getting back.'

'Oh, okay.' My mood dipped with disappointment.

He smiled, eyes twinkling. 'Has it got icing?'

'Yep.'

'Liam's chestnut and turnip stew or your chocolate cake? Hmm.' He slung an arm around my shoulders. 'I think I'll be late.'

WE WERE in the little kitchen when Artair found us. I was perched on the counter top, Quinn at the breakfast table; we were both laughing as we juggled utensils between us. His brother strode in and snatched a toast rack from the air.

'Quinn, I expected you back three hours ago.'

If we hadn't been so good at juggling that would've been enough to send things crashing to the ground. I was delighted to see, however, that we adjusted and Quinn deftly ended the routine, placing the objects on the table. I was left holding two tangerines.

'Artair, you didn't really meet Linny earlier. Linny, my brother, Artair.'

'Hi.' I waved jauntily, knowing that would needle him.

'Have you forgotten the rules on the Maledicta?' Artair snapped, ignoring me.

'The curse is suspended so I guess that is too,' said Quinn.

'No offense meant,' Artair shot this in my general direction, 'but the rule is put there for your protection, Quinn. You're at the critical point in your path, so are the people our father has sent to help you. If you're around dark magic, it might well be enough to tip you in the wrong direction. It's tempting that way. We can't afford for you to fail.'

'Why is it, I wonder, that people say "no offense" just before they launch a pretty insulting comment?' I asked the air as Artair was still avoiding me. 'I mean no harm to Quinn.'

'It's the curse, not you, I'm worried about.' So Artair had finally deigned to address me directly.

Quinn's brother was making me feel like a leper. We had treated them badly in Medieval times, making them ring bells to warn of their approach and live apart. They were driven off with stones if they came too close. I slid off the counter. 'Thanks for celebrating with me, Quinn.'

'Linny–'

'It's okay. I'm tired. That's a new thing for me – being tired on my sixteenth birthday. I think your brother has some things he wants to say to you. I'll see you around.'

Quinn took one look at his brother's granite expression and gave in to the inevitable. 'Thanks for sharing the cake with me. Sleep well.'

I wondered, as I went up to my bedroom, if we would've kissed goodnight had Artair not been there. Maybe. I wasn't sure what Quinn and I were now but I thought it might be the beginning of a friendship at least.

A CLEAR BUT cold day dawned near the end of the holidays. I was feeling more caged than ever watching the seabirds fly over, careless of boundaries. I'd not seen Quinn for over twenty-four hours as he'd had what he called a 'retreat' with his team, mental preparation for the coming battle, he'd explained somewhat cryptically.

He refused to divulge exactly what that meant, claiming it was Sidhe business and shouldn't involve me if I kept out of it. I don't think he quite understood me yet.

I returned to the snowman I'd built on my birthday and made some repairs.

'How's Snow Quinn doing?'

Once again Quinn had managed to surprise me with his silent arrival. My heart did a little tumble of pure joy. 'He's good, thanks. I've given him a makeover.'

Quinn gave me a quick brush of a kiss, both of us not quite sure of the new rules between us. 'I think we should make him a Snow Linny so he doesn't get too lonesome out here. It shouldn't take long.'

'Is that a crack at my less than giant size?'

'Did I say that?' Grinning, he began rolling the first snowball.

We made a fine job of my snow sister, complete with willow twig hair and shiny pebbles for eyes.

'Let me warm your hands,' Quinn said when we'd finished. I held them up and he rubbed them vigorously before slipping them inside his coat. 'How've you been? I couldn't stop thinking about you yesterday. The guys gave me grief for it.'

Lonely. 'Fine.'

'I missed you. I got you some shells from the beach. As you can't go there, I thought I'd bring the beach to you.' He showed me a handful of perfect little white shells.

'Thank you.' I transferred them to my pocket, knowing already these would become one of my treasures. 'I'll have to ask Sian to show me how to make them into something.'

Quinn pulled a wry expression. 'If she knows they come from me, watch she doesn't do something to them. I don't think hedge witches like us Sidhe much.'

'You don't say?'

We began walking towards the dining hall. I could almost convince myself we owned the whole place, the lord and lady of the castle. It was going to be very strange when we had to share it with others again. Looking up at Quinn, who also looked quite content to stroll across the sports fields with no one else in sight, I realized that I had been so caught up in my own drama, I'd stopped wondering about the lives of others. Quinn's life. That was incredibly selfish of me.

'Tell me, Quinn, what's it like being a Sidhe? You say you're not human. What's the difference?'

He took my hand and swung it gently between us. 'The power, I suppose; that changes us.'

'So is it like a genetic mutation – another evolutionary branch?'

'You mean are we a kind of *homo magicus*? I like that! To be honest I don't know. We eat and drink the same things as humans; on average we live a little longer, but few survive over a hundred and twenty. Our training and our magic together make us...' He paused.

'Hard to detect?' Like a predator, I thought.

'Yes. Nothing's been spotted in a laboratory when we've had blood tests or treatment but I'd think the magic has a way of hiding from over-interested scientists. I think you can tell us apart better by what we can do.'

It seemed quite abstract to me, this power he sometimes talked about as if it were separate from him, more like a good friend. 'So what's it like, having power?'

'What's it like being an expert juggler and gymnast?'

'Tumbler. But that's hardly the same.'

'Those are powers too, pretty cool ones. Like with them, you have to practice magic and respect its limits.'

'But it must make you feel superior to the rest of us being so powerful? What can you do with it?'

He stopped and turned me to face him. 'Nothing to hurt anyone else, not if I'm using it properly. Maybe it did make me arrogant, till a certain person halted me in my tracks with a well-placed knee when I used her in a spell without her permission. I think I need you around to keep me humble.'

'I have to break it to you, Quinn Ramsay, but you're not there yet.'

He laughed and we started walking again.

'See, you're doing just fine taking me down a peg, or two hundred.'

20

THE SIDHE INVASION

A few days later as a thaw took hold, the other students started returning. From the silence of the snowfields and empty corridors, the school was suddenly bursting with noise and people, the streams in the grounds gushing with meltwater. It was a hard adjustment for me. I hadn't expected to see any of them again.

Sian sought me out on her return. I was hiding in my bedroom to avoid meeting so many all at once and answering awkward questions as to how my holidays had been. She gave me a long hug then held me away at arm's length. Her grip firmed; she gave me a little shake.

'Right, I'm back now. You aren't facing this alone anymore.'

I wasn't sure if I should admit that I'd spent quite a bit of time with Quinn over the past few days since he came back from his retreat. We hadn't talked about the curse but we had chatted about many other things – my memories, music, families, growing up Sidhe – as we tried to understand each other's lives. We'd walked the grounds holding hands when we thought Artair wouldn't notice. It was a confusing friendship; sometimes it felt like we were involved in something deeper but neither wished to admit it. With so many ranged against us, so many reasons why it wouldn't work, so many historical hurts on my side against the Sidhe, it was impossible, wasn't it?

'I'm so pleased you're back. It's a relief to see you, Sian.' I gave her another hug. 'I'm worried I won't be able to avoid leaving the school much longer. I refused every invitation so far, which was okay as it was vacation time, but what happens when there's a school trip or something?'

'Jack and I will have to run interference.' Sian marched up and down the carpet, burning off some of her nervous energy. 'We'll keep an eye out for you – watch your back.'

'Have you found out anything more about how to break the curse?'

'Mom says she thinks she's got a lead. An old hedge witch in New Orleans might know something so she's going down there next weekend. They talked a little on the phone and apparently it is about unwinding it slowly, pushing the magic from you.'

'Conall said it was in every cell.'

'Conall?'

'One of Quinn's men, the guys he's got camping in the woods.'

There was a quick rap on the door and Jack burst in. 'I was spectacular!' He did a kind of pirouette and collapsed elegantly on my beanbag chair.

I had to laugh. 'You're always spectacular to us, Jack, but what do you mean in particular? Skiing?'

'No, I suck at skiing. It turns out that ice skating is my jam.' He pulled out his phone. 'I got Dad to take a video as I was sure no one here – apart from you two gorgeous people

– would believe me.' He showed us a little clip of him skating backwards, only falling twice.

'So you had fun?'

'It was fantastic. You must come with me next year, especially if your horrible parents abandon you again. So, how was your birthday, sweet-cheeks?'

'Quiet.' I exchanged a look with Sian.

'That's no good. We'll have to go to Rockland next free day and I'll treat you to a movie with the biggest popcorn they sell.'

'Jack.' Sian put a hand on his shoulder. 'Linny can't leave.'

'You mean her parents have grounded her?'

How to explain to Jack? 'I am grounded – that's more apt than you know – but it's because of something from my past.'

'You're not making sense.'

'I can't explain because you wouldn't believe me.'

He pummeled his forehead. 'Not you too. It's enough I'm friendly with one witchy person. I can't lose you to that stuff. I thought you were the sane one, above superstition. Listen, you two,' he leant closer as if imparting a big secret, 'none of it is real!'

'Can you just go with the idea that if I believe it then something bad might happen by the power of suggestion? That's rational, isn't it?'

He groaned.

'And help me not to leave the school grounds, no matter what?'

'Fine, fine. But get Sian to make you a string of garlic or another bracelet so we can go and see that movie.'

'It's not that easy.'

'Nothing ever is with you two.' He sat up. 'So?'

'So what?'

'Have you heard the news?'

'I've been avoiding news recently.'

'There are ten new boys – ten! Three in Eaglestone, three have been put in Hawkfield, three in Falconbury and one more to our house. I met him downstairs. He said his name was Conall Jedburgh and I think he's a friend of Quinn.'

Camping must have ended with a revolt among Quinn's men. Wet slushy weather was probably worse than the hard frost of before.

'I've never known so many new students arrive in January,' said Sian, looking rather alarmed for us both.

'Ah, yes, the new guy explained that,' said Jack easily. 'He said their old school went bust when the principal ran off with the accountant, taking the money with them. The students all had to disperse to new places quickly and Mr Collins said ten of them could be squeezed in here. They are mostly in my year, though I think Conall said he is in yours.' Jack went to the mirror and ran his hand through his hair. 'He's got these really cool little spike dreadlocks. Do you think my hair would do that with enough gel?'

'No,' Sian and I said in unison.

'Aw, I think I can really rock that look.'

I batted him over the head with a pillow. 'Moron!'

He thumped me back with a cushion and we ended up rolling on the floor until he tickled me into submission, finding the place on my ribs which he knew would reduce me to jelly.

'Stop it, stop it!' I gasped.

'Say you love me best in the world!' demanded Jack. 'Jack is the best – go on, say it!'

There came another quick knock on my door, then it opened to reveal Quinn and Conall standing in the corridor.

'It's Times Square in here,' said Sian, giggling at the ridiculous picture we made. 'I thought we were the "out" crowd?'

Quinn looked past Sian to see Jack and me in what must have looked a very compromising heap on the floor. And so my two worlds collided before I'd had a chance to explain. Quinn's expression changed, reminding me that one of my first impressions had been that he had pirate tendencies. He certainly looked mad enough to start swinging a cutlass at poor Jack.

'So sorry to interrupt the grand reunion,' said Quinn in a tone that froze the room.

'Do you want us to come back later?' asked Conall, giving me a commiserating look.

'No, it's fine.' I pushed Jack off me and got up, feeling guilty even though I knew Quinn was wildly misinterpreting what he had seen. 'Come in. Hi, Conall. I hear you've joined Crowthorne?'

Jack put the pillow down with exaggerated care. 'You know each other already? Linny, what have you been up to during the holidays? Your messages have been way too uninformative.'

'Conall, you met Jack earlier. This is Sian.' We were all avoiding involving the thunderous Quinn.

My friend was eyeing Conall with not a very welcoming expression. 'Hello.'

Conall took a step towards her then smiled broadly as he gauged her powers. 'Ah, the source of Linny's interesting jewelry choices.'

'Don't encourage her. She'll be making you wear weeds too,' said Jack. 'Linny, I just need my copy of *Great Expecta-*

tions back.' He moved behind Quinn and Conall in the pretense of choosing a book from my shelf. He started a pantomime of wiggling eyebrows and pointing to Quinn and me, then fanning himself.

Subtlety, thy name is not 'Jack Burne'.

Conall came to my rescue. 'So Sian, you make those *charming* bracelets yourself? It would be an honor to wear one.' Conall smiled even more widely as he saw Sian's shock at politeness from someone she considered an enemy.

Jack tucked a book under his arm. 'You don't know what you're letting yourself in for, Conall.'

'Oh, but I think I do.'

Jack edged to the door, unnerved by the still silent Quinn. 'Right, I'm outta here before Sian starts weaving – got to unpack. See you later.' He escaped.

'Are you Sidhe here to make trouble for Linny?' asked Sian, going straight to the point.

'No. Are you?' asked Conall.

'I'm her friend!'

'So are we.'

'The Sidhe aren't friends to people like us. You have your own agenda. Why are you here if not for Linny? Why have you invaded the school?'

'Conall can't tell you, Sian.' Quinn finally broke his silence. 'But it's nothing to do with you or Linny. Just keep out of our business and we won't interfere with yours. At all.'

Was he telling me that whatever had started between us was already over just because he misinterpreted what I'd been doing with Jack? He really could be a foolish Sidhe prince sometimes.

'She's under a death curse thanks to your lot in case you have forgotten,' said Sian. I appreciated the vinegar tone in my friend's voice. 'She can hardly keep out of your business.'

'I haven't forgotten. I'm trying to find out if there's anything we can do for her. In fact, I'd appreciate a word with her now.' Quinn gave Conall a speaking look.

'Oh, right. Sian, would you show me around the house?' Conall headed for the door.

Sian raised a brow at me.

'I'm fine. You can go.' I wasn't really sure I was fine but whatever Quinn felt he had to say was better just between the two of us.

'All right, Sidhe, I'll show you around,' said Sian to Conall.

'Thank you, hedge witch. So where do you keep your eye of newt then?'

'With the toe of frog, of course.'

I could hear them exchanging good-natured insults as they went down the corridor. If they didn't watch out they'd end up liking each other.

'So you've moved the posse in, lock, stock and barrel?' I said, seeing if we could get past the Jack moment without an argument.

Quinn revolved the silver ring on the longest finger on his right hand. 'The magic thinks the dark Sidhe are also gathering so I wanted to bring my men closer for emergencies. I see you were very pleased to see your friends too.'

'Yes.' I folded my arms. Apparently, the row was coming anyway.

'You and Jack – how long's that been going on?'

'Excuse me?'

'I thought we...well, clearly I was mistaken. I might not be used to human relationships but even we Sidhe know that you should only carry on with one person at a time.'

'You call that carrying on? With Jack?'

'How else do you explain you being on the floor with him putting his hands all over you!' His eyes flashed with blue fire.

'You're jealous – of that?'

'What do you expect me to be? Delighted? I thought we were friends –'

'We are.'

'And maybe more than friends. But now I'm thinking that I got you completely wrong.'

'You didn't,' I said quietly. He was winding himself up into a temper and I was not inclined to follow him.

He paced to the window. 'Even the magic said you were the one I should be with – told me to try to understand you – and look how well that's turned out. I don't understand a thing!'

I held up a hand to stop him digging himself deeper into this hole of jealous indignation. 'Quinn, if I came upon you and Conall having a friendly wrestling match in the common room, would you like me to assume you were seeing each other?'

'No! Don't be absurd.'

'It's no more absurd than what you are accusing me of. What you have with Conall, that's what it's like for Jack and me. He's like a brother and he thinks of me like a sister. We were just...' I shrugged, trying to find the right word, 'playing, I suppose you'd call it.'

'It didn't look like that. He had his hands all over you.'

'Because he was tickling me! Do Sidhe not tickle each other?' The thought made me smile even as I asked the question. 'Don't answer that – you are so not the tickling sort. But humans are.'

He ran his fingers through his hair, awareness dawning

that he had made rather a fool of himself. 'He's just a friend?'

'One of my two best ones so there's no "just" about it. If you'd paid any attention to me last semester you would've seen how it was. And when you get to know him better, you'll realize that I'm not his type.'

'I was surprised when I saw you with him, I have to admit. I hadn't caught that vibe from him before.'

'You added two plus two and made thirty-seven thousand.'

He cleared his throat. 'Is this the part where I have to say sorry?' He looked about as keen as a cat shown its bath.

'Yes, and you'll have to be extra especially nice to Jack. He's going to be too terrified to come out of his room in case you are waiting to rough him up.'

'I don't rough people up.'

'No?'

'I get my minions to do that for me.' If he was cracking a joke, then he was getting back to being his normal self.

'I'll tell Jack he needs to employ his own minions then and they can have a minion face off – settle it without involving either of you.'

Quinn groaned and sat down next to me on the bed. 'I jumped to the wrong conclusion, didn't I?'

'Just a little.'

'It's because I don't know what I'm doing with this kind of thing.'

'A relationship with a human?'

'Yes.'

'It can't be that different from what you are used to. You know what to do with magic – you talk to it.'

'That's part of what I do, yes.'

'The magic talks back to you?'

'Yeah.'

'So talk to me. Don't guess at what's going on in my life. Get to know me. For a start, you can tell me how you talk to the magic, what it feels like.'

He shrugged. 'I just feel it. It's like slipping underwater and being surrounded by it.'

'That must be amazing to experience. Is it everywhere or only in one place?'

'It's spread out across the grounds but there are stronger patches. You've found one of them.'

'Have I?'

'The holly bushes. The magic told me you'd been a frequent visitor there.'

'The holly fortress makes me feel peaceful.'

'Light magic – that's what you're sensing. It's accepted you despite everything. Artair doesn't believe me, he imagines the magic would reject you, but it's true. So, step two on the Linny plan of getting to know you better, let me ask you something. How are you today?'

'Now I've stopped you doing damage to an entirely innocent boy? I'm okay. I'm just waiting for the next crisis. You gave me a brief taste of one just then.'

He grimaced. 'Prince of over-reaction sitting right here.'

'You called it. As for the next crisis, I'm not sure which direction it's going to come from.' I was acutely conscious of the small gap separating our hands where they rested on the bedcover. 'And you?'

'Happier now the team is under a roof. Should shut them up for a bit. You wouldn't believe how they moaned.' He shifted a little closer and let his little finger brush against mine. 'I was wondering: seeing how I'm not making great judgement calls today, what do you want to say about us to other people?'

'That we've become friends over the holidays?'

'I suppose that will do.' He didn't look entirely content with that suggestion.

'Are we anything more to each other, Quinn?'

'You tell me.'

'Argh! Stop with the answering questions with a question! That's so annoying.'

He brushed my hair behind my ear. 'I think we might be more. I'm irrational and jealous and I want to see you all the time – these are all signs according to my most reliable source.'

'Conall? What about the fact that I'm a carrier of dark magic?'

'Artair worries too much.'

'Or maybe you don't worry enough?'

'I just know that I want this.' He put his hand over mine. 'It's not logical or even sensible. I just feel it's right. The magic here agrees.'

I had all kinds of counter arguments lined up – that we would meet with opposition, that there was no future for us, as friends or as more. But I had lived many lives of no future; I had the philosophy of trying to grab what I could before it was whisked away from me.

'Okay.'

'Okay what?'

'Let's be friends and more. For now.'

He smiled. 'That's good enough for me. Later I'll show you that we Sidhe know all about tickling. We're not that different from you.'

It was only after he left that I began doubting. I'm a suspicious kind of person, taught caution over the centuries. Sian had warned me never to trust a Sidhe. I'd seen Quinn charm most of the school within a few hours of arrival; I'd just witnessed how quickly his mood could change; was I just being lured into the same trap? For what purpose? I carried a curse inside me that the Sidhe saw as a threat. Was this a way of neutralizing me so I wouldn't find a way of turning it against them?

Or maybe, another voice whispered, *he just likes you. Because you have to admit that you've grown to like him too.*

21

THE STRONGEST CHARM

My next crisis came from an unanticipated direction and in the middle of assembly.

'So Tenth Grade, I hope you spent your vacation revising for your mid-year assessments which start tomorrow.' Our head of year, Mr Tomlinson, then began his usual speech about the vital importance of these exams for our grade point average and the rest of our lives. He flashed up slides about the revision techniques we all should've been using and warned that if we didn't do well we might be asked to move to a different school with lower academic standards.

It truly was a shocking awakening. My books had all gathered dust in a corner of my room for weeks.

'Oh my gosh, I haven't,' I whispered to Sian.

'Haven't what?'

'Done a stroke of work. I thought I'd be dead.'

Sian gave a choked noise.

'Are you laughing at me?'

'In a horrified, oh you poor thing way. It's kind of terrible and funny – a real sting in the tail of surviving.'

You would've thought I'd ace school after having lived so many lives, but girls had only been educated recently, and the content and style of exams changed so much each time I went to school, it was like starting all over again. 'Did you revise?'

'Some.'

'Which means you did loads. I bet even Jack managed to do some work in between skating lessons.'

Sian squeezed my fingers. 'Come on, Linny, you've faced much bigger problems than this.'

The next few days were a nightmare. I refused to go out for one of my walks with Quinn as I had so much cramming to do and, even so, I still went into every paper like an actress in a play in which she doesn't know the lines. It was truly awful. The only exams that went well were the French and German orals and that was because I was fluent in both before I came to Green Drake even if a little old fashioned in my diction. At the end of the week I was a confused, exhausted heap of quivering brain cells, not a girl at all.

Quinn finally extracted me from my room on Saturday and took me for a brisk ramble around the grounds, to 'blow away the cobwebs' as he put it.

'Why are you taking it so seriously?' he asked, genuinely puzzled by my behavior.

'Is that a dig at the fact that I'm not able to leave school ever as things stand?'

'No, no, really not.' He looked sweetly flustered that I'd made that connection. 'I meant why worry about this little human thing?'

'Um, maybe because I'm human?'

He boosted me up so we could sit in our favorite tree, a gnarled oak with welcoming broad branches. Quinn had said it was another focus of the light magic, drawing strength from its spreading roots. From here we could look out to sea without me getting too near the boundary.

'Aside from the fact that I have my pride and don't want to come across as dumb, I can't afford to be asked to leave. You know better than anyone what that would mean.'

'Yeah, but I'd change their minds.' He wiggled his fingers in a sign for spell-casting.

'Still leaves my pride. Don't you have Sidhe tests that matter to you, or are princes exempt?'

'I suppose the struggle between light and dark is all we really worry about at this age – and being good at charms and the like.' He brought one leg up to his chest, as at home in a tree as an owl might be.

'Are you any good?'

He looked offended. 'Can't you tell? I defeated one of the three most powerful curses ever made by a Sidhe.'

'Achieved a temporary reprieve, you mean.' The wall shimmered in my gaze – my protection and my cage.

'Yes, but still, it's impressed my brothers and my dad, boosted my rep in Sidhe circles.'

'Are Sidhe families different from human ones? I mean I have a lot of experience with my kind.'

He flicked a twig to the ground.

'Come on, Quinn, what harm is there in telling me? I know so much other stuff already.'

'Yeah, I guess you do. Okay then. I have four brothers, all older than me. Fergus, the eldest, is the one expected to take over the kingship from Dad if all goes to plan.'

'It's not automatic?'

'Sidhe rules mean that it doesn't always go with first-born. It's fitness for the position that matters, more like being elected president.'

'So, if a family produces a Sidhe with weak powers, they're never allowed to take the top job?'

'Or if they openly practice dark magic. If that happens, other families can put in a bid to take over if they feel strong enough.'

'This sounds very familiar. We did things that way in Anglo-Saxon England.'

'I don't doubt though that Fergus will be up to any challenge. He's pretty impressive.'

'And your other brothers, besides the ever charming Artair?'

'Brodie and Paten. They're easier going than Fergus and Artair.'

'They could hardly be more uptight. No sisters?'

'There hasn't been a female Sidhe born for many years in my family. The birthrate in our population is about four males to one female.'

'What's wrong with the Sidhe?'

'When the light magic fled into wild places it sent the population out of balance.'

He was saying my father did that.

'My mother was one of the rare ones. She was born to a Sidhe couple and chose to marry another Sidhe – my father obviously.'

'Was?'

'She died giving birth to me – an unexpected complication. Some say it was a curse rather than natural. It was a huge blow to my father and brothers. They still miss her like crazy.'

'I'm sorry.'

'It's a long time ago now. I never knew her.'

'But you miss her too. Eight of my mothers died before I could remember them but I still grieved for them.'

He leant back against the trunk. 'I keep forgetting. Of course, you would know. There's little you haven't experienced.'

We needed to lighten the atmosphere a little. Grief had its way of sinking in the claws and not letting go.

'There is plenty I'd prefer to do without. Going through puberty fifty times but never really getting out on the other side – that's no picnic.'

'I don't imagine the original curse-maker thought about that. That really is cruel.'

'So what do the majority of Sidhe do then when it comes to choosing partners?'

'Most of us tend to have short-term relationships with ordinary people. Occasionally they stay together and then they bring that person over into our world. There are charms that work to make sure they don't tell.'

'That sounds like a kind of...kidnapping.'

He laughed. 'No, no, not like that. It's more like joining the secret services and the charm is just to help them not make a mistake – they choose it entirely of their own free will. They don't spend much time after that outside the Sidhe community so it's merely an insurance policy. It's for their own protection as much as ours as they would be dismissed as mad men and women if they started talking about their Sidhe lover.'

'Or be thought of as a poet.'

'There have been exceptions who slipped through the net, no major harm done. Take a look at the history of art and literature and you'll spot them.'

We let silence stretch between us. It wasn't hard to see that our relationship fell into the short-term category for him, not least because no charm would work on me and

Quinn would have to move on eventually when his job here was done.

'Quinn, what happens to me if you fail to protect the light magic here?'

'Ah. You've thought of that, have you? Failure isn't an option.'

'Failure is always an option. You'd better tell me.'

His eyes took on their chill cast, reminding me of Mrs Willowbrook's warning that no matter how attractive on the surface, an icy magic lay at the heart of every Sidhe. Even light could be cold without necessarily being good. The phrase 'seeing things in the cold light of day' came to mind.

'The boundary charm will stop working – that's woven with light magic linked with the power of the deadly nightshade.'

'Could you move me to another place and recast the charm?'

'If the well of light magic is polluted here it means the world will have a much bigger problem than the fate of one girl. And if it's gone dark, then I will be too, Linny. I'll not be able to talk to the light magic again and I will only be able to cast dark spells.'

'You'll be a dark Sidhe?'

'Yes.'

'That's not going to happen.'

'As I said, failure isn't an option for either of us.'

THAT WAS a chilling thought to take back to Crowthorne with me. Quinn had a meeting with his magic squad so I went to Sian's room. She was beginning a new patchwork, this one for Jack who had complained that she hadn't given him one of her special blankets for Christmas. He might not like the woo-woo stuff but he dug the craftsmanship, he told her.

'How's it going?' I asked Sian, gesturing to the blue patch she was sewing to a white one.

'Good. I'm putting protection charms into it like I did yours. With so many Sidhe around we need to make sure Jack's safe.'

I didn't want to spoil her mood by telling her that Quinn said hedge witch magic was no match for theirs. 'I don't think they're after him.'

'He's our friend and we both are potential threats. Who knows what they'll do if they wake up to the fact that we care about him?'

'Good point.'

She put aside her project. 'Linny, what are you doing with Quinn? I mean, I know he's attractive and charming, but that's all charisma. Not real.'

'His charms don't work on me, ha-ha.'

'He's used ordinary methods then – flattery, kindness. You were lonely, susceptible, left here on your own, and the Sidhe exploited that. You've got to be careful and guard your heart.'

'You don't think he might just like me?' It was horrible to hear my own doubts in another person's mouth.

'Sidhe don't think of us that way. We are blurred shadows of people to their daylight world of other Sidhe. Or better, they are like colonizers living among a native population they mildly despise.'

'Some Sidhe have long-term relationships with ordinary humans.'

'You mean the thralls? Did he tell you that they are silenced?'

'Willingly, he claimed.'

'Oh yes? And how could you test that if they can't speak about their situation any longer?'

'Oh.'

'Yeah, oh.'

'You…you think there's nothing about me that could attract a boy like Quinn? He is far out of my league, I realize that.'

'Stop thinking about it in human terms. He's not out of your league – he's not even playing the same sport. Sidhe don't do anything without an ulterior motive. He must want something from you.'

Sian was right. I was nothing special beyond a curse that wasn't even mine but theirs. 'I did wonder if it was their way of shutting me up? If I liked them I wouldn't talk about them to others.'

'Most people wouldn't believe you. And now the boys aren't camping in the woods, they don't even have to hide their presence.'

'I was thinking of Rowena. Quinn has hinted that she might be a dark Sidhe.'

'As I said, the difference they make between the two isn't clear to us outsiders. Magical bullies, that's what the Sidhe are.'

Hearing the conviction in her tone that she was in the right perversely made me wonder. Were her prejudices a little too black and white? Maybe she couldn't see straight on this subject because she had been taught by her upbringing that everything Sidhe was bad?

'I researched Rowena on the internet,' I said. 'There are plenty of news stories in the art and culture section about her exhibitions.'

'How far back?'

'About four years. That's when her career took off.'

'Did you find out if Mr Huntsman has ever been married?'

'I didn't think to look. How do we discover that?'

'I'll ask my grandfather. He likes that family history stuff.' Sian sent a quick email to him. 'All my family have said they'll help us.'

'I'm surprised your mom let you come back.'

She grimaced. 'It was discussed. At some length.'

'Ah. You had a big argument?'

'A difference of opinion. In the end it went to family vote and I just edged it. I told them courage was a more powerful magic than any charm we could work.'

'That's true: you're very brave.'

'I meant you, you idiot. I said that I was protected by your strength and they weren't to worry.'

I hugged my arms around my waist. 'I don't feel very strong.'

'Take my word for it: fifty lifetimes have given you one impressive backbone, Linny. I don't see you running away from anything you have to do.'

22

BOUNDARY ISSUES

O ur results came back and mine were far below my predicted grades. It was humiliating. I'd once been looked on as one of the stars of my year; now I was on report and scheduled catch-up lessons. If I didn't rapidly improve, there were mutterings that I might be 'happier elsewhere'.

No, I'd be dead elsewhere.

To put the icing on this very depressing cake, my parents chose this moment for their promised visit.

I met them on the step as they got out of their Prius. Both were tanned from their vacation but the strain was clearly written on their faces. Neither looked that happy to see me.

'Linny.' Mom held out her arms but I didn't hug her in return. I was concentrating on holding back my bitter feelings.

'Mom.'

My dad kissed me. 'Nice to see you.'

'Is it?'

'We've got an appointment with Mrs Rainbuck in twenty

minutes,' Dad informed me. 'Just time for a coffee.' So we were going to pretend everything was okay, were we?

Not wanting them to see any of my friends – Jack had threatened to tell them exactly what he thought of them – I took them over to the visitors' lounge in the main building where there was an espresso machine for guests. They chatted about inconsequential things while I fiddled with the controls.

I handed my mom a cup.

'So you're sixteen now,' she said archly.

The second cup for my dad sloshed into the saucer. 'Yes.' I tipped the overspill down the drain. 'Yes.'

'I told you it was all making a mountain out of a mole-hill. The teenage brain is like that.'

'Yes, you did.'

'So you're ready to move on.'

I gave a harsh laugh.

'You'll see the school counselor?'

'I've changed my mind about that.'

Mom shared a glance with Dad. 'You were right. She won't go through with it, even though she said she would.'

'Linny, enough is enough,' said Dad in that judge-like way of his when he's about to lay down the law.

'Mr and Mrs Grace?' Mrs Rainbuck had come to find us. 'Please come this way. Linny, do you want to be part of this?'

'Yes.' I couldn't have them plotting behind my back.

We trooped into her study and took seats opposite her.

She opened my file. It was quite thick. I could just imagine the indignant notes from my subject teachers. *Could try so very much harder.* 'Mr and Mrs Grace, your visit is very timely. I'm sorry to say that Linny didn't do very well in her mid-year tests. We're concerned about this dip in her progress of late.'

I hadn't told my parents about this yet. I slouched in my chair staring out of the window past Mrs Rainbuck's left ear. She turned around to check what I was looking at but there was nothing there.

'Linny, didn't you revise?' asked Mom.

'No.'

'Why?'

'Didn't feel like it.'

'Mrs Rainbuck, I apologize for Linny's attitude. Clearly, she's taken a strange way of getting back at us for our decision to leave her here over the Christmas holidays. But as I said for work reasons it was impossible to fit her in and we didn't want her to miss school.' Another change to the story: how versatile of Mom.

'I quite understand, Mrs Grace, but I can also imagine that Linny was feeling upset about missing out on what she would've considered a treat.' Mrs Rainbuck fiddled with the pens in front of her, awkward at giving my parents something of a lecture. 'She didn't join in any of the activities we laid on for the students who stayed behind. I'm afraid she was rather miserable despite our best efforts. She really wanted to be with you. Isn't that right, Linny?'

'I was okay. I survived.'

'See? I really would recommend a good counselor for her. She has issues that need dealing with if she is going to succeed in her exams.' She turned a page in my file and cleared her throat. 'I'm afraid there are also suspicions that she might be cheating in some subjects. Her English teacher thinks she is not turning in her own work.'

'Linny, is this true?' asked my dad gruffly.

'That's what Miss King thinks,' I replied.

'Have you been copying?'

'No.' What was the point of even trying to explain?

'We've put her on report,' continued Mrs Rainbuck, 'and arranged catch-up lessons for her just to get her back on track academically but I do think your idea of taking her for professional help outside the school is a good one. This situation is beyond our ordinary resources.'

'What!' I sat bolt upright.

Mom tried to take my hand but I snatched it away. 'We've made an appointment with a psychiatrist in Rockland for this afternoon. She comes highly recommended and is a specialist in adolescent mental health.'

'No, no,' I leapt up. 'Not going.'

'Linny!'

'No.' I made a dash for the door.

Dad grabbed my arm. 'You will stop this right now, Linny!'

'I told you it would come to this. Mrs Rainbuck?' said Mom.

'I refuse! Let go!' I screamed.

'I'll call the nurse. I think Linny needs something to calm her down. None of us like to see her so distressed.'

Screaming my refusal, I struggled in my father's grip as she murmured into the phone. The nurse arrived a few seconds later.

'Now, now, Linny dear, you need to relax. I've a little shot here that will help.' She pulled out a syringe. 'Just a sedative I use for students with panic attacks.'

'Get away from me!'

'Linny, you're upsetting everyone!' said Mom, looking embarrassed rather than alarmed on my behalf.

'I hate you – I hate you both,' I sobbed, but I couldn't stop the nurse from injecting me with her needle. It only took a few seconds to take effect and my head started to swim. 'You're going to kill me.'

'Don't be so melodramatic, Linny. We're trying our best to make you better. Let us help you to the car.' Mom took one side, Dad the other, and they steered me to the parking lot. I tried to pull away but I'd lost control of my legs – my feet wouldn't stop as I ordered them to do.

Sian and Jack came running.

'Mr Grace, Mrs Grace, what are you doing with Linny?' asked Sian, trying to pull me away from them.

'We're just taking her to an appointment at the hospital. Nothing that concerns you, Sian.'

Jack looked torn. My mom, of course, sounded so entirely reasonable if you took the curse out of the equation. 'But she doesn't want to go.'

'Keep out of family business, young man,' said my dad.

'She can't leave!' Sian's voice was shrill.

'You two, return to your class!' barked Mrs Rainbuck.

A car drew up in the staff parking lot and Rowena got out, camera bags slung over her shoulder. She could hardly fail to notice the crowd around me.

'Can I be of any help? I'm a friend of Linny's, Rowena Huntsman. My father's her housemaster.'

Maybe my parents would listen to an adult? It was my last chance. 'They're taking me beyond the boundary.'

'I'm sorry?'

'I'm under a Sidhe curse – it'll kill me if I go beyond the gates.'

Rowena looked puzzled, though I thought I caught a hint of understanding in her gaze. 'What are you talking about, Linny?

'Sorry, our daughter's rambling. The nurse gave her a sedative and it seems to have disturbed her reasoning processes,' said Mom.

'I am not disturbed!' I screamed.

'Please, Miss Huntsman, you've got to do something! She's serious!' begged Sian.

I remembered the term all the Sidhe seemed to understand. 'I'm a Maledicta – one of the three cursed sisters.'

'Linny, you're ill. Please stop talking like this.' Mom bundled me into the back of the car then slid in beside me. 'I do apologize, Miss Huntsman. She's not herself.'

Rowena bit her lip, at a loss how to stop them. 'Wouldn't it be better to wait here until she feels better? Let her explain what she means when she's clear-headed?'

'I'm afraid our daughter has never made much sense.'

'But you're clearly distressing her by taking her now against her will.'

Mrs Rainbuck hurried forward. 'I'm sure you mean well, Rowena, but you aren't a member of staff. You should leave me and Linny's parents to decide what's best for her.'

Oh no, oh no. Dad got in the front seat. I could see Jack holding Sian back as she looked set to lay on the road in front of the car. She was screaming at him, struggling in his grip, but he didn't know how serious this was. The Prius pulled away and we were heading down the drive.

I flailed out at Mom, then tried to find the door release. My hands were too uncoordinated. 'Stop! Please!'

'It's for your own good, Linny.'

I moaned, my vision was edged with black. I was close to passing out. 'You're going to regret this.'

'You'll thank us when you're older.'

I laughed. What else was left to me?

The trees of the avenue passed as Dad accelerated. I'd been here before – the last few seconds of life. I could see the gates ahead with their dragon statues on the pedestals. Dad slowed to allow time for the automatic sensor to open them.

And then he stopped. 'What on earth—?'

Twelve boys had appeared from the trees and were blocking the way. Arrows were aimed at the car and several wicked-looking knives. Quinn and Artair stood in the center unarmed but clearly with no intention of moving to allow the car past.

The cavalry had arrived. They looked more like outlaws but they'd do for me.

Dad opened the window. 'What the hell do you think you are playing at?'

'Turn the car around, please,' said Quinn pleasantly.

'No, I will not!'

Conall came to my door and helped me out. 'All right, Linny?'

I was shaking. 'They've drugged me.'

'Sit down. I'll see if I can do something.' He sat me on a bench by the gates and put my head between my knees. I could hear the argument gaining volume over in the car. My mom had joined in.

'Young man, you are getting yourself in very hot water interfering between us and our daughter! She has to go to hospital,' she said in a shrill tone.

'Well now, that's where we disagree. Linny needs to stay here.'

'That's preposterous!'

'No, it's not. It's the only thing she can do for the moment.'

'And you're armed! Does the headteacher know about this?' blustered my dad.

'Now, sir,' said Quinn, giving the signal for the weapons to be lowered. 'I know you're furious and genuinely worried about your daughter so I'll forgive the fact you've dosed her with something and given her the fright of her life.'

'How dare you talk to us like this!'

'Quite easily. It's a gift of mine. Now just listen to my brother and me. Soon you'll not feel in the least angry and quite happy to allow Linny to stay here as long as she needs. We're going to part friends and you're not going to bother her again until she calls you.' The two Ramsay brothers began murmuring in that old language of theirs. The air thickened with magic. With my eyes closed, I could almost see it too in my mind's eye. My skin felt like crystals were forming on the surface as power crept over it, as delicate and beautiful as frost on fallen leaves. Then the words stopped and peace returned, settling over us with goose-down softness.

'Okay now?' asked Quinn. 'You understand?'

'Yes, we had a very nice visit with our daughter and we're going to go home content that she is in the right place,' said my dad. 'Good to meet you.'

'And you, sir. Safe journey back to New York. Oh, by the way, you'll forget this conversation entirely as soon as you get beyond the gates.'

'Yes, of course, I will. Goodbye.' Dad started the car again and drove out of the gates. I could see Mom in the back looking distinctly glassy-eyed.

Quinn came over to where I was sitting, sat beside me and pulled me onto his lap. 'That was close – too close. We almost didn't get here in time. I was in freaking double Math at the other end of the building when the magic warned me. I've never moved so fast in my life.' He hugged me. I could hear his heart beating rapidly and he was trembling as he came down from the adrenalin rush. He'd managed to sound so calm for my parents when really he'd been struggling to contain his fear. 'I don't know what I would've done if I failed you. Linny, don't do that again.'

'Do what?'

'Scare me like that. I...I need you too much. It's like there's a connection between us that would kill me if it were broken.'

I burrowed my head as far as I could into his embrace. He felt so safe – my only refuge in the mad world I lived in. *I love you*, I thought. 'Thank you,' I said aloud.

'No need to thank me, darlin'.' He was hoarse with emotion. 'We're here to help if you're having boundary issues, aren't we, Conall?

'That's right. We're Linny's border guards.' Conall draped his coat over my shoulders.

'Is she okay?'

'I can't counter the drug because of her resistance to magic but I think it will clear out of her system in an hour or two. The best thing for her is rest.'

'Artair, could you clear up memories in the school, please? Liam will show you the way. Who was there, Linny?' Quinn pulled me on his lap so he could keep his arms around me. He let me rest my head on him.

'Mrs Rainbuck and the nurse.'

'And?'

'Sian and Jack, but they'll not make trouble. You don't need to do anything to them.'

'Quinn?' asked Artair.

'She's right. The hedge witch and Jack Burne are on Linny's side.'

'Rowena Huntsman also turned up.' I tried to make myself sit up but I couldn't. 'I told her about me.'

'That's...not good.'

'I didn't think I had a choice.'

'I don't know what she'll make of it, finding out that

we've got a Maledicta here, but we can't go anywhere near her to change her memory.'

'But you said the boundary charm protects me from the curse, and the curse blocks other magic, so aren't I covered?'

'From any magic she might try on you? Yes, but it would still have been better for her not to know.'

'Stating the obvious now?'

'Yeah, sorry. Let's get you back.' He stood up, helping me stand with him.

I swayed on my feet. 'You won't always be here, will you? One day something like that will happen and I'll be dead.'

He swallowed, expression bleak. 'We were here today. Let's concentrate on that. I'm not letting you go, Linny. No matter what it costs.'

23

POKER FACE

Conall was right. I had recovered by the evening, the sedative having been a mild one. The attraction of staying on my bed had also faded. I know Sian had warned me about the genuineness of Quinn's feelings but I couldn't help being grateful and eager to see him again. He'd saved my life twice now. That had to mean something, didn't it?

I brushed my hair, leaving it loose. Checking what the mirror could tell me about my ordeal, I went with a little mascara to try to brighten up my features.

'You've never seen this before,' I told myself, 'sixteen and almost two weeks.' My face hadn't had long enough to look any different but the reflection did bring home the fact that I was in uncharted waters as far as growing up was concerned. I had become so familiar with what went before sixteen I'd stopped marveling at anything I did. Not now though.

Love, not for a family member, but for a boy. Was that what this sensation was? I'd had crushes before, imagined romances with characters from stories, but nothing this real.

Did love also feel very much like fear with a big dose of suspicion as to why Quinn was giving me a second glance? I couldn't relax into it. There were no emotions anywhere in the sentimental range for me – no hearts, flowers, and romance. If anything, I felt like I was walking a tightrope twenty feet up at Bartholomew Fair with no safety net and lots of people betting on me taking a plunge (that was a fifteenth century thing – you had to be there).

No descriptions I'd read of love had ever described it like this. Maybe I was fooling myself?

And that wouldn't be the first time. I'd tricked myself into believing happiness was possible for me on far too many occasions. I should be more cynical.

And yet...and yet...

I went downstairs, deciding to leave my doubts sitting in front of the mirror.

Sian and Jack immediately came to my side.

'You all right? Close call, hey?' Sian gave me a hug.

'Your parents are the pits,' said Jack.

'They mean well,' I managed. 'I have it on reliable information I'm a difficult daughter.'

He was still angry on my behalf. 'You're sixteen now. Your wishes should count for more than they did today.'

'I know, Jack, but I think it'll be okay. Quinn had a word with them.' I met Sian's eyes. She would know what I meant.

'Speak of the devil...' Sian nodded towards Quinn who had just entered with Conall and Charlie. Charlie was carrying a plate covered by a warming lid.

'Hey, Linny, I persuaded the chef to send you your meal as you missed out,' said Quinn. 'Feeling up to eating?'

A far too big a smile was on my face. 'I think I can manage something.'

Quinn gestured to Charlie to set it down at the card

table. A couple of younger students obligingly made way as he took it over.

'He's doing his lord and master thing again,' I murmured to Sian and Jack.

'And don't you just love it?' said Jack, grinning.

Leaving them to find places in the more comfortable armchairs, I went over to the table. Conall produced a knife and fork from thin air, Quinn a glass of water.

Charlie shook his head. 'These guys are amazing, aren't they, Linny?'

'They're certainly something.'

'Then again, you're the demon juggler. I would never've guessed that before Quinn arrived.'

'We all have our secrets. How was your vacation?'

I let Charlie chat while I made inroads on the chicken and rice dish Quinn had picked for me. It was a good choice, easy to eat and not too spicy for someone just coming back from sedation.

'Did I hear that you'd had a run-in with Mrs Rainbuck?' Charlie asked when he'd reached the end of the story about his time in Cancun.

'It was nothing,' said Quinn quickly.

'Just I didn't do well in my tests,' I replied.

'Wow, Linny Grace losing her geek girl status. Welcome to the company of the ordinary people.' Charlie chuckled. He was a famous last-minuter when it came to study, always squeaking by, but with style so that no one called him on it.

'I'd really love to join you.'

'In that case, Poker? Come on: you always say no.'

I began to shake my head but Quinn was there before me. 'You promised to teach me, Charlie. Got time now?'

'Sure – if Linny and Conall join us. It's no good with only a couple of players.'

'I'm sure you can find someone else to take my place.' I made to get up.

'I'd really like you to play, Linny,' said Quinn.

I found myself saying, 'Okay then.'

Hang on: if his charisma couldn't work on me, why did I still fall in with his plans?

Because you really want to, came the somewhat humiliating answer.

'I won't make a big noise about it but this is a day to mark in the calendar: Linny is the last hold out in the Crowthorne common room. I think I've played everyone else.' Charlie shuffled the cards. 'Okay, Linny, do you know how to play?'

'I've watched you fleece the freshers enough, Charlie.'

'Ouch and there she is – the sharp girl we all know and love.' He dealt the first hand, explaining the rules to Quinn. Conall said he already knew them.

'So what do we bet?' asked Quinn.

'Not money, promises. You write them on these slips of paper that I just so happen to have prepared earlier.' Charlie laid them on the table with four pens.

'What kind of promises?' Quinn popped the nib of his biro in and out a few times, considering his options.

'Got to be something that's got value to all of us so no promise to smooch us or stuff like that.' Charlie gave me a wink. 'Though maybe we three can all agree we'll take that pledge from Linny if she likes.'

'I think we'd better play by the regular rules,' I said before Quinn punched him.

'Yeah, I think I'd be happier with that,' said Conall, casting a wry look at his friend.

Quinn gave him a bared tooth smile that was nothing to do with humor. 'I'm sure you would too.'

'Charlie means things like cleaning football boots or running errands,' I explained, attempting to move the conversation on from smooching.

'You could promise to do your juggling thing again, Linny. That was so cool,' suggested Charlie. 'Quinn could bet his card tricks. Conall, do you do anything like that?'

'Oh yeah, I'm full of surprises,' said Conall.

'Write them down then.'

We each composed a series of promises and then the game got underway. Some of the nuances of the modern game were different, but I caught on quickly. Both Quinn and Conall folded fairly quickly on the first hand, guessing that their cards weren't good enough to win. Charlie and I kept going though.

'Are you sure, you understand the rules, Linny?' asked Charlie, glancing down at his cards then at me. 'You're going to lose a lot so early on if you have a dud hand.'

Quinn rubbed my arm. 'You feeling up to this? It's been a hard day for you. Maybe Poker isn't a good way of relaxing?'

'No, I'm sure.' I gave them both a brilliant smile. 'Time to show what you've got, Charlie.' I had a full house to his three of a kind. I pretended cluelessness. 'So does that mean I win?'

'Yes, you won.' Charlie pushed the slips over to lie in front of me. This had the advantage that I could now bet other people's promises rather than my own.

Quinn gave me an astute look. 'Beginner's luck, Linny?'

'You would think that. I prefer to imagine I might have an instinctive talent for this.'

Charlie perked up, believing he'd found a rookie overly confident after winning her first hand. 'You'll find, Linny, that experience does count for more in the end.'

I played carefully after that, bowing out early when I wasn't sure of my cards. Charlie stopped wondering about me, though I could see Quinn was still suspicious.

'Two more hands?' asked Charlie, looking up at the clock. He and I had the majority of the promises.

'Sounds good.' This time I went in for the kill. Luck was with me on the deal and I had the makings of a four of a kind. The turn of the cards was in my favor and I went head to head with Conall on the final round of betting. He'd put in all his promises so was going for broke. When he revealed his hand, my four of a kind far outstripped his flush.

In the final round, I was dealt a really rubbish collection of low cards in a scattering of suits. But in Poker that doesn't matter. It is all about psyching out the other guy to make him think you are holding a straight flush, the highest-ranking hand in this game as we weren't playing with wild cards. Conall was sitting this one out, leaving me facing Charlie and Quinn for the final betting rounds.

I put in half my pile of promises, reserving only the ones I'd written.

Charlie squinted at the slips of paper. 'She's got that little smile on her face. She's feeling very smug, see it?'

'But she's only bet our promises, not hers, so maybe she's not so confident.' Quinn stayed in, putting in all but the last of his slips.

Charlie was gazing at me as if he wished he could climb inside my head. 'I don't know, she's having beginner's luck tonight. I got burned in the first round and I want to walk away from the table with something. I'll fold.'

The people nearest us must've alerted the rest to the unusual scenes going on at the Poker game. The room hushed as Quinn and I were left facing each other over the pot.

I dumped in all my remaining promises. 'Okay, Quinn Ramsay, are you going to match or fold?'

He looked at the promise he'd kept back – I recognized my own writing on a slip I'd lost in an earlier round – then he stared at the great pile in the middle. 'I'm not sure.' He raised his eyes to my face.

I held his gaze, hoping my smile was as infuriating as it had been in 1903.

He laughed then shook his head. 'My cards are rubbish. I fold.' He threw them in, revealing that he had at least a one pair and would've beaten mine had he called my bluff.

'Thank you, gentleman, for a most entertaining game.' I raked in my winnings and quickly scanned them. 'Ah, Charlie, looks like my hockey boots are yours to clean tomorrow after the match.'

Charlie hovered between annoyance and admiration. 'Tell us what you had in your hand, Linny.'

I quickly shuffled them into the pack. 'I know better than that, Charlie. You'll never find out now, will you?'

As I got up from the table I was surprised by a cheer from the onlookers. I had to have been the first person to beat Charlie in over a year.

'We have a new queen of the poker table!' shouted the hand-walking Alfie from Ninth Grade.

'Really not,' I said, backing out of the room. Uncomfortable with so much attention I hurried to put the promises away. Quinn followed and caught up with me in the hallway. He pulled me into the music room.

'You're not a beginner,' he said flatly.

'I never said I was.'

'You, Linny Grace, are a lowdown card sharp.'

'Is there any other sort?'

He laughed. 'When?'

'The circus – that really was the most interesting in many ways of my multiple lives. I was infamous among the acrobats. Dad trained me to look innocently confident and we took money off unsuspecting punters in all parts of the good old U S of A.'

'Why did you never play here then?' He backed me to the window seat and pulled me down to sit on his knee.

'Seemed like shooting fish in a barrel.'

He laughed at that – and carried on laughing. 'Poor Charlie.'

I smirked. 'Yep. Though he might not be half bad given a few more years.'

A slip of paper appeared before my eyes. 'I want to claim a promise.'

'Are you sure?' I showed him the fistful with which I had walked away.

'Oh yes. Read it.'

My handwriting, that was true, but the words had changed. *I promise to kiss Quinn.*

'I never wrote that!' I protested. I was happy to kiss him any time, he really didn't need a slip of paper for that, but this was about keeping to the rules of the game.

He shrugged. 'And here I was thinking you are a woman of your word.'

I turned the paper over but there was nothing on the other side. 'You did something to it.'

'Did I? Maybe words have a way of rearranging themselves around me, a kind of overflow of my natural Sidhe charm.'

'You...you cheater! Just because you can't use your powers on me, doesn't mean you can go around changing what I write!'

'But that's why I wouldn't bet my last promise even

though I suspected you were taking great shark bites out of all of us at that table. I could've walked away with the whole pot, couldn't I?'

'I'm never going to tell.'

'So pay up and stop complaining. You've got lots more promises of mine than I have of yours.'

Suspicious now, I quickly leafed through my slips. Somehow all of his had turned into *I promise to kiss you.* I'd just hit the jackpot: my own treasury of Quinn kisses to spend as I like.

'You don't play fair.' My grumbling tone wasn't very convincing.

'Whatever gave you the impression I was the least bit inclined towards fair?' He presented me with my pledge and pulled me closer. 'Time to collect.'

I grabbed one of the slips and hid it in my fist. He won this round but the second kiss would be mine.

24

DARK SIDHE

I needed to get my head straight, I told myself as I set out on a late-night ramble around the boundary walk. The school days of February were proving as horrible as I had feared. This was the first time I'd been able to get out all day thanks to my catch-up sessions and as soon as I got to my bedroom I just knew I had to be outside. It was like an itch that I had to scratch. I didn't want anyone with me, not Quinn with his confusing effect on my emotions, nor Sian with her mutterings of dire warnings, or even Jack who wouldn't get why I had a problem. He was happy on my behalf that I, who so far had scored a dating zero, seemed to have hit the ball out of the park by snagging the attention of the most sought-after boy in Green Drake. He and Quinn were getting on like best friends as a result. I think he saw more of Quinn than I did as they shared some classes.

As I walked, I reflected that it was probably foolish of me to go to the very length of the tether that bound me here but have you ever seen a panther in a cage at a zoo? It marks out a footpath at the wire, testing, testing, testing, just in case the path to the jungle miraculously opens up again.

I did the first part of the walk in silence, quieting my thoughts and concentrating on the beauty around me. Though the snow had gone, tonight brought with it a hard frost. It had already made blind eyes of the puddles as they gazed with milky cataracts at the stars. I stepped on one and saw the trapped bubble of air shift below the surface like the gauge in a spirit level. Funny how a carpenter's tool had such an ethereal name.

So was I now on the level myself?

Halfway around I decided I was and let myself start thinking.

Either I was in love with a boy who also had feelings for me, or I was an idiot being manipulated by a very clever Sidhe. How was that for the unvarnished truth?

More than that, my fate rested on something I didn't quite understand – the rescuing of light magic from the dark forces that threatened it. Quinn had never said exactly what this entailed, just that something really major was about to happen and that he was responsible for it. The boundary charm seemed part of his strategy because it kept dark spells at bay. I sensed there was something bigger at stake than I understood but I was not the only one good at keeping a poker face, hiding what I really meant.

As for my old companion – the death curse – that was still with me like a bird of prey hovering over a meadow waiting for me, the mouse, to make a move.

I paused by the section of wall on which Sian and I had sat so many weeks ago. Quinn said Sidhe under eighteen could talk to the power that lived at Green Drake. Could ordinary people do so too?

'Hello, magic.' There was no one to tell me I was being stupid. 'Thanks for keeping the bad stuff at bay. I hope Quinn can save you.'

Of course, there was no answer but I had a slight feeling that I had amused someone, or something.

'Okay then, I'll keep on talking to you because we're kind of in this together. Can you help me? I'd be really happy to save you if I knew what to do.'

Nothing came back to me but the whisper of wind through bare branches. Oh well. It had been worth a shot.

I started walking again.

Careful.

I'm not sure where that thought came from but I stopped and listened hard. I could hear talking, female voices.

Stay. Listen. This is why I brought you here.

I moved back into the shelter of a holly bush just in time to avoid the torch beam that strobed the path.

'There's still one of them out here, camping in the pine wood.' It was Rowena speaking. 'I wouldn't mind meeting him when he's on his own.'

Three people walking beside her laughed. I only recognized one but that was shock enough: Miss King. The other two were men. They were all wrapped up in hiking gear as if they were just returning from a much more ambitious walk than a stroll around the grounds.

'But the rest have moved into the school?' asked one of the men.

'Yes. There are eleven of them, but they're young. Apart from their openness to the power here they have few skills to worry us. No, it's the king's sons that are the biggest threat.'

'And greatest opportunity.'

'True. The older one is probably beyond turning but the younger one, now he shows promise because he takes risks.'

I backed into the bush. It seemed to want to shelter me, giving way without prickling.

'It's that girl, isn't it? The Maledicta. What a stroke of luck for us,' said Miss King. 'And to think I almost had her suspended for plagiarism when all the time she had lived through what she wrote. Ironic really. I was so angry with her.'

'I find her very interesting – an old soul in many ways but glaringly young in others.'

'What must that be like? Eternal youth, eternal life?' said the man who had not spoken so far. I caught a glimpse of a white beard and a glint of eyes in his hood.

'Dark magic is a gift. I don't think she realizes that. She's been brainwashed to think her curse a handicap. As a result, it's wasted on her,' said Rowena. 'It's a shame really as I think she shows promise.'

'So can we take it from her? Use it ourselves?' asked Miss King.

'I don't know.' Rowena paused a few yards from my hiding place. 'Can you sense that?'

I shrank still further in.

The teacher felt out with her palms like Conall did. 'Our counter charm is having no effect. It's strong magic the boy's cast, and the light magic wants to keep the barrier up. You can feel it wanting to kick us out, stopping us using our power.'

'Remember, we don't want the barrier down yet. We've got them all penned here. We've time to put our plans into place before the night arrives. Just widen a crack in the king's son's resolve and the light magic will leave him – this place will fall to us. The girl's the key. It must be why fate brought her to us.'

'She'll see us as the bad guys. She definitely doesn't like me.'

'We're on good terms. I'll try and convince her otherwise. Dark is not bad, nor is light good. If we can take the curse she doesn't want from her then surely that must be enough to sway her our way?'

Miss King shook her head. 'I think she might be in love and that'll make her stubborn. I see the two of them in each other's company all the time – the Maledicta and the younger son.'

'Then she'll need to be told the truth. We Sidhe don't love. We are stronger than that.'

They carried on walking and as much as I wanted to hear the rest of that conversation I couldn't risk it. One part of what I had overheard had shaken me to the core.

They could take the curse from me. They had no reason to lie about it as they hadn't known I was listening. What Rowena said fitted with what Mrs Willowbrook had found out from the old hedge witch in New Orleans. If someone was willing to take on the burden, they could unwind it slowly from you – a difficult and painstaking task, dangerous to both parties. The power couldn't be got rid of – even magic obeyed the laws of physics that matter cannot be created or destroyed – but I hadn't thought that anyone would actually want the curse. That man, though, had seen it as a form of eternal life.

It was really an eternal torment. I shouldn't pass it on to someone else.

But if they wanted it?

Didn't I have a responsibility to save them from themselves?

And keep on suffering myself? Wasn't it someone else's turn?

'Magic, what should I do?' I whispered.

Not what you are tempted to do, came the answer, though it was probably just my conscience piping up inconveniently.

'OH NO, HE'S COMING.'

I was on my way from German to History when I saw the familiar tousled head over the top of the crowd of students. I grabbed Sian's elbow and dived into the nearest classroom, the computer science lab, fortunately empty. I flattened myself against the wall.

Sian gave me one of her looks. 'What are we doing in here, Linny? You're not even taking IT as a subject.'

'Can you get out of the view of the window in the door please?'

Too late, the door opened. I crawled under a desk behind it so I was impossible to spot unless Quinn came all the way in.

'Sian, have you seen Linny?' asked Quinn.

I shook my head at Sian.

'Um, she's gone to the girl's bathroom, I think,' said Sian airily, pretending to check something in her bag.

Good one. Even Quinn wouldn't follow me in there.

'When you see her, can you tell her that this running away every time she sees me is getting ridiculous. I mean, what have I done? Is she trying to break it off with me and too scared to tell me?' He sounded bewildered.

Sian glanced at me. I shook my head again.

'Don't overreact, Quinn. She's just...busy...with her work. Got a lot to catch up on as she thought she'd be dead by now. You Sidhe only have yourselves to blame for that.' Sian knew that attack was the best form of defense.

'Sian...'

'Your kind did that, remember. Quinn, I've got to get to my lesson. See you later.' She walked out past him and firmly shut the door with them both on the far side so I was left alone in the classroom.

I crawled out from under the desk. The IT teacher came in carrying a mug of coffee.

'What are you doing in here, young lady?'

'Sorry, took a wrong turn.' I grabbed my bag and darted out. The corridor was emptying as people went into their classes. I made it to History only a minute late. Mrs Bailey liked me so didn't make a fuss as I slid into the chair next to Sian.

'You will explain,' whispered my friend.

Explanations had to wait until the end of the lesson. As it was now the lunch hour, we were able to linger in the classroom.

'You're avoiding Quinn?'

I nodded.

'Why? I thought you two were still in the starry-eyed phase?'

How to explain? Since I had overheard the dark Sidhe's conversation two nights before, I had avoided being alone with Quinn. I knew he would guess something was wrong and if he winkled out of me what they had said, he would probably feel duty bound to block my one chance.

'I think I'm bad for him,' I said instead. 'His brother' and Rowena, 'thinks I damage his ability to channel light magic. I'm doing him a favor.'

Sian gave me a long look. 'Turn around.'

I did as she asked. Sian tied another of her special braids into my hair. 'That's for defense against angry Sidhe boys who might want to get you back for breaking off with them.'

'I'm not sure I've exactly broken off, more that I've put some distance between us. You approve?'

'Linny, have I or have I not been telling you that your relationship can't work? I have to admit that I'm warming to Quinn and Conall as people – they saved you the other day after all – but I hate the fact that they are Sidhe. Quinn isn't good for you in the long term, and now it sounds like you aren't good for him. Don't let him change your mind. You stick to what's best for you.'

My heart was telling me contradictory things: on the one hand, I yearned to be free of this curse; on the other, I couldn't imagine continuing this life without Quinn.

'Thanks, Sian.'

'Don't worry, I'll help you keep out of his way. He looks like the sort of boy whose attention will move on to someone else pretty soon.'

I wasn't so sure because I sensed the strength of the bond that already connected us and in a place like Green Drake, it wasn't possible to avoid someone permanently. There were always opportunities, particularly when Quinn had recruited an unexpected ally.

'LINNY, I've finally finished your theme,' said Jack one afternoon as he passed me in the corridor. 'Do you want to hear it?'

'Duh!'

'I've booked the practice suite with the grand piano in the music block for seven. Meet you over there?'

'I could meet you at dinner and go across with you.'

Jack hurried off. 'I want to run through it first. Come at seven.'

Failing to remember that my friend was an old romantic

at heart, I went to the music block as arranged and was surprised to find an empty room. A score sat on the piano with a new title: 'Linnet and Quinn's theme'.

'Jack, you goose.' I messaged him, demanding his presence. To kill time while waiting I sat down and began playing. I recognized the first theme he had written but he had grafted on a mercurial melody that spun the fragile one into a soaring anthem. It was amazing, full of joy, but hardly an accurate portrait of what 'Linnet and Quinn's theme' should be – that should be jagged and broken, fraught with danger. Jack's version was a glimpse of an impossible might-have-been, not reality. My friend never thought ahead; he didn't recognize the brevity of the things we experience, even relationships. His music made us sound so much stronger than we were.

The door clicked closed. 'You've been avoiding me.'

'Quinn!' My fingers crashed on a discordant chord. 'Did you put Jack up to this?'

'I appealed to him as one heart-broken boy to another.'

'He's heart-broken?' How had I missed that? 'Who?'

'That's his story to tell, not mine. Move over.' Quinn sat beside me. I wanted to rest my head against his shoulder and just take in the scent of woods and starlight that seemed to accompany him but I couldn't be so weak.

'You and Jack plotting together – what's going on there?'

'We've become good friends since you've been making pretty blatant excuses not to see me. I found out that humans do this kind of thing all the time – agonize with mates over "is she, isn't she mad at me?".'

'I'm not mad at you.'

'Play the theme for me then.'

I stroked the keys. 'Jack's an optimist. You must've picked that up about him?'

'He's written a version of it as a duet.' Quinn reordered the sheets and showed me that Jack indeed had arranged it for two players. 'I asked him to.'

'Ask or told him with your persuasive powers?'

'Just asked. I'm learning that you don't manipulate mates if you want a real friendship with them. I'm on a steep learning curve in human ways.'

'Quinn—'

'It's hurt – you avoiding me. I didn't know that was what it felt like. Human relationships aren't easy.'

He said it like he was the first person to discover the fact. I almost smiled. 'I'm sorry.'

He played a few notes. 'Artair is pleased. He thinks I've cut you off. I didn't want to admit it was the other way around. Princes don't usually get rejected.'

'I wasn't rejecting you.'

'So what were you doing?'

'Thinking, I suppose. I needed space to do so.'

'And you couldn't just tell me?' He sighed. 'Play the theme, Linny.'

It was a simple enough request. I began and Quinn joined in after five bars.

'I didn't know you played.'

'Royal education. Nothing left out. I'm not up to your level but I can manage this.'

I'd purposely let a distance grow between us since hearing the dark Sidhe talk on their boundary walk but the melody collapsed that. There is nothing more connected than players sharing a piece of music, a single instrument. My fingers danced past his, his over mine, but we were together – literally in harmony.

We finished. Jack had done an inspired job. I had the sensation of flying up with the last notes, disappearing like the final firework of the display in a cloud of stars. I leaned forward and put my head on the keyboard. It was no good: I couldn't keep this to myself any longer.

'Linny?'

My eyes filled with tears. I didn't want him to see. This was love as I experienced it, this knife of emotion in my chest, more pain than pleasure.

'I can get free of the curse, Quinn, but it risks everything – you included.'

His genuine shock at least told that he hadn't known about my real reasons for avoiding him. 'What? How? My father said it was impossible.'

'I can hand it over to someone else.'

'But it's dark magic.'

'What if someone wanted it?'

'Who would be that crazy?'

I sat up and wiped my tears away with my wrist. 'Does it matter? Do I have to stay on this torture wheel if someone else wants to take my place?'

'I think it does matter. When dark magic is on the move, the balance is disturbed.'

Had he known it could be shifted but chosen not to tell me? A crack appeared in my already shaky foundation of faith. 'What about me, Quinn? I'm disturbed all the time and have been for centuries. When am I going to matter more than the balance to someone?'

He swallowed. 'You do matter.'

'But not more? Tell me the truth: do I matter more than that to you?'

'I...' His eyes were taking on their chill expression. Was that the real Quinn coming to the fore?

'You can't answer that, can you? I'm so confused. Is dark

really bad? Is light really good? Are you good? Are the dark Sidhe bad?'

'Why are you asking these questions?'

'Because I have to. I can't, *can't* carry on like this.' I pressed my fist to my heart. 'You wonder why I've been avoiding you? Don't you understand that I'm desperate? I think I've fallen in love with you but I don't know if I can trust you or even if your feelings for me are real. People are already saying I'm bad for you.'

'Who?'

'Your brother, even Rowena Huntsman...'

He gave me a betrayed look. 'You've been talking to her about me?'

How could he think that? I shook my head. 'Listened in. But if your feelings for me are real, where do they lead? Nowhere, because I'm trapped. I can't even kill myself to end this. I can't take it any longer – I'm not the Sidhe punchbag for some wrong committed centuries ago!' I swiped the music off the stand and stood up, hands clenched. 'Every other person on this planet has death as their absolute last resort to suffering, but no, not Linny. Linny has to keep coming back and going through the same cycle of realization, pain and loss because the Sidhe couldn't keep their urge for revenge in check!'

'Linny...'

'No, Quinn, I've been deluding myself, haven't I? I really hate your world and all it stands for but yet I'm betraying myself by loving you. That's why I've kept away from you – I hate myself for loving you.'

He moved towards me. I held up my hands to ward him off. 'You'd better keep back. I'm toxic – everyone agrees about that, light and dark Sidhe alike.'

'I don't – I don't agree.' Not allowing my protest, he

folded me to his chest. Why, oh why, did I like being there so much? 'I understand, Linny, I really do. Everyone has a breaking point and you've reached yours. You can't do another life. I hear you. But please, let me find another way.'

'There isn't another way. I've searched for centuries and this is the best there is.' My voice sounded lost in his chest. 'We're enemies in this – I want something you can't let me have.'

'That's not true, darlin'. Please believe me. What I really want is you and I think you want me.'

'That's not enough.'

'It is or it would be if you felt even half of what I feel for you. I've failed you by keeping a rein on my emotions, not wanting to scare you off. Everyone told me to go slow. But let me prove it to you the only way I know how. Let me in.'

Then he kissed me. It was heated, part punishment, part argument, not the gentle ones of the start of our relationship. He was annoyed and frustrated – but then so was I. I kissed him back, my impossible, unattainable boy. If only I could disappear inside him and hide there from the curse forever!

He broke away. 'How can you kiss like this and still say you don't believe in my feelings for you?'

'I—'

'Give me some of it.' He closed his eyes and put his hands on my waist under my shirt. 'I'll take it.'

'What are you doing?' I could feel a scorching twisting energy come out of my skin and into his palms. Violet light framed us. 'No!'

'You don't believe me so I'm doing this.' His eyes were open now but they were no longer cool, they were burning with the blue of the hottest part of the flame. He was taking dark magic from me, opening himself to it.

'No!' I shoved him from me, finding strength I didn't know I had. He fell over the music stool. The power snapped back into me – all of it, I think, though I couldn't be sure. What had we done? 'Not you. It can't be you.' I burst out of the room and ran. I kept running. People tried to stop me – Conall, Sian, Jack – but I dodged them with a dexterity I hadn't used since one of my lives as a pickpocket on the run from the law. I sprinted all the way back to Crowthorne, took the stairs two at a time, then banged on Mr Huntsman's door. Rowena opened it.

I held out my hands, palms open. 'I need you to take the curse from me. Can you do it?'

25

ONLY SOLUTION

'Linny, come in.' Rowena was talking as if a terrified girl had not just burst in upon her, jabbering about curses. 'I've just printed off those photos I took of you. Would you like to see them?'

I wanted to scream, beat my head against the wall, but, instead, I followed her. Mr Huntsman was washing up. He had a faraway look on his face as he swirled the dishes in the sudsy water.

'Father, I'm just taking Linny to my studio.'

'Of course, dear. You carry on.'

Rowena took me into a spare room that she had turned into her workspace and closed the door.

'You do not talk in public about curses,' she said severely.

'What?'

'You heard me.'

'I'm...I'm sorry.'

'My father is oblivious to that side of my life. I can't have you jeopardizing that.'

'Is he really your father?'

'Of course he is.'

'Is he Sidhe?'

'Don't be foolish.'

'Your mother?'

'Obviously.' She began shuffling the photos she had printed off. 'She went back to the Sidhe world with me but we kept in touch with Father. She prompted my father to take a job here. We thought it might come in useful one day. Look.' She put the picture of me on the bridge by the frozen waterfall on the desk.

'What have you done to it?' Behind me was a blaze of white light but I was surrounded by a dark cloud, my features blurred by it.

'When you told me that you were Maledicta, I developed this again, looking for magic traces. That's the camp,' she put her finger on the brightness behind me, 'and that's what you're really like.'

'I'm ugly – all that dark stuff pouring out of me.'

'You really think so? I thought you looked interesting.' She put some more photos down, candid shots of Quinn and his men. They all came out as gashes of white lightning taking the shape of boys. 'Oddly, I can't seem to capture the older one, Artair, though I've tried.' She pushed two images closer – the one of me and one of Quinn. He looked like a white-robed angel in a stained-glass window, the warrior kind. I looked like one of the devils they used to paint on church walls in Europe before those images were whitewashed out by the Reformation. I was never going to be able to have him no matter what I did, was I?

'I don't want to be like this any longer,' I whispered. 'Please take it away from me. Please.'

'Sit down.'

I took a seat on a wooden chair, feeling sick and hopeless. Rowena leaned on the side of the desk.

'I don't think you understand what this is about.'

'I heard you talking to Miss King and your friends. You can remove the magic, someone else can have it, this eternal life of coming back.'

'And dying.'

I nodded. 'I will do anything to get free of it. Please just tell me you can help me.'

'I suppose this is the part where, if I were the villain, I'd hold out false promises and get you to sabotage the light Sidhe's protection of this place,' she mused, flicking aside the images she had shown me.

'Why do you want Green Drake so much?'

'I want its power – and that's the only thing that has any value to us. We don't want to spoil it; we just want to harness it. The light Sidhe think the only way is to leave Green Drake untouched. We believe its destiny is to become part of us again.'

'But turned into dark magic?'

She nodded. 'But dark is not bad, it's just different.'

'What about the balance?'

'It will be restored when magic is back in its rightful place – in the Sidhe and not out in the fields and hedgerows. Magic needs to be contained in us, not roaming in the wild to do whatever it wants. We took years to achieve that until that fool Lihtan got himself killed and sent it running for cover.'

'Will you hurt Quinn if I give your side the power that's in me?'

'I have no intention of hurting anyone.'

'And me – what happens to me?'

'If someone siphons off your curse? I don't know, to be

honest. Worst-case scenario is that you'll die – but really die. Not come back. Isn't that better than what you've got now?'

Her bedside manner left quite a lot to be desired. 'And best-case scenario?'

'We take the power and you are free.'

'And Green Drake?'

'That isn't really your concern. It's between us and the light Sidhe.'

I thought of Quinn and his dangerous promise that he would find another way. He'd almost cracked himself wide open trying to prove to me that he loved me. Yet what would that have achieved? Just swapped our places and I didn't wish that on him. He'd done it out of impulse rather than as a considered gesture. He had probably already realized that it couldn't be.

The dark Sidhe, however, wouldn't be harmed by the power of a dark curse; they were already awash with it. Wasn't it forgivable that for once in my many lives that I put my needs first? I knew Rowena wasn't telling me everything, she fully intended to carry on this war, but couldn't I risk a little side skirmish of my own?

'What do I have to do?'

'I'll need to find a volunteer who wants the curse. Then on the night of the equinox we'll do the exchange.'

'I thought it was a slow unwinding? That's what an old hedge witch said.'

'Not the way we do it. You'll find we're rather more capable of handling this level of power than a hedge witch.'

I shivered. Rowena seemed so matter-of-fact about it. She wasn't pretending to be my friend now; she wasn't hiding the fact that the outcome for me was uncertain. There was no hand rubbing and cackles of manic laughter to warn me off. It felt more like listening to a hospital specialist pronouncing on the correct form of treatment for my disease. Possible side effects include death. 'On what day does the equinox fall this year?'

'We'll mark it at midnight on 20th March.'

That was the date when the length of the day and the night would be equal. The equinox shifted around a little depending on the solar cycle.

'And it'll be just the dark Sidhe and me? It won't involve Quinn and the others?'

Rowena shrugged. 'I won't deny that you'll make us stronger and that will aid us in our struggle with them over the future of this place, but no, it won't involve the light Sidhe at all.'

'Okay, right, let's do this then. I'll wait to hear if you've found someone.' I swallowed. 'They should know it isn't easy being cursed.'

'I'll make sure they understand. And Linny, keep this just to ourselves, all right? The light Sidhe will try and stop you. They need you to carry on suffering to keep the balance. But our side, we don't see the point of torturing an innocent. Things change and every punishment should have an end.'

I stumbled back to my room, terrified and elated by what I had done. My motives were horribly mixed – selfish, selfless, I couldn't tell the difference – but maybe, just maybe, I'd truly be free.

'WHAT HAVE YOU DONE TO QUINN?' asked Jack the next morning. We were having breakfast and our little trio was on its own again in the 'out' corner while Quinn's court buzzed around him. The photograph had shown me surrounded by a dark cloud, but I'd say it had settled over Quinn since our disastrous talk in the music room.

'It's complicated.'

'You argued, didn't you? I knew it! I knew you'd mess this up! Idiot!' He hit me over the head with a rolled-up school magazine.

'Hey!' I grabbed the magazine and hit him back.

'I told him he shouldn't press you but he wanted to get a clear idea of what you felt towards him. Poor guy: he looks heartbroken.'

I didn't think so. Quinn was flirting like mad with Genny and three other girls. He was in 'make Linny suffer' mode.

'Whose side are you on, Jack?' asked Sian, removing the magazine from combat. 'If Linny's broken off with Quinn, then you should be backing her, not blaming her.'

'But he loves her. It's the big one for him – I'm convinced about that. And she loves him, don't you, Linny? You just have a self-destruct tendency. I'm trying to save you from it.'

'Jack, please...'

'No, Linny, you listen to me.' Deprived of his magazine, he poked me in the chest. 'When you have a chance at happiness, you've got to take it. If you don't, he'll go off with one of those girls – Genny or Zoe – look, they're practically sitting on his lap! Do something or you'll miss your chance!'

'What chance have you missed, Jack?' I asked quietly. 'Why haven't you told us about that?'

He blushed. 'That's none of your business.'

'But it's fine for you to interfere between Quinn and me?'

He got up. 'You know something, Linny? Right now, I don't like you very much and I'm not surprised you've messed up with Quinn. You don't deserve him.' He dumped his tray and strode over to join in the crowd around his idol.

Sian sighed. 'Don't you get it? He's had a serious case of hero-worship for Quinn for weeks. He's been so jealous of you being special to Quinn that he's had to be super-nice about it.'

'Jealous?' I started laughing. It was what I did when I reached despair.

'It's not funny.'

'This isn't funny laughter. This is me wishing I hadn't been born. Oh, Sian, I just want this all to stop.' I lowered my head to my hands, temples aching.

Conall must've noticed the bust up with Jack. He approached and took the chair next to Sian.

'Problems?'

'Oh, no, life's never been better,' I said breezily, sitting up and forcing my face to assume its poker expression of innocent interest. 'Yours?'

'Besides having a commander in a continual state of rage?'

'Besides that?'

'Peachy. What happened yesterday, Linny?'

'You'd better ask Quinn. You're his friend, rather than mine.'

'I was hoping I could be friends to you both.'

'Yeah, I know, but in the end we all have to choose our sides, don't we?'

I got up and took my tray and Jack's to the clearing station. Sian came up alongside me.

'What are you not telling me, Linny?'

'Look, Sian, things are probably going to get ugly between Quinn and me. Best to keep out of it. It's light and dark Sidhe stuff. See how easy it is to hurt people?' I nodded at Jack.

'I'll only be hurt if you don't tell me stuff.'

Then prepare for a world of hurt, I thought, *as I can't tell you what I've agreed to do.* 'Thanks. I appreciate it.'

Sian took my elbow. 'So the 'Out' crowd is down to two.'

I looked back over my shoulder at Jack talking to Liam and Quinn, remembering I'd had a premonition that Jack would go that way. 'Seems to be. And it's my fault in part: I didn't realize he was jealous.'

'People do stupid things when they are. He'll be back when he's over it.'

'Will he?'

26

A DECLARATION OF WAR

Green Drake was angry with me. On Saturday, when I went to my usual sanctuary to keep out of the way of everyone, the holly bushes scratched me and wouldn't let me through.

'Oh, come on!' I shouted at them. 'Don't tell me you're blaming me too! I was trying to stop him taking over the curse. I had to make the deal! It was for his own good!'

It wasn't. You're doing it for yours.

'Who made you my judge, you...you well of useless, pathetic magic!'

I was losing it. I stomped over to the oak tree, but without Quinn to boost me up to the lowest branch, I couldn't reach it. I sat at the base instead, submitting to the discomfort of knobbly roots digging in. Even the placid old oak tree hated me, it seemed.

I shouldn't be surprised, I reflected. My entire week had been like that. I had mentally prepared myself for Quinn and his magic squad being hostile; I hadn't expected to be made an outcast by everyone else too. Sian and the dark Sidhe were the only exceptions, Miss King positively gushing whenever I said anything in class or handed in a piece of work. Our English set didn't know what to make of it.

Sixty minutes of being liked in English lessons didn't make up for the rest of the time of torment. It wasn't subtle. People pushed past me in the corridor, let doors swing in my face, knocked over my pile of books in the library, broke off conversations when I entered the common room. I had no idea if the order had gone out from Sidhe high command to make my life a misery or if they were doing it in spontaneous sympathy. Quinn's hurt could be seeping from him like the reverse of his charisma. The version of what happened that Sian heard circulating was that I had had a bust up with Quinn in the music room and thrown his feelings cruelly back in his face. The whispers that I was unstable had become something people now felt confident they could speak aloud. There was plenty of evidence to support it, including the damning fact that even my own parents didn't like or trust me enough to take me away with them at Christmas.

If I didn't have a sliver of hope that the end was near, I'd walk out of the gates myself.

Artair dropped out of the upper branches of the tree and landed at my feet. Just what I needed.

'If it isn't the last Boy Scout standing. How's camping?'

'Maledicta, what are you doing to my brother?'

'Not another one in the Quinn Defense League.' I curled up into a ball. 'I thought you'd be pleased,' I said from within my own huddle.

'I am pleased he no longer loves you.'

Ouch.

'But not pleased that his light is tainted. You've infected him.'

'Go away.'

'How did you do it?' A curved knife appeared in Artair's hand. 'Tell me!'

'What are you going to do with that? Kill me?' Horrible laughter bubbled up. 'Go on. Try.'

'I know I can't kill you this side of the wall but I can make you suffer.'

'Really? More than I already am?' I held out an arm. 'I dare you.'

The blade hovered between us, edge glinting with the coldest of lights. I met his eyes with my own; I imagine my gaze was filled with an ocean of pain that was way beyond what he could inflict. Bluff called, Artair lowered the weapon.

'Too much is at stake here. I told him we should've pushed you beyond the boundary, let the curse take its course.'

'Yeah, you should've done. See, I'm on to you now: light is not good; it's cruel, it has no mercy. You are all about extracting a penalty from the innocent. But it's too late. I know now how to end this farce and, frankly, if your gang are shaken by it, then so be it. You deserve it.'

He glanced behind him at the nearby wall.

'And if you toss me over that, I'll just come back with this knowledge a generation later. You won't know where I am but I'll know what to do. And believe me, I'll make sure I get my revenge on you and yours in the process.'

He stood up, expression one of disgust. 'You've given in to it, haven't you? The dark magic that fills you? You've borne it with courage but now you are a coward.'

I sprang to my feet, ready to take a swing at him if he came close enough. 'Don't you dare call me coward! If you had experienced what I have for fifty lifetimes, you might have earned the right to criticize, but you haven't. You've struggled with magic for what, twenty years? That's nothing. I've lost loved ones in terrible ways, so many times I've given up counting. I've died of plague, starved, been hanged, killed by fricking lightning, slaughtered by Vikings, murdered by my master when I wouldn't go to his bed – you name it, I've experienced it.' He'd shaken all the worst memories loose, ones I'd put away and vowed never to think about again.

Artair had the decency to look ashamed. Still he had to argue, so sure was he of his own righteousness. 'That was the past. This is now. You are making the wrong choice.' It sounded like he knew I'd gone over to the dark Sidhe for help – knew that this was more than about what happened between his brother and me. Maybe he could sense the change in me? Quinn said all his brothers were powerful magic wielders.

'Are you so surprised? I should've done it long ago – used the power that's in me to free me.'

'But not at the cost of my brother's life. We'll be fighting for our future in a few weeks' time. Yet doing what you're doing, you'll ruin him and pollute the magic here – and then the whole world will suffer. You clearly don't get how important this battle is or you wouldn't stand in our way.'

'I don't want anyone to be harmed, but you can't stand in my way either, Artair. This is my chance – don't you see that? I've been ruined so many times because of what someone else wants. Just once, why can't it be about me?'

He leapt back into the oak, staking his claim over the light magic it contained. 'Then we are at war, Maledicta.'

I walked away. 'Have we ever really been at anything else?'

·   ·   ·

IT RAINED that afternoon so I had little choice but to go back inside. I entered the common room and, trying not to look at anyone else, strode straight over to Sian. She was chatting with Genny but, of course, that broke up when I sat down next to them. Genny drifted over, oh so casually, to join Quinn, Conall, Jack and Charlie at the card table.

'I didn't see you at lunch,' said Sian.

I shrugged. 'Yeah well.'

'You're not eating properly again.'

Utter misery had that effect on me. 'I don't feel hungry.'

'I snuck out a roll and an apple. Eat it.' She took them out of her craft bag and pressed them into my palm.

I played with the wrapper on the hoagie, finding it difficult to imagine actually swallowing. 'You know, I think this is possibly the bottom of the barrel for me. I wondered when I would reach it.' I kept my tone light, but Sian must've heard the bone-deep bitterness. 'There was this time when my sister died of TB – that was bad – but at least I never doubted she loved me and I followed soon after, coughing up my lungs – not a good way to go, believe me. Then there was the memorable occasion when my village burned down my hut and turned me out into the forest in winter. I starved but the end was kind of peaceful. I think I probably died of exposure – just faded to white though my fingers and toes were black with frostbite. Before that there were the Vikings – how could I forget the Vikings? They weren't the picturesque heroes of the movies you see – no horns on their helmets, no hearty berserker battle cries. No, they crept in under darkness and dragged us to the beach to bash our brains out. That's not all they did.'

'Linny—'

'But do you know what, I was never despised like this. Disliked, feared, blamed for something I didn't do – that's happened before – and often I deserved it. But now? I am sick and tired of being thought the one in the wrong, the one being selfish. Why can't it be my turn for some justice? Why do I have to keep on being the victim? I'm just so, so angry with...with everybody and everything!'

Sian was about to take my hand but she reared back. 'Linny, what's happening to your eyes?'

'My eyes?'

'They're changing color – going black. Stop it! You can't do magic in the middle of the common room.'

The shelves behind me began to shake, books and magazines falling to the ground.

'What's happening? An earth tremor?' asked Charlie. The card table was rattling like a pan lid on simmer. Quinn grabbed it but that only made it buck. He turned to look at me.

'I don't do magic.' I made to take Sian's hand but she snatched it away as if I'd burned her. 'Sian, help me!'

Cracks were appearing in the ceiling plaster. A lump fell down, narrowly missing two students sitting on the sofa. Catching Conall's attention, Quinn jerked his head in my direction.

'Sian!' I begged my friend, but she was backing away.

'You're flaming out. Stop it, Linny!'

'I can't stop what I don't understand!'

Everyone was now looking at me as even my last friend deserted me. I could feel Green Drake protesting, trying to evict my dark magic but the curse swirled about me, looking for a weakness to enter the well of light. It wanted to take over, to blight.

Quinn and Conall strode across the room and each took an arm.

'Don't let her go!' Quinn warned his friend though I

could see that it was agony for them to touch me. I was burning with black fire. They pulled me out of the room. Of course, they were going to take me to the gates and push me out. I felt almost relieved. My pain would be at an end for a time and Quinn would be safe.

'You're going to have to renew the boundary charm when I'm gone, don't forget – plant more nightshade berries,' I said hoarsely. Lights were dancing around my head – pretty patterns like blue fireflies. There was a shrill noise in my ears.

'You're not going anywhere,' said Quinn. He sounded furious with me.

'Can you stop this? I'm not doing it on purpose.'

'We didn't think you were. You're out of balance.'

I told him what he could do with his precious balance.

He ignored my bitter words. 'Conall, call the others. Send Liam to change memories in the common room.' He dropped my arm when we reached the entrance to the holly fortress and made a call. His palm was blistered. 'Artair, I need you.'

'Not him.' I held out my hands, fascinated by the violet shimmer on my skin as the flames flicked and danced. 'That's all I need – the guy who wants me dead. Am I losing the magic?'

He reached to stroke my hair but sparks drove him back. 'No, it's just coming out to play – and Green Drake doesn't like it. You've got to rein it back, Linny.'

'I don't think I want to.' It was so beautiful in a twisted way, so strong, like a storm oversetting trees and beating crops flat. My anger was magnificent.

'Then, darlin', I'm afraid we'll have to make you.'

'You can try.' I didn't want to bow to anyone. I wanted to

shoot into the air like a firework display and burn the whole place down.

The magic squad arrived at a run, no Liam – he was off changing memories – but Artair came in his place.

'It's her doing this, not the dark Sidhe?' asked Artair. Holly leaves were sparking, going brown and dropping around us.

'Yes, it's her. I don't know what set it off. She doesn't seem to have any control over it. It's possessing her. She's fading in and out.'

Oddly I wasn't afraid. I felt immensely powerful, scornful. 'Jeez! You don't know what set me off? Of course you don't, because you haven't the slightest idea of what it's like to be me! I am furious – spitting mad – that's what's the matter. But I'm so done with being sad, depressed, regretful. I'm done with love. All I can feel now is anger.' A branch ripped from a nearby chestnut tree, span in the air and speared to the ground right between Quinn and Artair. They didn't flinch but held their position. I laughed. 'Look how brave you all are! You are so fricking perfect.'

Artair exchanged a look with his brother. 'I don't think it's her speaking now. She's given in to the dark magic and that's speaking through her. The curse was made in anger, wasn't it?'

'It's the dark Sidhe – they've done something to her,' said Quinn.

'Are you so blind, Quinn Ramsay?' I took his shirt in my hands and shook him. The fabric singed under the pressure of my fingers. 'It was never them that did anything to me – it was always your side. You cast the curse, you condemned me! Your king strode into the hall and killed us – my sisters and me – and we'd done nothing – nothing! I'd even felt sorry for Lihtan and tried to stop the hunt. Finch was only eight!'

'Linny—'

'And you – you let me fall in love with you and then you punished me.'

'Quinn, there isn't time for this,' snapped Artair. 'It'll have to be you. I can't transform here.'

I didn't understand what they meant, but they dragged me through the holly, uncaring of scratches on any of us. They put me in the middle of their circle. I looked up: grey plumes of smoke billowed from me, obscuring the stars.

'Linny, listen, you've got to switch this off, okay, this anger?' said Conall.

I couldn't see Quinn any longer. 'Where is he?' I needed him even though I felt I might hate him now.

'He's here, he's trying to help you, but you've got to help him. Please.'

The white light was growing in the clearing. It was coming from the boys like it had in Rowena's pictures. That meant I wasn't really violet. I was a blurred shadow. Full of ugliness. That was what the camera saw. I swayed, eyes rolling back in my head.

Conall caught me and laid me down on the leaf litter, face to the cloudy skies. 'Hurry, Quinn, we're losing her,' he called. 'The dark magic's killing from inside – breaking the boundary charm's protection.'

Artair stepped away from his brother and I could see Quinn now. He was burning white more strongly than any in the circle, apart from the black edge to his feathers. Feathers? What was I seeing? He was Quinn, yes, but he was also an owl. A boy who was an owl and an owl who was a boy. I thought he flew to me and let his wings surround me –

or were they his arms? I had to be dreaming this. They felt so soft, so right.

Come back, Linny. Don't let the dark magic take you. Don't ruin this place in your anger. It was like the voice I sometimes heard walking the grounds, but this time it sounded like Quinn too.

It's both. Quinn and I are one.

'I want this to end. I can't be the Maledicta any longer.'

We know.

And I knew then that I had been heard and understood in a way that no one had ever done before. It was no idle complaint I made. Quinn and Green Drake both acknowledged that I'd reached my limit.

That was enough to reverse the tide. I felt the anger shrink, turn to sadness, to a more familiar despair. The curse retreated to its old place in my bones, my cells, my soul, fire extinguished. I was understood but they also knew I was beyond their aid.

I came back to my senses still surrounded by Quinn's arms.

'Leave us please,' he told his men. 'And thank you – for coming. I won't forget you risked your own lives for her.'

Artair nodded. 'I'll make sure Liam got everyone. We'll clear up her mess.'

They left the holly fortress, strangely subdued.

Quinn shifted so he could sit with me, my back to his chest. 'So, Linny, what are we going to do about you?'

27

SUPERNATURAL

'Y ou're not taking this from me, not again,' I said, trying to break free.

'Calm down, I won't. That stunt in the music room – that was stupid of me. Artair has made me very aware of that. I almost ruined everything. Dad nearly pulled me off the mission.'

'If you realized that, why have you punished me for the last week?'

'What?'

'The pushing and shoving in corridors, the accidentally spoiling my work, leaving the room when I enter?'

'I haven't done any of that!' He looked indignant at the suggestion.

'Your minions have. Don't tell me you haven't noticed?'

His jaw clenched. The wretch hadn't even been aware of the hell I was living through. Someone's charisma had been well out of line.

'And you stole one of my best friends!'

'Jack thought that if he came over to me, you'd have to follow.'

'Then he thought wrong.'

'Yeah, we were getting that message. His confidence has been dented. He thought he knew you.'

'But he doesn't believe in any of this.' I made a gesture meant to encompass everything happening at Green Drake. 'He doesn't have a hope of understanding me.'

'But he knows you need me – he's got that right. And I need you. Linny, there's a place inside me that only you can fill. Without you I feel half a man, half alive. We've got to find a way for us.' His chin rested lightly on my head.

Hearing such beautiful words, I could feel the temptation creeping over me again, the weakness that told me to be with him at all costs and lose my chance.

'Quinn...'

'Linny.'

'I think I'm going to betray you.'

'I know.'

'And Green Drake.'

'It knows.'

'I'm not strong enough to resist. I'm sorry but I'm just not strong enough to do this again.'

'Don't be sorry. We understand.'

'Please don't be understanding. Shout at me. Tell me I mustn't.'

'How can I? We looked inside you just now; we saw.'

'You did?'

'Knowing that you've reached your limit, who are we to stop you? It would be going against nature. Don't worry, I won't tell the others, just let me keep them safe. As long as the magic and I understand, you've no one else you need to explain yourself to.'

This boy was forgiving me in advance. He knew I was going to sell him out to his enemies, possibly unbalance him enough to send him over to dark magic, pollute the well of light, yet he was not going to lift a finger to stop me. He was just going to let me do what I had to do. This was love. I needed no further proof. Even if Rowena didn't believe that the Sidhe could feel it, I knew they did.

We rested in silence for a few minutes. The usual noises of the night resumed. An owl hooted away in the distance, reminding me of the extraordinary things I had witnessed.

'What was going on with the owl, Quinn?'

'You saw that, did you?' He rubbed his cheek against my hair, needing to be as close to me as I did to him. 'It's how the magic sees me.'

'So you become a real owl, or was it a vision?' I snuggled into him, deciding talk of magic was easier than discussion of the future.

'What's real, what's a vision?'

'You're answering a question with a question again.'

'Magic is natural – just an extreme form of nature's power.'

'Super-natural?'

'Exactly. I am not just the person you see on the surface.'

'I like your surface. Very much.'

He smiled. 'Good to know. But I'm also what's inside. When I'm open to the magic, make myself absolutely vulnerable to it like a newborn in a mother's arms, that side of me is visible.'

'That's why my first father was able to shoot the Sidhe boy who was your light guardian?'

'Catastrophically wrong place, wrong time,' agreed Quinn.

'So...so I could've killed you – used the curse to harm you despite the boundary charm?'

'Interesting question.' He scratched his chin. 'I didn't

really think about it, but yes, I suppose you could've done, theoretically, because we were working on the level of pure magic energies rather than spells. The boundary charm was failing as you let go.'

'Didn't think about it!' I sat up. 'You've got to take better care of yourself, Quinn!'

'I knew you wouldn't turn the power on me – blacken a few leaves, throw a few branches, but at heart you were still mine, not the curse's.'

'You shouldn't trust me.'

'Say that as much as you like but I've decided I will.' His face bore a stubborn expression, two little lines chiseled above the bridge of his nose.

'I'm not worth that.'

'You are to me – and to Green Drake.'

Sitting in the middle of my favorite place in the grounds – a spot I'd nearly destroyed with my anger – I felt a great swoop of sadness. 'How are you going to protect this place?'

'On the equinox we're going to hold the fort. I'll be changed like you saw me tonight, and I'll surround Green Drake as best I can with my power. The others are here to guard me.'

'And the dark Sidhe?'

'I imagine they'll be doing a very similar thing but from the outside, bashing away to get in, trying to drain off the power for themselves. One of them must change to challenge me for possession of this place. But we have an advantage: they can't practice dark magic in here.'

'Then what?'

'Then it's a battle to see who is the stronger.'

'And if I've given them my curse energy. I'm inside the boundary – I'm full of dark magic – won't that tip the balance in their favor?'

'Linny, that isn't your fight.'

'That's why you are all so unhappy to find me here, isn't it? I'm like a...a bomb about to blow up in all your faces. I nearly did so tonight.'

He turned me to frame my face in his hands. 'Not your fault – not your war. You do what you have to do and let me worry about the rest.'

WHEN I RETURNED to Crowthorne with Quinn, we found everyone but Sian and Conall had gone to bed. There was little sign anything momentous had happened apart from some new cracks in the ceiling.

Sian threw her arms around me. 'I'm so sorry, Linny. I shouldn't have backed off.'

'It was a good job you did, hedge witch,' said Conall, 'or you'd've been burned to a frazzle. Our girl here was cooking on gas.'

'He means dark magic energy,' I explained, collapsing into an armchair. Quinn pulled me up again then rearranged us so I was sitting on him.

Sian's raised brow was her only comment on our reconciliation. 'How did you stop it?'

'It's a Sidhe thing,' replied Conall. 'If we tell you, we'd have to kill you.'

'What!'

'He's teasing, Sian,' I said quickly. 'They held me together until I calmed down. Green Drake helped too.'

'You're on first name terms with the school? That's a new level in your weirdness, Linny.'

'Not the school buildings, the old magic here. And yeah, we chat from time to time. At least I think we do. I might be imagining it.'

Quinn tightened his arms around me. 'I did not know that. I sensed that Green Drake feels attached to you but to talk to it?'

'Only young Sidhe talk to magic, Linny,' said Conall.

'Well, maybe you Sidhe don't have the monopoly on that after all,' said Sian, shooting him a whiplash of a look.

'I expect being the bearer of the curse for generations has altered you,' said Quinn thoughtfully. 'I'll have to talk to our elders about that – see if they've heard of a similar case.'

'Maybe they'll be able to locate my sisters that way? There are two other incendiary devices potentially wandering around the world. It would be better if we were all defused, or at least found, wouldn't it?'

'You think they're still alive?'

I rested my head on his collarbone, calmed by his stroking of my arm. 'I have no evidence just a feeling.'

'What were their names, Linny?' asked Sian.

'Wren and Finch. Our parents loved the birds that came to our garden so called their daughters after them.' I remembered the stone walls covered with roses, the grassy suntrap where my mother used to sit with her ladies, the birds singing in the cherry tree.

'And your name has stayed the same?'

'The language we spoke changed but the bird kept coming up. I've always been named after a linnet by all my parents.'

'The magic probably pushes them that way,' said Quinn.

'It's like I always look the same.'

'Why try to improve upon perfection?' His eyes twinkled, knowing he was laying it on too thick.

'If you think perfection is muddy brown hair and grey eyes.'

'Hair the color of chestnut and eyes like a stormy sea.'

Conall laughed. 'You see where our ruling family get their power from, Sian? It's flattery of the rest of us, pure and simple.'

I WAS JUST RETURNING from lessons the following day, when Mr Huntsman stopped me in the hallway.

'Linny, my daughter would like to see you. She says she has news for you.'

'Oh.' A small part of me had been hoping that she wouldn't be able to find a volunteer and then I'd be spared the responsibility of going ahead with my betrayal of Quinn and the light Sidhe.

He patted his pockets absentmindedly. 'I hope you two aren't plotting anything? Rowena was always in trouble as a little girl.'

'No, nothing like that.'

'I'm glad you've made a friend of her. We all need friends. I don't know where I'd be without my fellow lepidopterists.'

I had a mental image of him at the bar with other butterfly collectors, sharing secrets about where to spot the rarest species, laughing, relaxed. It was odd to think of teachers as ordinary people. Mr Huntsman was a lonely man, I felt. 'Where can I find her?'

'She's mounting an exhibition of her photos in the school hall.'

I put my coat back on. 'Thanks.' Best to get this over with.

I took a moment in the doorway before I disturbed Rowena at her work. She was lining up the frames of her wildlife pictures. They were amazing. She must've had a trip out to the islands because she had captured the seals lying on the tiny beaches, flippers raised in the manner of languid students answering a question in class. Urgent little puffins patrolled their grass burrows like top-hatted doormen at the entrance of exclusive hotels. My favorites though were her photos of frosted leaves, so close you should see the individual ice crystals. Surely someone with such a vision of the beauty of nature wasn't evil? As she said, neither dark or light was good or bad, they were just different.

You know better than that, whispered Green Drake.

Rowena looked up. 'Oh, Linny, I thought I felt someone come in. What do you think?' She gestured at the pictures.

'They are wonderful. It's a stunning display.'

'You made an interesting display of your own last night, I think?'

I blushed. 'Yes, I got a little bit angry.'

'What stopped you leveling the place?'

'Have I that much power in me?'

'That and so much more.'

That was all I needed. 'I suppose I controlled it just in time.' I hoped she wouldn't press. I couldn't let her know that Quinn and Green Drake were aware of our plans. If she understood how far they'd seen inside me as part of calming me down then she would realize I had hidden nothing from them.

'As I said: very interesting display. I suppose my father passed on my message?'

'About you having news? Yes.'

She beckoned me to join her in the window alcove where she had stacked her spare frames. The school hall was smaller than the dining room, built later and including a stage with red velvet curtains for performances. The oak beams and ornate white plaster of the ceiling molded into wreaths of flowers and fruit reminded me of a seventeenth century palace, the kind of place King Charles I of England would have strode around with his spaniels barking at his heels. They'd been drafty buildings but we'd thought them the last word in modern comfort at the time.

'So, I've very good news for you. I've found a volunteer to take your place.' She gave me a wry smile. 'I was surprised at the interest. I was inundated with applications once I spread out the word. Any of my fellow Sidhe reaching the end of their lives thought another chance was better than facing the end.'

'They don't know what it's like.'

'Who's to say that they will experience it in the same way as you have? They'll be choosing it willingly – going into it with eyes open.'

'I suppose so.' They'd learn differently after a few centuries. 'Who have you picked?'

'A good friend of mine. He lives locally and was the first to put his name forward. In fact, he offered even before you asked.'

The white-bearded man from the overheard conversation.

Yes, that's him. I don't like him.

I glanced up at Rowena, hoping she wasn't aware that I was talking with the old magic that surrounded us. I could sense it kept away from her. It thought her a bully.

Aren't all Sidhe bullies? That's what Sian thinks.

Not all.

'So, are you pleased?' Rowena was puzzled by my silence.

'Yes, yes of course.' Inside I was dying just a little. Another step on the way of betrayal.

We forgive you.

I don't forgive myself.

'Good. I'll tell him we are still on for the equinox.' She packed away her nail gun, then put the rejected frames in a crate.

As I watched her, a hitch suggested itself to me. 'Rowena, how are we going to do this? Other people's magic doesn't work on me inside the boundary and if I go outside the curse is immediately triggered.'

She bunched back her hair, tying it in a red scarf. 'I have taken that into account. It's not a problem.' She put her coat on.

'How so?'

She pulled on her gloves then met my gaze. 'It's not us doing the magic, you see, but you.'

28

KING OF THE SIDHE

J ack had forgiven me. Seeing me back together with Quinn, he joined Sian and me at our lunch table.

'Seen the light, hey?' he asked.

'Something like that.' I couldn't help but smile at his accidentally perceptive remark.

'Did you like my theme?'

'Jack, you know that it's excellent – inspired. Are you going to put it in as course work?'

His mouth turned down like he'd eaten something sour. 'I'm not sure I want Mr Browning to maul it with his usual scathing comments.'

'Get Quinn to talk to him,' suggested Sian. 'He might change his tune.'

'I'll see.' I had a feeling Jack wasn't going to make his private gift to us public without a lot more persuading. 'I suppose you've both heard?'

'Heard what?' I asked, occupied by slicing my banana on top of my cereal.

'Quinn must've told you?' Jack looked puzzled.

'Er, no?'

'His dad is coming for a visit this weekend.'

'His dad!' squeaked Sian. 'You're joking?'

'What's the matter with you?' Jack turned to me. 'I'm sure he's going to be a nice guy. I mean Quinn is. He's bound to take after him.'

We were expecting a visit from the king of the Sidhe. I felt sick, memories rushing in of my one and only meeting with a predecessor. Why hadn't Quinn warned me? 'We'll see, I suppose.' There was always the option that Artair took after him.

'He won't like you if you meet him with that stunned rabbit look on your face. You've got to sparkle, show you're good enough for his son.' Jack fluttered his hands, a gesture suggesting I lacked the required razzmatazz for a Ramsay.

'Believe me, I don't think he'd want any sparkling from me.'

Sian snorted, her juice going down the wrong way.

I CORNERED Quinn on the first chance I got him on his own. It happened to be in the library so I pulled him up from his desk and marched him into a neglected corner in the Philosophy section. This was where old books came to die.

Quinn looked about him and raised his eyebrows. 'Looks promising: you, me and no one watching.' He moved in for a hug.

I held him back. 'Why didn't you tell me your father was coming?'

His hopeful expression changed to one of chagrin. 'You found out about that?'

'Of course I did. You should've told me yourself. I had to hear it from Jack.'

He dug his hands in his pockets. 'I was going to tell you but I was hoping I could put Dad off.'

'And have you?'

He shook his head. 'No, he's announced he's coming Saturday morning.'

'Is this about me?'

'About you, about this situation – he says he's not feeling good about it.'

I gave a hollow laugh. 'I bet the reports from Artair have not been glowing ones. "Quinn's hanging out with someone who almost blew the place up with dark magic." What should I do? Keep out the way?'

'I don't think that'll be possible. He has a way of getting his will. If he decides he wants to meet you then that's what'll happen.'

I folded my arms. 'No, it won't. He can't use his magic on me.'

'It's not magic. It's a parent thing.'

'And a king thing?'

'I suppose but I don't think of him like that. He's just Dad.'

'And what are you going to tell him?'

Quinn looked annoyed. 'This is my battle, not his.'

'What if he wants me removed?'

'He's not like that.'

'He's a Sidhe king; you're his son; he might well be like that this time.'

I DECIDED I couldn't worry about Mr Ramsay's arrival. That's what happens when you have too many things that make you anxious: some have to drop away and you concentrate on the major ones. I'd say hello when he arrived then make myself scarce – yes, that would be the best policy. Going missing would make me more conspicuous and probably prompt a search by the magic squad.

Saturday morning, I practiced my royal greeting in the mirror. 'Hi, your majesty.' But he wasn't my king. 'Hello, sir, nice to meet you.' That was better. I put on a little bit of makeup to distract from my ashen face and pale lips. My hand shook so I had to take it off again and try a second time. 'If you think about it, you're older than him,' I told myself. That brought a smile. 'There you are: Linny's game face. Let's go rub shoulders with royalty.'

Quinn said his father was due at eleven. I found Quinn waiting at the gate, his men around him. Even though he was pretending not to be, I could tell he was extremely nervous. He had these little tells, such as fiddling with his gold earring and digging hands in pockets. He'd made light of it but it wasn't beyond the bounds of possibility that his father would make sure I was removed from the equation so Quinn could fight undistracted – 'removed' of course being a euphemism for 'killed'. There was little I could do about it, just as I had been powerless against the Fey King striding into my family's castle centuries ago. The king was the most powerful Sidhe, I a mere immortal.

Jack and Sian stood to one side under the shelter of the porch so I joined them.

'Quite the welcoming committee,' I murmured.

Jack beamed at me. 'Quinn asked all of his best friends to be here.' I could see he was thrilled to make the grade.

'What do you think? Helicopter? Limo?' I scanned the skies. 'Can't hear anything.'

'Is he rich then?' asked Jack, innocent of the regal background to Quinn's family.

Sian nudged me. 'I think that's him over there.'

A man was coming on foot down the drive. He was wearing faded jeans, a leather jacket and he had a guitar strapped to his back, a modern troubadour. Mirrored sunglasses hid his face but his silhouette was unmistakable.

'Oh my gosh, oh my gosh, oh my gosh,' intoned Jack. 'Quinn did not say he was the son of Shay Ramsay!'

We were looking at one of the world's most celebrated singer-songwriters, almost as famous for his intense privacy as his string of hits. I hadn't made the connection but of course it was there in the lanky frame, the shock of black hair, and blue eyes that gazed out from many an album cover.

'Quinn seems not to tell us quite a lot. Did you know this, Sian?' I asked.

'Uh-uh. I think my oldest sister has all his music. She has no idea.'

'You can ask him for an autograph later.'

'But he's –'

I elbowed her. 'I think somehow your sister might overlook that.'

Shay Ramsay had reached the gate and handed off his guitar to Conall so he could hug his son. Laughing, they rocked to and fro, clearly at ease with each other. He then shook hands or slapped palms with the rest of the squad. I wondered where Artair was. I would've expected him to be here, particularly if this was going to turn into an execution.

Quinn turned to us. 'Dad, these are my new friends: Sian Willowbrook, Jack Burne and Linny Grace. They've made me very welcome at Crowthorne House.'

'Hey, guys, nice to meet you,' said Shay. He didn't offer his hand but gave us a friendly kind of wave. 'Thanks for making my son welcome in his new school.'

'Mr Ramsay,' I said stiffly, braced for the blow.

'Shay, please. Or Seamus if you must.' I couldn't tell, thanks to the glasses, but I was fairly certain he was studying me. So would I be if I were him and knowing what he knew about me.

'So, Dad, what do you want to see?' asked Quinn. 'We've an hour and a half before lunch.'

'I want to see everything. Let's do the circuit.'

Okay, so that was over. I exchanged a relieved glance with Sian and we headed for the house.

'I meant you three too,' called Shay. 'I'd like your new friends to show me around. I expect they know the place better than anyone.'

Jack must've seen our hesitant expressions. 'Stay here – I'll get our coats.' For him this was like his Christmases and birthdays rolled into one to be asked to conduct Shay Ramsay around the grounds. 'Quinn, do you want me to fetch yours?'

'Thanks, Jack, but I'm fine in my fleece.'

Once he'd gone inside, Shay crossed to Sian. 'So, hedge witch, are you going to make trouble for us?'

'If I can.'

Sian's feisty reply was met with a roar of laughter. 'Hey, I like this one. I can see why you're friends.'

'I wouldn't call us friends exactly,' she came back.

'Better and better.' Shay rubbed his hands. 'Keep 'em coming, darlin'.'

It appeared that there was nothing Sian could say to annoy him so she shut up.

I took Quinn aside. 'Is he really the same Shay as, you know, THE Shay?'

'Yes.' Quinn sounded resigned.

'Doesn't he have the king business going for him? Why have another career?'

'He has to earn a living, Linny. Fairy gold is a myth. How do you think he paid to place us here?'

'I don't know.'

'A new single released last October.'

'And you didn't tell us?'

'No.' His gaze shifted away from me.

'Why? Do you realize how much kudos you would've earned?'

'That's the point. People change around me when they find out.'

'It's not enough that you have your charisma and your Sidhe royal status?'

'They don't know about that.'

'I bet they sense it. So that's not enough to make them act differently?' I put my palm on his cheek to turn his gaze back to me.

He covered my hand with his. 'That's about me though, isn't it? My influence on them. I don't want to be known as just one of my celebrity father's sons. He's worked hard to keep us out of the limelight.' He kissed my fingertips.

Jack was back, handing Sian her patchwork jacket. Shay was now admiring the eclectic garment to which all her sisters had donated a square.

'He can see the hedge witch magic on it. He digs that kind of thing,' said Quinn with a smile.

Jack handed my coat to Quinn, who held it up for me to slip into. I batted his hands away before he started buttoning it.

'I'm not five.'

'No, you're sixteen. I'm not likely to forget.'

Shay clapped his hands. 'Okay, guys, let's get this show on the road.'

The magic squad headed off back to their houses as

we began the familiar walk around the boundary. Sian, Jack and I deliberately let Quinn and his father pull ahead.

'They must have lots to catch up on,' Jack said. 'Shay's been on tour this winter – Australia and Japan – that's why Quinn was here over Christmas. Just think – a rock star for a father! I'm in awe.'

'We would never've guessed.' Sian took his arm.

'I feel like we've got music royalty visiting! What is everyone going to say when they see him at lunch? Charlie is going to be so mad he went on the school trip to see *Hamilton* and missed this.'

We were walking clockwise around the walls and reached the dragon gates. Shay stepped beyond them to look up at the statues.

'Linny, do you want to come here and tell me about these?' He was baiting me. I bet he would love me to solve his problem by killing myself that way.

Jack rushed over. 'Mr Ramsay—'

'Call me Shay, Jack, Shay.'

'Linny's got this agoraphobic problem, doesn't go beyond the gates. I can tell you about them.' He started reeling off the school story about when they were put there and the number of times they'd been stolen by a rival establishment a few miles up the road.

I turned my back on Shay.

'He's just testing you, like he did Sian,' said Quinn softly.

'It was cruel.'

'I didn't say he would necessarily be nice to you. That's my job. Come here.' He hugged me to him and brushed his lips over the crown of my head. 'Take no notice of Dad. He's far too used to getting his own way.'

'That's really interesting, Jack, thanks. Linny, what can

you tell me about this place?' Shay reentered the grounds and held out a hand to me.

'He won't bite.' Quinn nudged me over to his father so I rested my gloved hand in the crook of Shay's elbow, barely touching. We began walking again, Quinn running interference with Sian and Jack so our conversation could take place uninterrupted.

'I can't tell you much that you don't already know, sir.'

'I'm not going to get you to call me Shay, am I?'

'No, sir.'

'There's one thing I don't know: why are you with my son, Maledicta?'

I made to remove my fingers but he put his free hand over them, capturing them.

'I'd prefer it if you didn't call me that.'

'It's what you are – a title of sorts. You've borne it with honor for centuries I hear.'

'Not really. I've just muddled through.' I looked anywhere but at him; his eyes were too like Quinn's. Funny though, I would swear that the man who made me feel so uncomfortable was having the opposite effect on Green Drake. The old magic loved him. I could almost hear it purring. We slowed by a patch of star-like wood anemones, white petals with a yellow center, framed by a little plantation of silver birches. I hadn't expected to be here to see them this year.

'My son loves you.' Shay was gazing at them too.

'I know.'

'There's a tradition in the Sidhe that we don't love.' He waited for me to comment.

'Yes. That's what I've been told.'

'But it's false, Linny. Only those consumed by an appetite for power dismiss as worthless something that is far more precious. They don't understand love because it looks like weakness to them.'

I thought of Rowena and her confidence that her way was better than that taken by the light. 'The people who think like that – they're not evil.'

'No, indeed – at least not all of them. Half my court are dark Sidhe. For them magic is about holding tight to power, rather than creating something beautiful with it. But they are pitiable; they spend their lives wanting the wrong thing. Surely you of all people know what is worth valuing in any life?'

'Yes – yes, I think I do.'

He turned to face me. 'So what is worth it?'

'Love, friendship, kindness goes a long way too, and loyalty.'

'Have you experienced all those?'

I nodded. I was afraid that the lump in my throat was the prelude to tears.

'And their opposites?'

'Trust me, they come along more often.'

He brushed the back of my hand, satisfied by my answer. 'I'll tell you something that I tell few people. I loved my wife, Quinn's mother. I'd do anything to get her back but I know that I have no power strong enough to work that spell even if I took over every well of light magic in existence. Sometimes the lesson taught by life is acceptance of what we can't change. It could make us bitter, or it could help us grow as people.'

I looked away. Was he suggesting that I should just lie down and accept my fate? 'But if you could change it? If you could bring her back?'

'Then I'd have to ask myself if the means honored her

memory. She wouldn't want to be brought back at any price. Our love was better than that.'

OUR WALK ENDED up in the music block. Jack was keen to show Shay that the school had excellent facilities. We went into the largest practice room, the one with the grand piano.

'Jack writes songs,' said Quinn.

'Do you now?' Shay took a place on the music stool. 'Play me one.'

'Oh, I've nothing good enough to show you.' Jack flushed bright red.

'He wrote Linny and me a song. It's amazing. He arranged it as a duet.' Quinn leafed through the files of student compositions on the shelf until he found Jack's. 'You should try it, Dad. It'll help you understand.'

His father gave him a measuring look. 'I probably understand more than you think, Quinn.'

'Just give it a try.'

'Are you up for this, Jack?' Shay turned back to my friend.

'Absolutely, sir, er, Shay.' Jack spread out the sheets. 'Don't expect too much, please? I know Quinn and Linny like it, but you might hate it.'

'Now why would I do that? I trust my son's taste.'

They began playing. Sian moved to Jack's shoulder to watch while Quinn came to stand behind me, arms around my waist.

'I think it's even more beautiful this second time,' he murmured.

And it was. I closed my eyes, letting Jack's clever music lift me out of my poor confused body and float me in a realm where I was better than I was, purer.

'That's how I see us exactly,' said Quinn.

I wished I could see us that way too. I was too conscious that I was letting down my side of the harmony.

Sian gave them a round of applause when they finished. 'Wow, Jack, I didn't know you'd composed that. Why did you keep it from me?'

'It's only just finished.' He gathered up the music, his blush having hardly subsided.

I prayed that Shay would say something encouraging. He could dash the young composer's hopes for good if he said something critical or dismissive.

Shay held out a hand. 'Can I take a copy of that?'

'What? My music? Oh, oh, of course.' Jack bundled it into his outstretched palms.

'Do you write lyrics?'

'No. That's not my thing.'

'I had an idea as we were playing. Do you mind if I try writing some to fit your music?'

'Mind? Oh my gosh, it would be an honor.'

Shay gave him a wry smile. 'I don't suppose you have an agent?'

'An agent?'

'He's at school, Dad. He has teachers, not agents,' said Quinn dryly.

'I'll send you the number for a good one.'

'I'd get independent advice if I were you, Jack. Dad's well known for driving a hard bargain when it comes to business.'

'That's why my recommendation will be a good one. You want a lion not a lamb.'

Sian wafted Jack with a score. 'Don't you faint on us, Jack.'

'I'm in shock,' he moaned.

Shay patted his shoulder. 'I'm looking for a ballad for my next album. I think this might be it.'

'You're joking?'

'Deadly serious.' Shay got up from the piano stool to look over at us. '"Linnet and Quinn's Theme". It's going to be a tribute to one of them, I think, but I don't know which yet. We've got a hell of a fight on our hands.'

'Sorry? I'm not following.' Jack scratched his head. 'You want to change the title?'

'You'll let me talk to your agent?'

'The agent I haven't got yet? Of course!'

'Great. You've an amazing gift, Jack. Keep on composing no matter what happens, okay?'

29

EQUINOX

I'd never been one to wish my life away knowing how short it would be, but I found myself wanting the weeks between Shay's visit and the night of the equinox to pass so I could just get it over with. I felt like a driver in a skid on a wet road, aware she's on a collision course but all I could do was close my eyes. I think I was afraid I'd listen to my second thoughts. I was ruthlessly optimistic on the surface: maybe it would go smoothly; I would live free of the curse; and the power I gave the dark Sidhe would not be enough to beat Quinn. We'd have our happily ever after.

But would he still want me knowing what I'd done? If I were in his shoes, what would I think of someone who didn't put me first?

Both Quinn and Green Drake had gone very quiet on me. We spent a lot of time together, and I do mean all three of us, sitting in our oak tree just waiting. There was no more that needed to be said. I was accepted, forgiven.

And I hated myself.

'Dad's come through with some lyrics. I think he's

serious about Jack's song,' said Quinn, idly braiding a lock of
my hair. Sian had continued to add her beaded charms, not
happy that I was still with a Sidhe. Quinn said he liked them
– they gave him a buzz like the fizz of sherbet in the mouth
when he brushed against the beads.

'Jack said Mr Browning fell off his chair when Jack told
the class that he'd entered into negotiations with your dad's
label.' I revolved the ring on his finger. He had lovely hands,
much bigger than mine but elegantly shaped. A musician's
hands.

'And what do you think? Having our song out there?'
asked Quinn.

'I hadn't asked myself that. He's not kept the title,
has he?'

'He's saying that depends on us.'

I hadn't missed the barb in Shay's comment about a tribute. It was the closest he got to accusing me of endangering
his son and the world's balance. He knew that I wouldn't be
able to bear hearing the song again if something happened
to Quinn and it was my fault.

'Quinn?'

'Linny.'

'I've been thinking—'

He kissed me to stop me speaking. 'Don't. This time is
your time, okay? I thought we agreed that?'

I was about to kiss him in return when I saw that Artair
had joined us. Quinn groaned.

'So Dad sent you back?'

'You've been away?' I asked.

'Missed me?' asked Artair straddling the branch.

'No.'

'Yeah, he sent me back. He said you'd need me
tomorrow.'

The equinox.

'It's all in hand, Artair,' said Quinn.

'It isn't and you know it. Sorry, Linny, but Quinn, seriously, why are you still with her? Didn't Dad order you off? I told him to tell you to separate yourself from the touch of the curse magic. It saps your will.'

Quinn tightened his hold on me but he needn't. I wasn't going to cede the branch to my least favorite member of the Ramsay family.

'He didn't say a thing,' said Quinn. 'In fact, I think he liked her.'

'It's not about liking or not liking, it's about surviving.' Artair was so furious he was fairly steaming despite the chilly day. 'I'm not talking here just about you and your path. This is the biggest challenge you'll ever face and yet you're playing sweethearts with her. You know what's at stake; I don't get why you're risking it all for a human!'

'Artair –'

'No, Quinn, you have to do your duty tomorrow. Face it: if this source of light magic is polluted then things have got so bad we risk a chain reaction across the world. The balance will become more and more out of kilter. It'll be harder the next time, and harder, until light magic is endangered, then extinct. All that will be left will be dark magic wielders; all lightness and joy will go. What will the world look like then?

'So I repeat the question, why are you still with her?'

Quinn's mouth had thinned to a determined line. 'The magic doesn't mind.'

Artair sighed, looking exhausted, older than his years. 'I remember what talking to the magic is like. It's too kind if anything. It tends to like the wrong people. You have the same weakness.'

'Linny is not a wrong person.'

'I'm afraid that's exactly what she is and she knows it too, don't you, Linny?'

'That's enough, Artair,' said Quinn, a snap of command in his voice. 'You've made your point but this is my choice, my time. Please, leave us alone.'

'Okay. Linny, don't think you'll feel forgiven if you do this and survive.' Artair dropped to the ground and walked moodily away.

'I've already told you that you're forgiven,' said Quinn. 'Don't worry about him. He has never loved anyone like I love you. He doesn't understand.'

I murmured something but I had the feeling that Artair was talking about me forgiving myself, not the judgement of others.

THE DAY of the equinox arrived – the day that would decide all our futures. Rowena asked me to meet her on the drive at eleven thirty that night. She explained that most of the dark Sidhe would be outside the boundary to do their part in the exchange. I was to come to the gates.

That was a relief for me because I was fairly certain Quinn and his men would be holding their ceremony in one of the most precious spots, the oak or the holly fortress on the far side of the grounds from the drive.

'What are you up to, Linny?' asked Sian as she caught me putting on some warm clothes.

'Nothing.' I tied my hair back with one of her beaded charms.

'Your expression doesn't say nothing.'

I hugged her. 'Sian, stay inside tonight, okay?'

'Why?'

'Things are...moving.'

'What things?'

'I can't explain until the morning but it's good, necessary, I promise.'

Sian noticed the day I had circled on my calendar. 'Of course, it's equinox. Quinn's going to be out there too? He's found a way of helping you?'

'Yes.' It wasn't a lie. He was aiding me by not stopping me. 'But it's a Sidhe spell: you'd better keep well away. You... you'll still be my friend if it doesn't quite go to plan?' No, no, it had to go to plan. Quinn would be okay; he'd save the world's balance.

'Of course I will, you idiot.' She tweaked the beaded braid tying back my hair. 'Don't make it sound so drastic. I had my doubts about him but I'm convinced now that he really won't let any harm come to you. Tell him to consider binding the boundary charm to you so you can carry it in your skin – a locket containing deadly nightshade berries might work.'

'Yeah, I'll tell him.'

Jack came in with a dazed look on his face. 'See how much they offered me.' He showed us the sum from Shay's lawyer.

'Oh my gosh, you'll never have to work again!' said Sian, attention mercifully distracted from me.

'I'm not sure about that but I think you will never need to take out a student loan,' I said forcing a smile. 'That's amazing.'

'You think I should accept it?'

'Duh!'

'Yeah, yeah, I should. I mean Quinn's dad is hardly likely to be swindling me.' Jack drifted away without even giving me the chance to say 'goodnight'.

'Do you still think all Sidhe are toxic?' I asked Sian.

'The jury's out but I think it might return a more favorable verdict if Shay Ramsay really does go through with this deal. There's a problem though.'

'Oh?' My heart missed a beat. What did she suspect?

'If the others hear about Jack's music career, our "out" crowd is suddenly going to be the height of "in".'

QUINN and I met by arrangement in the porch. We walked hand in hand as far as we could go before we had to separate.

'You're shaking.' He hugged me, putting his forehead to mine.

'Why aren't you?'

'I am – inside. I'm worried that they're going to kill you doing this. I just couldn't bear that so you mustn't let them. You shouldn't trust the dark Sidhe; their bargains always have a sting in the tail. Be watchful.'

'Please don't worry about me. A real death would be a release of a kind.'

'Not for me.'

'I'm more anxious about you and what this'll do to you.'

'Don't be. Linny, if the worst happens, you are not to blame, remember that.'

'What worst? Are...are you saying that it's not just about turning you to a different path?' I'd been telling myself that he'd just become like Rowena and she seemed okay: harsh, power-hungry but alive.

'I'm not becoming a dark Sidhe. Green Drake and I have agreed we will stick together on this. The world can't lose another well of light magic. Too many have already fallen. We'll fight it all the way to the end.'

'Quinn!'

'I know what you thought but we don't agree with you. Dark magic isn't just different from light; it's captivity, exploitation, twisting.' His blue eyes glowed with a knowledge that was far beyond anything I'd gathered in all my lifetimes. I hadn't really realized how wise he was under the charming exterior. 'We don't want to live like that. What kind of existence would that be when we've known love, freedom and kindness? Go now. Green Drake and I wish you well. You have our blessing – our love.' He pushed me gently away. 'You'll be late.'

I stumbled down the path. 'Quinn?' I turned but he had already gone.

He hadn't kissed me goodbye.

Maybe that was just as well. I would have felt a complete Judas.

What was I doing?

Steps dragging, I made myself walk up the drive and past a bonfire that no one seemed to be tending. Rowena stepped out of the shadow of the gatepost, dressed in a long black coat. She appeared relieved to see me.

'Good, Maledicta, you came.'

I rubbed my arms. 'What's with the coat?' She looked so different from her usual fashionable self. I wanted to turn and run.

'We have our ceremonies – tradition. Don't be alarmed.'

'Rowena, where did all those people come from?' It was hard not to be alarmed when I now saw that hundreds of people were waiting just beyond the gates all dressed in similar robes, a huge bonfire on the road behind them casting their faces into shadow. There were two more fires just by the wall on the right and left of the dragon statues. I was reminded of some twisted gathering of the old Benedictine monks in their black habits, gathered for a service, but I'd never seen them conduct one in such a dark place and time.

'Not Rowena tonight, Maledicta. I am the Hunter – and these are my dark Sidhe allies.'

'There are so many of you!' I thought of Quinn and his ten men, eleven with Artair. They were hugely outnumbered. 'This isn't fair.'

'Who said anything about fair? That's not how we fight.'

'What's...what's going to happen?'

Rowena checked the skies. 'We're waiting for the half-moon to show. That's when the light and dark sides are in balance. We'll focus our power to allow for the barriers to be lowered. Simon will then come through the gate and take your hands. You'll let go of the dark energy inside you and give it to him.'

'How do I do that?'

'You did it the other night. Do you recall what happened then?'

'I was angry.'

'Then get angry. You have a lot to be angry about.'

But I didn't feel angry tonight. I felt grieved, ashamed. 'Okay.' It wasn't okay. Not in the least.

'Once the exchange reaches half way, Simon will then be strong enough to start pulling the power from you. He won't be able to stop, even if it's not going so well.'

Side effects may include death.

'And then?'

'When you're free of it, I'll make sure you get back home but it might be a little later. We have other business tonight. And here they are: right on time.' Her eyes were steely as she looked past me. Quinn and the light Sidhe were coming up the drive. Why did they have to be here where they could see my shame, my betrayal? They'd shed their usual coats and jackets and were dressed in silver grey shirts edged with bird footprints; Quinn's was longer than the others, exactly like the robe worn by the Fey King – the man who had done this to me.

I shuddered as I remembered the pain of the curse, and each subsequent terrible death. I could be free of that in a few minutes. Why was I wasting my concern on his descendant?

Because he is my soulmate and I love him, whispered my heart, or was it the magic? *Let past grievances remain in the past. You can't hold on to bitterness without it twisting you.*

The light Sidhe stopped at the edge beyond the first bonfire and formed into a circle around Quinn. None of them were looking at me. They had to be under orders from Quinn to leave me be. They ignored the jeers coming from the dark Sidhe beyond the gate; they moved like dancers following a well-rehearsed choreography.

I had to try something to save him. 'Rowena – Miss Huntsman – Quinn said the fight tonight might kill him.'

Rowena smiled – but it wasn't a nice expression. 'So he knew you would be here? I did wonder after the king paid a call and didn't intervene. The boy must be very arrogant if he thinks he can beat us even with your power on our side.'

'You said you wouldn't harm him.'

'I said that wasn't my intention. If he gets in our way then we can't be responsible if he becomes collateral damage.'

That was when I knew I couldn't go through with this. I'd probably known for days but I'd pigheadedly carried on the same track as I hadn't wanted to admit I was giving up my chance. 'I'm sorry, Miss Huntsman.'

'What?'

'I...I can't.' I took a step away and towards the light Sidhe.

Rowena's face underwent a strange transformation. All pleasantness fled and I was looking at a person of implacable will. A shadow came over her – something with wings – a kestrel. The night grew darker and hotter. Sweat beaded on my brow then trickled down my face to my neck like I was standing by the open doors of a furnace. The power was pulsing from her, not the bonfire at my back.

It's how the magic sees me, Quinn had said when I asked about the owl. The magic was showing me Rowena.

You're her prey, Green Drake whispered.

'Don't tell me – you changed your mind because of love?' sneered Rowena, casting a scornful look at Quinn who stood quietly only twenty feet away, head bowed. Why wasn't he looking at me?

'Yes. For love.'

She gripped my wrist. 'I'm afraid it's too late. You made a pact with me and you've entered our circle. The process has already begun.'

'What circle?'

She gestured to the fire behind me, then to the ones lit to our right and left. 'That circle. The magic – even the light magic here – isn't allowed to let you leave until this is done.'

I wasn't taking her word on that. 'Quinn, I'm sorry! I'm not going to do it!' I turned and ran towards the bonfire behind me. I'd join the circle of light Sidhe, seek their protection so I couldn't be used against him.

Don't! screeched Green Drake. *You'll break me.*

I stopped at the very edge of the circle. Quinn raised his eyes to mine and shook his head slightly.

'Quinn! Please, I'm sorry!'

He closed his eyes, face etched with sorrow. None of the

light Sidhe looked at me. They kept their eyes on their commander. He knelt and they began chanting softly. Snow fell in their midst but I couldn't feel the cool touch of their magic, only the heat of Rowena's.

Rowena yanked one of Sian's friendship beads from my hair and threw it into the bonfire. It exploded in a crimson shower of stars. 'You really should've asked to read the small print, Linny. I would've thought fifty lifetimes were enough to learn that lesson.'

I faced her. 'I'm going to die, aren't I?'

'Probably. I did say. It's about time, though, isn't it?'

The people beyond the gate started a counter-chant. They lit torches from the fires, passing the flame along the line until I faced a blazing wall, hundreds of brands all burning so I could not hide my traitorous self in the shadows. I was sickened by my own act. Why had I persuaded myself that there was no difference between the kinds of magics?

Because you wanted to believe that. Green Drake was still accepting me, still forgiving.

I've made the wrong choice. I'm going to die, and doing so I'll destroy you and Quinn – damage the world.

You wanted death.

Not like this.

Then make another choice. Green Drake was getting fainter, almost as if it was fading away already.

I looked up over the trees. A half-moon had risen. I felt a jolt of power in the earth and a wall of silver-white magic shot up from Quinn and his men. The light Sidhe were fighting back. But I had so much dark magic inside me – an ocean – enough to swamp this place in an ugly tidal wave.

Then I understood: I was the fulcrum on which the balance rested. I wasn't a side skirmish. I was the decisive battle. I think we'd all known that but only I had fooled myself into thinking I was able to hold myself apart from this. It was my world too that they were fighting over.

'Simon, can you get through with your powers intact?' asked Rowena.

The white bearded man I'd seen once on the path tested the boundary. 'Yes.'

'Our donor is a little reluctant. I'm going to need your help with her. Remember, Maledicta, you cannot leave the circle until the exchange is done. You might as well get on with it. Think what a relief it will be to have it all over.'

She was voicing thoughts I'd had for weeks. That was another reason I'd let myself fall for her promises that this would solve my problem. Simon took my arm, Rowena held the other side and they propelled me up to the middle of the gates, the center of the circle they had made.

'Good, the king's boy is vulnerable now.' Rowena pointed to Quinn as he crouched on the ground. A vast swirl of power funneled up from his shoulders like a tornado balancing on his back. Wind whipped and tugged at the trees but it was curiously still in the space between the bonfires. Quinn's magic formed an owl-shaped break in the cloud and hovered over us, pearly like moonlight. Lightning flickered from the edge of his wings. Bells pealed in Green Drake tower and nearby churches.

'Cover your faces!' said Rowena.

Those who weren't yet wearing their hoods put their head in shade so none of the light magic would fall on them.

Forgive me, Quinn. I tipped my face back, bathing in the magic Quinn was shedding over all of us, human, light and dark Sidhe, without discrimination. He was holding nothing back. It was the most beautiful thing I'd ever seen – a wild dance as the earth celebrated its natural power, channeled through one who did not want to use it for selfish ends.

'See, we can't have power spilling over everything like this – being wasted,' said Rowena as if the sight that I found so awe-inspiring was a blasphemy against good order.

Hope fluttered back to take up its perch in my heart again after such a long absence. I understood finally what the magic wanted. It had kept it even from Quinn but at this point I was closer to it than it was to its protector.

All right, magic. I'm listening.

'Simon, see if you can pull the curse from her. She needs to be angry.'

'Yes, Hunter.'

'I'm not angry. I'm at peace.' And I did feel safe, flying beyond their reach – they couldn't catch me now. The owl swooped, brushing me with wing tips. Flakes of snow drifted, penetrating the dark circle. The dark Sidhe ducked, some screamed, as if the flakes burned rather than soothed.

'He's winning. Take the girl's power!' ordered Rowena. She clicked her fingers and Miss King and another dark Sidhe rolled two bundles out into the middle of the road. Not bundles – Sian and Jack, bound and gagged.

'No, no you can't! Let them go!' My illusion of comfort crashed to the ground. The light owl soared out of reach, unable to help.

'Of course, but only if you hand over what you agreed.' Rowena's nail tipped my chin towards her, point digging in. 'I thought we'd need a bargaining chip so I arranged for these friends of yours to join our party.'

Lying in the dirt, Sian looked furious, Jack terrified.

I went down on my knees, reaching towards them. 'It's okay, Jack,' it wasn't okay, 'I'll get you out of this! Sian, I'm sorry.' She had to have guessed from our conversation that I had made this devil's bargain and lied to her. I'd betrayed them both.

'Hurt them – show her we are serious!' yelled Simon.

Miss King pushed her palm towards Sian. Violet light arched from her fingers to hit Sian in the chest. She screamed. Jack had struggled free of his blanket and kicked the teacher's ankle. The other captor seized his hair and pulled his head back, exposing his throat.

'We don't need two, do we?' he growled, a knife in his hand.

'No!' My scream split the night. The light magic faltered as Quinn opened his eyes to see what was happening in the gateway.

'Good, good.' Rowena beckoned two acolytes to support her. 'We're almost there. This is my time.'

'You must be feeling really angry with us?' said Simon, raising me from my knees and squeezing my wrist in his bony fingers. He looked in his eighties but he had the strength of a much younger man.

I could feel the dark magic bubbling up, violet sparks bursting from my fingertips. I could save my friends if I used it, blast all the dark Sidhe to kingdom come. No, no, I had to control it. There was no one tonight who could stop me flaming out if I let go. I'd destroy everyone and everything.

'She's getting warmer!' said Simon triumphantly. 'That's right girl – push it out at me. Make me suffer.'

'If I do give you this, you'll suffer more than you could possibly imagine.' I gritted my teeth. 'I should give it to you just to punish you.'

'Linny, you mustn't,' shouted Sian.

'That's right. You hate us,' hissed Simon. 'We hurt your little friends. If you don't hand this over, we'll make them feel more pain. Do you want them to feel pain?'

The power inside me surged, beat against my will, howled.

You're better than this, whispered Green Drake. *You know what to do.*

The chanting grew louder. The sky darkened and the outstretched wings of the owl were now fighting with the sharp claws of a kestrel, grappling, losing. Quinn could not concentrate with his friends in peril and, even if he did, the balance was shifting away from him as my curse crept from my body into Simon. Dark magic was on the move. Thunder rolled across the skies and the wind picked up. Rain fell, drops hissing as they hit the ground, scorching the earth, burning our skins. Rowena was on her knees, held up by two of her companions. She was making the change to her dark self, becoming completely vulnerable. I would never have a better opportunity. If I hesitated I would be too late.

'Sian, Jack, I really do love you!' I shouted against the noise of wind and thunder. 'Quinn, I'm sorry I ever started down this path. As for you....' With a swift move, I had Simon bent over, his grip released. The knee had worked again. 'Right. See you all in about thirty years or so.'

I stepped through the gates.

IN-BETWEEN

A SPELL OF SLEEP

I woke up.

No, this can't be right.

I took a moment to work out where I was – not lying between the gateposts and yet not in my bed either. It hadn't been a dream. Looking up at the dawn sky above me, branches edging my vision, I realized I was wrapped in Sian's rug and resting on a pile of leaves. A posy of wood anemones was in my hands, held together by one of her friendship bracelets. Quinn's ring sat loosely on my finger.

So you're awake.

What happened?

I could sense that the magic was deeply pleased about something. A little breeze blew caressing me with a confetti of last year's leaves. *Look around you.*

I sat up. Quinn was sitting on the ground nearby, leaning back against the log I'd once dragged into the holly fortress. He was asleep but his face was streaked with tears.

They think I'm dead? I asked. Why else would they have laid me out like this?

Yes.

Am I?

The magic laughed – I don't know any other word for it. It wasn't a human noise but a chatter of water over pebbles, the cry of wild birds, the drum of hooves on hollow ground. *No. I've sent them all to sleep.*

What? All?

Yes, everyone within the boundary of the school wall.

Don't tell me you've made a thorn hedge grow up overnight too?

Go and see.

What about Quinn?

Don't worry about him. I'll look after him. He needs his sleep. He fought hard last night and thinks he lost you. The magic showed me a glimpse of the light and dark battling in the skies, a wash of white cancelling them both out for a moment, then Quinn coming back to himself, only to be presented with the news that I'd sacrificed my life. Artair carried my body into the clearing and placed it with great tenderness on the leaves the others had gathered. Quinn had been in despair, kneeling by my side, his brother clutching his shoulder in desperate comfort. My heart clenched in sympathy.

Trust me. Quinn needs this sleep.

I nodded. I'd trusted the magic this far and would always do so now. I draped Sian's rug around Quinn and shifted his ring to my thumb so I wouldn't lose it. I then pushed through the holly barrier and walked to my favorite patch of wall.

Go up.

I pulled myself to the top and stood there. Compared to the quiet within the boundary, the world was busy outside.

The meadow grass was fluttering in the wind, the waves breaking on the shore throwing spray into the air.

No thorns, I told the magic, *at least not any that weren't here already.* I sucked a little scratch picked up from a bramble.

Go to the beach.

What?

Go on. If magic could be smug, this was. *I thought you decided to trust me?*

All right. But if I die, I'll blame you.

No, you won't.

I wasn't sure if that meant I wouldn't die or I wouldn't blame the magic. I decided it didn't matter because I was already jumping down.

Nothing happened. No bolt from the blue. No heart attack or invasion of hostile forces ready to ambush me. I walked through the meadow with its spring flowers just opening to the daylight and reached the edge of the dunes. I waded up through the sand and marram grass, slid down the other side to arrive on the beach as the sun edged over the horizon. The sky blazed hot on the eastern side, cool blue overhead, still dark in the west. The shore stretched for glorious miles either side of me. In the distance a little party of seals had swum ashore and lay on their sides waving at me.

Okay, they weren't waving at me – that's just what they do – but I waved back just in case.

Is this real?

Yes.

Wait – how can I talk to you out here beyond the boundary?

That's down to you.

What did I do?

You restored the balance. A great wrong can only be equaled by an extravagant act of self-sacrifice. You gave up your one chance for Quinn, your friends, and for the sake of the wider world.

And for you.

Yes, and for me. I needed you to do that but I couldn't tell you or it wouldn't have been from your free will. If you'd made the wrong choice, then I would have died and the rot spread from me to all the other sources of light magic. I won't forget what you did.

And the curse?

It changed – or I should say it went back to what it should've been all along. Light magic. It now sits around me, stretching, connecting.

I had an image of roots spreading underground, reaching out to other wells of light magic. I remembered Rowena's view of magic, how she had wanted to appropriate it for her kind. *Is it – are you – out of dark Sidhe control, free, unconfined?*

Yes.

That's good.

I rather thought so.

So I righted my father's wrong?

Oh no, you couldn't do that. He did nothing wrong. He made a mistake. It was the Sidhe king who committed the wrong. Distraught at the loss of his favorite son, he turned light magic into a terrible dark curse. The Sidhe destroyed the balance themselves, not your father.

I sat down on the sand and let the grains trickle through my fingers. *My poor family. All the years living under a curse and taking the blame for someone else's wrong.*

By loving a descendant of the one who did so much harm to yours, that's how you began to restore the balance. And the boy didn't do so bad himself, sacrificing his needs to yours. Cherish that, Linnet. Your relationship is in balance. And now you are free.

The magic and I – for that was what it felt like – walked, then ran, then tumbled on the sand. We visited the seals, skipped stones in the waves, and drew pictures on the flat wet margin where the tides were retreating. We celebrated life. I didn't have to ask. I knew that I was completely emptied of the curse. Not a shadow was left in my body or my soul.

A gull shrieked overhead, calling me back to all my other questions.

What's happened to everyone else?

Go see.

I jogged across the meadow and climbed back inside the school. It was still early, only just after seven, but usually there would be someone up and about, a groundsman walking his dog or a delivery van unloading at the kitchen doors, but today it was silent.

When you said all, you meant all, didn't you?

Yes.

I crossed the drive. The ashes of the bonfire Rowena had built in the middle of it were cold.

What happened to the dark Sidhe?

When you gave up your chance to break the curse, the boost in light magic meant the ones outside couldn't enter and those who were already here didn't feel very welcome.

What did you do?

I caught an image of the dragons on the gate turning from stone to flesh and breathing fire on those hundreds gathered near them. Rowena, Simon, Miss King – they all fled, jumping in their cars and heading as far away as possible. They hadn't expected the kindly light magic to turn on them.

Dragons? Really?

Just an illusion, but a good one.

You, Green Drake, are a bit of a showman.

That's why we get on so well, Miss Poker Champion-Juggler-Acrobat.

I entered the dining room and pushed through the double doors to the kitchen. Three members of staff slumped face down at a table, a late-night game of cards still set out in front of them, a bottle of whisky hardly touched. I took a quick look. The pastry chef was going to win the hand if she didn't entirely throw away her good cards. I explored further, opening the pantry door. The chef's cat was asleep on the warm top of the boiler. A mouse slumbered not far away, half way through eating a piece of cheese in a trap that had not yet sprung.

We have mice?

Naturally. That's why there's a cat.

Feeling a great affinity for the mouse's predicament, I lifted it out of danger and put it in the hedge outside the kitchen door – with the cheese, of course. I noticed on my way back in that the spider on the web hitched between bushes was also still. The birds in the beech near the feeder were not fluttering around the gardener's gift of sunflower seed heads as they normally would be at daybreak, but asleep on their twigs.

I don't do things by halves, said the magic proudly.

I walked through the silent school. It was empty, not even the dust motes settling. I then visited each of the houses. All the students were asleep where they had been at midnight, some in bed, some snoring in front of the computers they should've switched off at curfew. Even the screens were on sleep mode. Only the magic squad weren't in their rooms.

Where are they?

Keeping vigil for you with Sian and Jack.

I'd left Crowthorne until last. My friends were in the common room, Sidhe, hedge witch and ordinary boy all curled up together fast asleep. I put a wood anemone in Sian's hand and kissed Jack on the cheek.

They'll be all right?

They had a scare and they're sad but you'll set that to rights.

I will.

Jack has some adjusting to do.

Poor Jack. He doesn't believe in you.

No he doesn't, but he is in touch with me through his music. Tell Sian she won't reach me by that path even though her mother said she should try. Her crafts are the way to go for her.

So that was why Sian insisted on taking music when she had no talent for it. Oh dear. I'd have to break that to her very gently.

Leaving them sleeping, I went back outside, my feet bringing me back to the holly fortress.

This isn't going to last a hundred years, is it? I asked only half joking.

Only if you neglect to wake the prince with a kiss.

I get to break the spell?

This is the twenty-first century, Linny. Even magic moves with the times.

Laughing, I ran the final stretch back to the holly clearing. The branches seemed eager to part for me, sharing my joy.

And there he was. My prince. My Quinn.

I knelt beside him and brushed at the tear tracks on his face.

What do I do? I asked the magic, afraid of getting it wrong.

Oh come on, Linny, you know. Just kiss the boy. That's how this is supposed to end when I get to tell the story.

So I kissed the prince.

32

LISTEN

'Wake up.'

Quinn's cobalt blue eyes fluttered open. It took a moment for him to process what he was seeing.

'Linny?'

'Yes.'

'You're alive? This isn't a dream?'

'Yes – and no, no dream.'

His shoulders quaked and he began to sob. 'You were dead.'

'Technically, I think I might've been in-between with the light magic.'

He crushed me to him, hands searching my back, my neck, my hair. 'You're warm – you're here. You smell of...of salt.'

'I've been to the beach with the magic. We went for a little stroll.'

'How can this be real?'

'I think the magic had better explain but for now I have a bone to pick with you.' I stroked his cheek. His face, his smile, his voice had become so necessary to me. Did he know that?

'About what?'

'Where's the glass casket? And dwarves. I wanted at least seven.'

He began to laugh, which was what I had hoped.

'Or at least put me up at the top of a tower. But do I get that? No, I get a pile of moldy leaves and a bunch of flowers.'

'They're very nice flowers, best I could do at short notice.'

'Pathetic.' I tucked one behind his ear.

'And the leaves aren't moldy.'

'Decomposing – you have to admit that.'

'Well, it is spring – that's what they do.' He got up and wrapped us both in Sian's rug. 'The curse?'

'Completely and utterly gone. It's become light magic.'

'How can that possibly have happened?'

'Don't worry; it's how it should always have been. The magic informs me that the balance always changes. That is what nature does. A place like this adjusts and right now it's a good time to be light magic. Oh.' I slipped the ring off my thumb and put it back on his finger. 'This is yours. Maybe, if you haven't changed into a frog, you can get me one of my own in a few years' time when we're ready.'

With that he gave a great shout of laughter and spun me in a circle. The world whirled, the branches danced, the sun spotlighted us as a beam slanted across the boundary.

WE HAD to hurry back to Crowthorne, thinking we should break the news I'd survived before other people got up to start their day. We walked in hand in hand to be greeted by shocked looks from a silent circle of mourners.

'Wow, now I know what the ghost of his father feels like in *Hamlet*,' I quipped, a little awkward now the moment had arrived. I pointed to my chest. 'How can I put this? Not dead.'

That was the signal for something approaching a rugby scrum of hugs. Jack cried, Sian yelped and wriggled past Conall to get at me. Even Artair could be heard clearing his throat a few times and discreetly wiping a sleeve across his eyes.

'Guys, give her room,' said Quinn, managing to sound quite at ease with the whole Linny's-not-dead scenario. They should've seen him fifteen minutes ago.

I took hold of Jack. 'Are you okay? Those people last night didn't hurt you?'

'We should've called the police – had them arrested.' Jack hugged me fiercely. 'I don't know what they did to you – to us – but it was a violation of our human rights. I think they must've drugged Sian and me – we saw all sorts of weird stuff. Dragons and things. Do you think we need a blood test to see if it's out of our system?'

'Jack, that was magic.'

'Linny, there's no such thing. Let's call the police.'

'Let's not.' I held on to his arm. 'The magic has dealt with them.' Green Drake gave me a nudge. 'Jack, you don't really believe that it was drugs. You might just have to accept that there are more things in heaven and earth...'

He groaned. 'Than are dreamt of in my philosophy? Okay, okay, stop it with the Hamlet references.'

'Why? I saw the very first performance.'

'Look, just let me pretend a little longer, okay, while I adjust to a whole new level of weirdness?'

I couldn't help doing a little mischief. 'You'd better hurry up because Quinn's dad is the fairy king.'

'Stop it, stop it.'

'And the boys here can all do spells.'

'And you'll be telling me next that Sian's weed bracelets also work wonders?'

Quinn came to my side. 'Jack, if you prefer, I can help you forget all this. You can go back to how you were.'

Jack looked around the room. 'But everyone else will be in on the secret? Conall? You? Sian? Linny? That would be like you all going to the coolest party in town, leaving me in Boringsville. I'll stay as I am, Quinn. You need someone level-headed among you, someone rational.'

'Thank you.' I kissed him on the cheek. 'Yes, we need you.'

MY FRIENDS WERE PLOTTING SOMETHING. I wasn't born yesterday – I was born many yesterdays, as I liked to point out to Quinn, but even with this clinching argument, he wouldn't tell me what was going on.

On Sunday, he suggested, far too casually, that we go for a stroll on the beach at sunset. This had become one of my favorite places over the last week since equinox, a reminder that I was no longer trapped by any boundary, that my life was not limited except in the normal way.

I looked round the common room but Jack and Sian were absent. Charlie was luring some new victims over to the Poker table. He saw me watching him.

'Want to join us?' he asked, not very enthusiastically.

'It's okay. We're going for a walk,' I said pleasantly.

He grinned in relief. 'Great. I mean, er, don't do anything I wouldn't.'

'Well now, that gives us a lot of latitude I'd say,' said Quinn, stealing a quick kiss from me.

We passed Mr Huntsman humming happily to himself as he nailed up another of his butterfly pictures in the hall. There was no talk now of giving his collection away to be hidden in a museum vault. Instead, he was spreading it across the school so we could all enjoy the photographs.

We took a winding path to the wall, enjoying the long shafts of sunlight streaking across the playing fields. The girls in the basketball team, who practicing on the courts, looked like they were dancing with the giant players of their shadows. We passed through the library garden and I noticed that the prissy maiden statue, reminder of my Victorian flower seller humiliations, had become hidden by ivy so it now looked as though she had sprouted a green glossy beard. Smiling, I decided I'd tell Quinn that story from my past later.

Quinn gave me a boost onto the wall then sprang up beside me. He jumped down and I followed, landing in his arms in a cheesy gesture that made us both chuckle.

'We're getting quite good at this romantic stuff, aren't we?' he said.

'When we're not laughing at ourselves.'

'Oh no, especially then. That's the best part. I was looking for someone to laugh with me.'

We set off across the meadow, following the path I'd beaten into the long grass with my frequent trips this way.

I remembered some not so welcome news I had to give him. 'Thanks for inviting me to your home at Easter, but Mom and Dad have decided they should have me at theirs.'

'How do you think that's going to be?'

'Awkward. But the twins will make it fun and I suppose I made it difficult for my parents to cope with me. They weren't entirely wrong about that.'

'They just handled it badly.'

'Yes. They perked up when I said I was hanging out with Shay Ramsay's son. They'll be angling for free tickets next time you see them.'

'I think I can find a few for them. Besides, Dad's got a big house in Manhattan near Central Park. I can tell him we should spend Easter there so you can come around when it gets too much at home.'

'Thanks, that makes me feel much better.'

A V-formation of wild swans flew over, their wings making that distinctive sound like squeaky boots, which was at odds with their breathtaking beauty.

'Linny, I've been talking to Green Drake,' said Quinn.

'Oh? So that's why you've been cutting class – don't think I hadn't noticed.'

He swung my arms easily. 'I told you, I don't worry about little human things like exams and lessons.'

'Tell that to your dad who's footing the bill for your tuition. I got a feeling he might not share your view.'

'Ah, rumbled.' He grinned. 'Okay, I'll sit next to you in the catch-up lessons.'

'I'm not sure either of us would get much work done.'

'We could have an agreement: a kiss for a homework turned in.'

'That might prove enough to turn my academic record around.'

'Linny, don't you want to know what the magic told me? It's quite amazing.'

'Spill it then.' I thought I knew what he was going to say because the magic had been speaking to me too.

'It says you are something new – a human that can talk to it. That is why it has picked you as its guardian, not like Lihtan who contained it within himself, but a new sort, a kind of champion or spokesperson. It says you won't lose touch with it when you reach eighteen like we do and you'll be able to communicate with it wherever it is strong.'

'That's just as well because under some calculations I'm more like seven hundred and fifty.'

'Just think, I'm dating an older woman.'

I elbowed him. 'I hope that won't be a problem for the Sidhe?'

'Me dating an old lady?'

'No! The guardianship passing to a human.'

'Some won't like it but Dad says that any change is usually met with horror by conservative elements in his court – that's until it becomes the new normal. Anyway, we haven't got a leg to stand on in this case. The magic explained about the Sidhe being the ones at fault, casting the curse and disturbing the balance. It says that light magic continues to be at risk because your sisters are still suffering unfairly. It told me we have to find them.'

'It's been telling me the same. It thinks without the three of us coming together as guardians the curse will never really be reversed and continue to have the power to undermine the light. I was going to ask you to help.'

He pulled me to the top of the dune. 'I will, but for now, there's something else we've got to do.'

We'd arrived on the shore and I was surprised to find many people had already gathered there. Quinn's dad was standing with Artair and three strangers; Sian and Jack were in the middle of a crowd of women: Sian's mother and what looked like all of her sisters.

Quinn must've felt my resistance. 'Come on, don't go bashful on me now.' He tugged me over to Shay. 'Dad, we're here.'

'Linny, I don't think you've met my other sons. Fergus,' Shay gestured to an austere-looking young man, smartly dressed in a navy-blue suit that seemed out of place on a beach. Fergus had black hair like his father, Artair and Quinn, but his own dark brown eyes.

'Linny.' Fergus held out a hand. The charming smile that came over his face when I shook it made me realize that he wasn't really severe, just shy.

'This scallywag is Brodie.' Shay ushered forward a golden-haired man with twinkling light blue eyes. Laughter did not look very far from the surface with this brother.

'Dad, is that the way you introduce me to my brother's girl now, for shame?' He leant forward, going for a kiss rather than a more formal handshake. 'Don't believe a word he tells you about me.'

'Sadly, it'd all be true,' quipped the remaining brother. 'Hi, Linny, I'm Paten, the good-looking one.' To be fair he was handsome, with his riot of chestnut curls and green eyes like a putti angel grown up to be very naughty indeed. However, he didn't have Quinn's vagabond charm. No one came anywhere near Quinn in my eyes.

'Nice to meet you all at last,' I said, hoping they wouldn't hate me.

Shay gave a signal and his sons moved into place in a semi-circle around him, including Quinn, leaving me standing on my own.

'Mrs Willowbrook?' called Shay.

Sian's family took their positions providing the other half of the circle.

'Linny, you must be wondering what all this is about. It's been brought to our attention – forcefully I might add,' Shay nodded towards Quinn, 'that our family has done yours great wrong.'

'Oh.' I realized that this was developing into something of a formal apology. 'Mr Ramsay...'

'Dad or Shay, take your pick.' He folded his arms, looking like his son at his most stubborn. 'But not Mr Ramsay.'

'I think I've had rather too many dads to call you that.'

'Shay it is then.'

'Mr...Shay, you don't need to say sorry. You aren't to blame for what happened.'

'But we are responsible. Our blood carries that as one of its inheritances. So I have called the Willowbrook family, respected wise women, to see that this is done properly. Do you accept them as representing your interests in this dispute?'

I glanced over at Sian and her family. 'Yes.'

Mrs Willowbrook gave me a no-nonsense nod, her suspicion of the Sidhe clearly still alive and well. Sian's sisters, bar the one I had down as the star-struck Shay fan, looked equally wary.

'And what about me?' piped up Jack.

Shay's expression softened. Clearly, Jack had won himself another friend recently. 'You, Jack, are here because there always should be a Doubting Thomas. Magic should be kept on its toes by those who question it, or don't even believe in it.'

Jack cast a nervous look around him. 'Good, yes, I'm glad that's clear then. You're all utterly crazy, of course, to put your faith in this stuff.'

'The question is, though, will Linnet Grace accept the apology of the current Sidhe king and his sons?' Shay went down on one knee, head bowed; his sons followed suit.

'Oh my, I don't know what to do.' I put my hands to my mouth.

You can come up with something better than that, Linny,

mocked the magic. *Don't make them wait when they're doing so well.*

'Right, so, er...' Quinn glanced up and smiled in understanding, giving me the reassurance I needed that I couldn't really mess up in his eyes. 'Yes, I, Linnet Grace, accept your apology. Please...all rise.'

Shay got up first then closed the distance between us to give me a kiss on the brow. 'Thank you.' His sons then copied the gesture in age order. Artair gave me a second kiss on the cheek. We'd become friends since I was no longer imperiling his little brother. I'd grown to appreciate his tough line on protecting Quinn. After all, I'd do anything too to make sure he was safe.

Quinn was the only one to deviate from the ceremony. He gave me a long kiss on the mouth, the kind that took my breath away and made my skin tingle.

'Come on, break it up,' said Jack. 'Some of us don't want to spend all night standing around on the beach waiting for love to have its way.'

Quinn ended the kiss but didn't let me go. 'Satisfied?'

'For now.' I looked back at his lips.

'I meant the apology.'

'Oh that. Yes.'

'Mrs Willowbrook, are you content that an apology has been made and accepted?' asked Shay.

'Yes, er, Shay, we are,' said Mrs Willowbrook.

'And as part of our restitution, I give my word that we will seek Linny's sisters, Wren and Finch. Our apology will not be finished until their curses too are lifted. The world will not be safe until the great wrong is righted.'

I felt a huge wave of happiness mixed with relief – with the resources of the Sidhe king behind us, surely it wouldn't be long before we found my lost sisters?

But you have to hurry – they don't have long left, said the magic.

What do you know?

Only that they have to be rescued – and soon – or it will be too late for them and the magic they carry.

Quinn rubbed my chilled arms. 'I heard that. We'll start looking right away, I promise.'

'Thank you.' That was the best I could do for them now – far more than I had ever been in a position to do in the past.

'All right, that's done.' Shay clapped his hands and rolled his shoulders, breaking into the serious mood that had come over us all. 'What do you say to a barbecue on the beach and the first performance of Jack's new song?'

'It's not just mine,' said Jack, embarrassed, 'you wrote the words.'

'What've you called it, Dad?' asked Quinn as his father picked up his guitar from where he had left it resting on a nearby rock.

'Well, Jack and I discussed this.' Shay strummed, checking his tuning. I thought how millions of fans around the globe would've mortgaged their houses to buy entry to a private concert from Shay while none of us had had to do a thing. 'I've tried to keep you out of the public eye, Quinn, and I don't think Linny would like the attention either, so the world is going to know it as "Listen to the magic"; all of us, though, will know it is really called "Linnet and Quinn's Theme" just as Jack intended.'

'"Listen to the magic"?' said Quinn smiling into my eyes. 'I'd say that is very good advice.'

ABOUT THE AUTHOR

Joss Stirling is the author of the best-selling *Savants* series. She was awarded the Romantic Novel of the Year Award in 2015 for *Struck*, the first YA book to win this prestigious prize. Her first adult novel, a psychological thriller, *Don't Trust Me*, came out in 2018.

A former British diplomat and Oxfam policy adviser, she now lives in Oxford.

For more information, please visit
www.jossstirling.co.uk

ALSO BY JOSS STIRLING

38545179R00165

Printed in Great Britain
by Amazon